THE GOLDE

By
E. PHILLIPS OPPENHEIM

P. F. COLLIER & SON COMPANY
NEW YORK

THE GOLDEN BEAST

—

BOOK ONE

CHAPTER I

ISRAEL, first Baron Honerton, famous in commercial circles as chairman of the directors of Fernham & Company, Ltd., the great wholesale chemists, Lord of the Manor of Honerton Chase, in Norfolk, sat at the head of the long black oak table in the banqueting hall of the ancient and historic mansion which he had bought, as the auctioneer described it, " lock, stock and barrel ", two years ago. One of the shrewdest financiers in England, a multimillionaire, in all the ordinary affairs of life a grim materialist, he was liable at odd moments to strange fits of abstraction, to mental wanderings almost akin to those of the visionary, during which the appearance of the man himself seemed to become transformed. Of his type he was a person of fine presence. He was tall and slim, even to lankiness. He had still a wealth of grey hair, fine, though harshly cut features, overhanging eyebrows, a pitiless mouth, eyes generally keen and hard, but filled at such times as the present with a curious, unearthly light. Even his attire seemed part of the man. He wore conventional dinner clothes, but cut after some ancient and unrecognisable pattern, the waistcoat high, the coat loose and double breasted like a smoking jacket. His collar was of the fashion of a hundred years ago; his black tie little more than a wisp. Yet, although his father had been a small master tailor, and his mother had served in a fish shop, he alone amongst that company had the air of having come to the place which was his in life.

The background and the setting of the feast now in progress were alike perfect. Honerton Chase was one of the show places of the world, and inside as well as out it was architecturally unique. There was nothing of the vandal about Israel Fernham, Lord Honerton. He had, as a matter of fact, a taste for beautiful things at least equal to the last hopelessly bankrupt owner of the great house he had acquired. The sombreness of the walls with their fine oil paintings and occasional choice pieces of armour had remained untouched. The tapestries which covered the north side of the room had even been left unrenovated lest any charm of the old colouring should be lost. The servants who waited were the best trained of their order; the butler had known royal service. Glass, silver and flowers were alike perfect. The guests! — It was his contemplation of the guests, most of them members of his own family, which had sent Israel, Lord Honerton, off into one of those mysterious fits of abstraction. There were three sons of the house and their wives. There were two daughters, both married, with their husbands. There were two Englishmen whose birth and breeding brought them well and aptly within the setting of the picture, but whose reputations were tarnished, and who had spent the best years of their lives slipping from the places which they should have occupied in the social world. Then, there was the youngest son of the house, on whom his father's eyes had rested longest; a young man only just down from Oxford, dark, clean-shaven, reputedly clever, the sole inheritor of his father's lean face and deep-set eyes; the sole inheritor it seemed too, in those slowly ticking moments of revelation, of the traditions of his race.

The babel of conversation around him rose and swelled. It was a family party amongst people with whom family meant intimacy, unbounded kindliness, and a decided gift for light conversation of the chaffing order. There was a great deal of champagne being drunk by the women as well as by the men — more than a great deal of noise. Once his father's eyes strayed towards Cecil's glass. He, alas, was as the others, the flush already creeping into his cheeks, the gleam in his eyes no longer one of intellect. Some of the men and the women, too, were already smoking cigarettes, although the dinner was only half served. The laughter now and then was uproarious.

Through it all Israel, host of the gathering, sat still in his trancelike mood, his wine glasses empty, a tumbler of water by his side. It was one of many moments of bitterness, when his eyes saw the truth and the judgment of his brain, unbiassed by his affections, spelled out the condemnation of these, his own brood, the children of his blood and bone. They were his sons, but he knew that the hand of luxury and evil living had laid its slur upon them. They all carried too much flesh; their mouths had loosened. Money, wine and pleasure were claiming their own. And the women — there was a vein of idealism in the nature of this man who watched so sorrowfully, a touch of those sterner joys of renunciation handed down to him from the great forefathers of the race from which he sprang — the women filled him with a sense almost of shame. Judith's shoulders were disgracefully bare, the look in Rebecca's eyes — " Becky ", as every one called her — as she flirted with the young alien by her side, seemed to speak of modesty cast aside. Leah, once his favourite, was quieter only because she was devoting herself with more absorption to the offerings of her father's wonderful chef. Her uncovered shoulders were almost colossal, her laughter, when she did pause to join in what had become less a conversation than a stream of chaff, was louder than ever. Alone of all the boisterous company, Rachel, his youngest daughter-in-law, showed occasional signs of shyness and discomfiture.

Although with no knowledge of it at the time, it was the last of these embittered periods of clear-sightedness in which Israel, Lord Honerton, was ever to indulge. He pursued his train of thought to its unhappy end. He looked back to his youth of poverty, remembered those days of cleaner fasting, the days when purely family joys sufficed, when the reading in the Synagogue brought a living message to these others as well as to him. He felt the passing of all that was picturesque and spiritual in life. They had gone — his four millions remained!

A servant entered the room and whispered to the butler who presently crossed to the other side of the table and leaned over Cecil.

" John Heggs, the keeper, is here, sir. He wondered whether he could have a few words with you."

The young man received the message curiously. He turned sharply around and there was a gleam in his eyes almost of apprehension.

" Heggs! " he repeated. " What the devil does he want? "

" I understand, sir," the butler explained, " that he was anxious to discuss the order in which the coverts should be taken to-morrow."

Cecil's face cleared. It was a particular vanity of his to direct the shooting on the days when others besides the house party were invited. He nodded acquiescence.

" I'll come out at once," he assented. " Quite right of Heggs! I wanted to see him about the long spinneys before he sent the beaters out in the morning."

He rose to his feet.

"You'll excuse me, Dad," he continued, quickly, as he passed his father's place. "We ought to have a topping day to-morrow. They'll be tame enough for even Rudolph to hit — that is, if we can get them to fly at all."

There were roars of laughter and a volley of chaffing reminiscences. The two strangers exchanged glances. Under cover of it all Cecil left the room, and strolled across the great hall, out towards the back quarters, preceded by one of the footmen.

"Heggs is in the far room, sir," the man told him, "not the ordinary gun room."

"What the mischief's he doing there?" Cecil demanded irritably and with a momentary return of that first impulse of uneasiness.

"There's a map of the estate there, sir," the servant reminded him. "He was studying it when I left. I think his idea is to have three partridge drives after lunch."

Cecil pursued his way down the stone-flagged passage. The room which he presently entered was in a wing almost cut off from the rest of the house — a large apartment with stone floor, deal table and plastered walls, used many years ago as a dairy. Heggs the keeper was studying a map which hung upon the wall, a blackthorn switch in his hand. He turned round at Cecil's entrance, and touched the place where his hat, which reposed upon the table, would have been.

"You wanted to see me, Heggs?" the young man asked.

"I wanted a word or two with you, sir."

"Hurry up, then. I'm in the middle of dinner. I should like the birds ——"

"We'll talk about that presently," Heggs interrupted.

Cecil, son of Israel, Lord Honerton, stared at the speaker in amazement — amazement which turned almost in a second to fear. Heggs was a man of over sixty years of age without much physique, but he had the hard clean complexion and bright eyes of the careful liver. His hair was grey, his expression, as a rule, entirely benevolent. He was a very ordinary product of the soil, a man who loved his glass of beer, his friends, his occupation, and was supposed to know more about the hand rearing of birds and the ways of vermin than any keeper in Norfolk. It was plain, however, at this moment, that he was thinking of other things. What those things were Cecil Fernham probably knew. At any rate he made a quick movement towards the door and, finding it frustrated, opened his mouth. With surprising quickness it was covered by Heggs' horny hand.

"You know what I'm here for," the latter said. "You can guess what I'm going to do. If you hadn't come to-night I should have done it to-morrow in front of all your friends. If I had a son I'd have let you two have it out. But he's in Australia. You can squeal if you like. They won't hear you, and if they interrupt before I've finished, you'll get the rest another day."

Cecil Fernham struggled and did his best to call for help. Neither proceeding availed him very much. With the first fierce plunge his beautifully laundered white shirt was ripped from the studs, and his collar torn. Presently graver things happened. Heggs was a kindly man and humane where his fellow creatures were concerned, but he was cruel to vermin. The affair would

probably have been brought to its natural conclusion —
Cecil Fernham would have spent a fortnight in his room,
owing to some regrettable accident, and Heggs would
have accepted one of the many other places always open
to him — but for a slight and untoward incident. A
scullery maid passing down the passage heard something
of what was happening. She rushed, breathless, into
the kitchen. There was a stampede of servants along
the passageway and Heggs heard them coming. The
thought that he was to be robbed of one single blow,
baulked of one single second of the punishment he was
dealing out, for a moment maddened him. As the door
was being opened, he lifted the half-insensible body of
the young man whom he had been castigating, a grim
and unpleasing sight, held it over his head as he might
have done the carcase of a fox, shook him and flung him
on to the floor, which was unfortunately of stone. Then
he turned to the door, passed through the little throng
of servants, not one of whom showed the least desire to
stop him, and out through a back exit into the park.

John Heggs conformed to type up to a certain point,
and at a certain juncture in the psychological tree
departed from it. On reaching home, he presented
very much the appearance of a man who has got through
a disagreeable piece of business and means to forget it.
He completed a task upon which he had been engaged
earlier in the day — cleaning a couple of guns which
had been sent down for that purpose from the house.
Afterwards he poured himself out a tumbler of beer,
glanced into the kitchen to see that the woman, who
came in to look after him since the days of his widower-
hood, had prepared his breakfast, and finally filled a
pipe, found the local paper, and sat down in his easy-

chair to await events. He was on the point of retiring
for the night, when the long expected knock at the door
came. In response to the invitation to enter, his old
friend and companion, P. C. Choppin, the local policeman, crossed the threshold. Choppin, who had been
disturbed in the act of going to bed, was wearing his
official trousers, but an old tweed coat and a hat. The
gravity of his manner, however, atoned for any irregu-
larities of toilet. He closed the door firmly behind him
and there was an ominous jangle in his coat pocket in
which he was feeling.

"This is a very bad job, Mr. Heggs," he said
gloomily.

Heggs folded up his paper and rose to his feet.

"It's none so terrible, Choppin," was the undisturbed
reply. "I've just gi'en one of them young varmints up
at the house sum'at that he deserved. I'm willing to
go to jail for it, though, if it's their wish."

It is doubtful whether this was not the moment of
P. C. Choppin's life. He realised that it had fallen to
him to convey the fell tidings. He was not an ill-natured
man but he was carried away by the enormity of his
news.

"You've broke his neck, Heggs," he announced solemnly. "He's dead! He were stone dead when they
picked him up!"

Heggs looked a little dazed.

"I didn't go for to do that," he muttered, half to
himself.

Choppin shook his head mournfully.

"You ma'un put 'em up, John Heggs," he said. "I
hurried here before the Sergeant from Fakenham, who
be on the way. I thought you'd rather it were a
friend."

The handcuffs clicked on Heggs' wrists. For the first time in his life P. C. Choppin had arrested a murderer.

John Heggs, notwithstanding a strong recommendation to mercy, was hanged by the neck until he was dead, and Israel, Baron Honerton, sat outside Norwich jail in his automobile and listened to the tolling of the bell as one who hears music. As he gave the word to drive off he found himself surrounded by a small but hostile crowd. It was a matter of common report in the City that but for his tireless efforts the jury's recommendation to mercy would have had due effect. They had heard, these people, of his frequent visits to the Home Secretary. There were rumours that he had threatened a withdrawal from the political party to which his entire adherence had been given, if any measure of leniency were shown to the condemned man. They closed in upon him now menacingly and the words they shouted were not pleasant to hear. Yet, for the first time since his son's death, Israel smiled. He let down the window of his automobile and looked out into the driving rain.

" Is there any one who wishes to speak to me? " he asked.

There was a volley of catcalls and abuse, sounding oddly enough against the background of that slowly tolling bell, but no single person accepted the challenge. Israel was on the point of giving his chauffeur orders to drive on when a girl came from the edge of the crowd and approached the automobile. She was young, good-looking in a somewhat quiet manner, neatly, even fashionably dressed. She advanced to the side of the automobile and looked in at its occupant.

" Are you Cecil's father? " she enquired.

" I am," he assented.

She pointed to the jail.

" He was my father," she said.

Israel scrutinised her from underneath his heavy grey eyebrows and there was neither interest nor pity in his face.

" It is you loose-living women," he declared, " who bring death in amongst us. Do you realise that it is for the gratification of your lust that I have lost my son and you your father? "

She answered him quite calmly. She was obviously a person of education. She was, also, undoubtedly possessed of a rare gift of restraint.

" What about your son? " she asked. " He was my first lover."

" That may be so or it may not," he rejoined. " A wanton has no knowledge of the truth. Are you here to beg from me? "

For the first time she showed some sign of emotion. Her eyes were lit with anger.

" Money! Money! That is all you and your breed think of! " she exclaimed passionately. " You buy your pleasures, your wives, and you would buy your way into heaven if there were such a place. It is perhaps as well that your son died. He would have grown like the rest of you."

" He bought you, I suppose," Israel remarked.

She took off her glove deliberately, removed a small platinum ring from her finger and threw it into the bottom of the car.

" That is the only present I ever had from your son," she announced — " the only one of value I was ever willing to receive from him."

"What do you want from me?" he demanded abruptly.

The bell had ceased to toll. The crowd of people were slowly dispersing. One or two policemen had put in a casual appearance. There was still every now and then, however, a menacing shout, and once a stone struck the back of the car. A brewer's dray, passing, spattered her with mud. She waited until it had gone before she tried to speak.

"I came to remind you of what you already know," she said. "Of you two men —you and my father — it is you who are the murderer, not he. My father has died at your hands a shameful death. I found him reading the Old Testament when I paid him my farewell visit. He was reading your code — 'Life for life, eye for eye.' Something like that, isn't it?"

"Well?"

"I have not come to threaten you," she continued, "but I am here to tell you this. For the deed which you have permitted to take place this morning you and your race will suffer. My father killed your son by accident; you murdered my father with foul and beastly premeditation. You bought his death with your money. This money shall spread itself like a foul cobweb of hate and decay over you and your family of whom you are so proud."

He looked at her unmoved, cold and stern, his eyes steely, his tone, when he spoke, bitter.

"So you are a prophetess," he sneered.

She leaned a little forward so that her face was framed in the place where the window would have been. The rain glistened upon her cheeks and clothes, her perfect self-control seemed for a moment disturbed by some new emotion.

"Why not?" she demanded. "You come of a race who have trafficked generations ago with soothsayers and the magicians. Have you never heard that there is just one moment in a woman's life when she may see a little beyond the world — a little above it? That moment is with me now. It is your son's child, drawing near to life. You are an old man, and you will not live to see the things of which I tell you, but nevertheless they are true. The millions for which you have toiled are changing already into the poison which will bring your people to nought and worse than nought. The fear of it is in your heart already. You will never lose it. You will die in your bed and not on that shameful scaffold, but your heart will be as heavy as his because, like all others in those fading moments, you will see the truth."

As quietly and unobtrusively as she had come she turned and passed away. The old man sat in his place and watched her. She walked, notwithstanding her dripping state, with dignity and self-possession. He pulled up the window and muttered a brief order to the chauffeur. Somehow or other he felt baulked of the sullen joy with which he had entered upon the morning. Ghosts rode with him.

During the afternoon, Israel sought his wife in her sitting room. She was a large lady, addicted to post-luncheon repose, and neither the persuasions of her more modish children, nor the stern disapproval of her husband had ever succeeded in preventing her from adorning herself by daytime as well as night with a great profusion of costly and glittering gems. Her husband stood and watched her for several moments. By some irony of fate he found his thoughts wandering back to the day of their marriage — she, a slim, half-frightened

child, with dark eyes still holding a touch of the visionary. This was what his wealth had brought; the result
of forty years of luxury! She opened her eyes slowly
and returned his gaze.

" What is it, Israel? " she asked, a little peevishly.

" It came to my mind to ask you a question," he
said. " This girl of Heggs', do you know anything
of her? "

" Know anything of her? " Lady Honerton gasped.
" Would I be likely to, Israel? She never lived here.
She only visited once that summer."

" But since — you have made enquiries? "

" Not I! " was the indignant response. " What do
you mean? Has she been to ask for money? "

Israel shook his head, moved away, and his wife once
more closed her eyes.

Israel made his way to his library, a room of solemn
magnificence, yet somehow imbued with a touch of its
new owner's austerity. He sent for his butler.

" Groves," he said, " you have lived in this neighbourhood all your life."

" All my life, your lordship," the man assented.

" I should like you," Israel continued calmly, " to
tell me what you know of the young person, Heggs'
daughter."

" Very good, my lord," Groves replied. " There was
— your lordship will pardon my asking — there was no
reprieve? " he added, with a note of anxiety in his tone.

" There was no reprieve. Heggs was hanged at eight
o'clock this morning."

The man stood for a moment without speech. His
master read his thoughts with grim resentment.

" The young lady, my lord," the former proceeded,
" was a very superior person. Heggs himself came from

a family of yeomen — gentlemen farmers they call themselves. They have lived in these parts for generations.
The young lady won scholarships and went to college
and Oxford University. She was very clever and very
gifted. She was — if your lordship will pardon my
saying so — very much esteemed here."

"Do you know where she is now?" Israel enquired,
after a moment's pause.

"I have no idea, my lord. She has not been seen in
these parts for some time."

His master dismissed him with a little wave of the
hand, and presently wrote a letter to his lawyers. In
three or four days he received a reply.

17, Lincoln's Inn.

DEAR LORD HONERTON,

We have carried out your instructions and have
been in communication with the young lady, who, as
seems natural under the somewhat shameful circumstances, has changed her name. We regret, however, to
inform you that she declines in the most absolute and
uncompromising terms to hold any communication with
any member of your family. We may add that there is
no indication of her being in any financial distress.

Faithfully yours,

FIELDS, MARSHALL & FIELDS.

Israel had received the letter after dinner one night
and had taken it to his library to read. Slowly he tore
it to pieces and threw them on to the fire. He stood
there with his hands behind his back, wrapped in
thought. Through the half-open door came the brazen
sounds of jazz music from the latest and most expensive
gramophone. Some of the family had motored down
from London in luxurious motor cars " to cheer up the

old people." He could hear the sound of their heavy
footsteps upon the polished floor, almost the sound of
their breathing, the high-pitched voices, shrieks of
laughter, the popping of corks — for the family of
Israel, Baron Honerton, preferred champagne to all
other wines and drank it at all hours. A wave of something almost like nausea swept through his mind. He
felt a sudden giddiness, staggered towards his easy-chair
and rang the bell.

That night, Israel, Lord Honerton, died.

CHAPTER II

JOSEPH, second Baron Honerton, was, unlike his long defunct father, in no sense of the word a dreamer or an idealist. He had finished a very excellent dinner, a meal which would have evoked the strongest remonstrances from his physician had he been present, before he even thought of disengaging himself for a moment from the conversation of the honoured guest on his right and taking a self-congratulatory glance down his sumptuous dining table. The room itself was unchanged since Israel, the founder of the family, had sat in his son's place thirty years ago; the tapestries perhaps had grown a shade softer, the walls in their dark perfection a trifle more mysterious, the faces which gleamed from the half-seen canvasses a thought paler. Three decades of years, however, had made little change in a room whose atmosphere was the growth of centuries. It was the guests, the men and women seated around the table, who marked the progress of time. This was no family party such as would have been dear to the heart of Israel. In thirty years the new Lords of the Manor had grafted themselves upon the soil they had purchased. It was a tolerant age where social qualifications were concerned, and, after all, a son of Joseph had been in the Eton Eleven and was doing well to-day in the Embassy at Paris, apart from which, Judith, the younger daughter, was without any rival the beauty of the season. Great painters approached her humbly for sittings. Very desirable young men had sought her and her millions. She had only one drawback, as many of those in her immediate circle had already discovered. She was amazingly and unpleasantly clever. Her father's eyes rested for a moment upon her beautiful face, with just the same contented, self-approving pleasure with which he would have contemplated some *objet d'art* which he had bought that afternoon at Christie's. They passed from her to his only surviving brother, Samuel — an irritable dyspeptic, out of health and temper with the world — whose presence was some faint concession to the spirit of the departed Israel. They passed over a little row of well-dressed, well-bred people with complacent indifference, rested for a moment kindly upon his wife at the other end of the table with her elaborately coiffured white hair, parchment skin, and brilliant eyes, and finally lingered, with something nearer real affection upon the handsome yet rather obtrusively Semitic form of Ernest, his younger son, who had just entered the business. It was a company with which any host might be satisfied, a son and daughter of whom any father might be proud. No wonder that Joseph, second Baron Honerton, pulled down his waistcoat over his rotund stomach and felt nothing of that wild unhappy impulse which thirty years before had spelled the grim writing on the wall to Israel's haggard gaze.

"I can't tell you how much Frederick is looking forward to his shooting to-morrow," the Marchioness, who was seated on his right, observed. "Our own pheasants this year have been so disappointing. The fact is we don't rear nearly enough birds, and haven't been able to for years."

Her host nodded sympathetically. It was not a pleasing gesture, as it drove his second chin on to his collar. He had learned many lessons during the passing of the years, and with a conscious effort he omitted all mention of his standing order for ten thousand of the best eggs.

" We'll try and give the Marquis some sport," he
promised genially. " I'm shooting myself to-morrow.
I've been looking after things the last two or three times,
but my boy's taking that on now — good sportsman,
Ernest."

" How very unselfish of you," his neighbour purred.
" I hear great accounts of your elder son, Lord Honer-
ton. They tell me that he will be First Secretary at
Paris, if he stays there, before many years have passed."

" Henry's a good lad," his father admitted, " and
his head's screwed on all right. I sometimes wish we'd
had him in the business. Still, one can't have it all
ways."

" I should think not, indeed," the Marchioness assented. " You ought to be very proud of your children,
Lord Honerton. There wasn't a person at the last
Court who didn't declare that Judith is the most beautiful girl who has been seen at Buckingham Palace for
years. My boy Frederick was in the Throne Room on
duty. He could talk of nobody else — couldn't remember what he had to do in the least."

Lord Honerton glanced down the table.

" He seems to have recovered himself now," he remarked.

" Frederick is always at his best when he is with some
one he really likes," his mother confided. " He's a dear
fellow though elder sons are rather an expense," she
sighed. " Polo and all those things cost so much money
nowadays. I am afraid there'll be nothing of the sort
for the younger boys. We thought of trying to get
Dick into a good business where he could make some
money. What do you think, Lord Honerton? "

Her host became a little less expansive. There were
plenty of millions to be made in the great Fernham

business, but they were most distinctly to be made by members of the Fernham family. Clerks and managers and travellers were all very well, but he had a shrewd idea as to the outlook of a woman like the Marchioness who was seeking a commercial career for her son. There was no room for anything in the least ornamental at the Fernham Works.

"It depends whether he's got it in him or not," he remarked in a noncommittal sort of way. "As a rule the man who makes money in commerce is the man who has inherited the instinct for it. I can't imagine Lord Frederick, for instance, or any son of yours, holding his own nowadays in the commercial world."

"Unless he were helped," the Marchioness murmured.

"There are only two sorts of help," Lord Honerton declared. "One is the giving of an opportunity. That's all right, but it isn't worth a damn unless the recipient's got the right stuff in him to make use of it. The second kind simply means providing an income which the recipient doesn't earn. I call that charity."

The Marchioness was a little ruffled. The worst of these princes of commerce, she decided, was that they had no sensibility. She was preparing to change the conversation when an event happened which to just three people in the room — to Lord Honerton, his wife, and Samuel, his brother — was possessed of a peculiar, almost a sinister significance. It was the lifting once more of a forgotten curtain of tragedy. A servant had entered the room and whispered to Martin, the impeccable butler. The latter, with a brief nod, had moved to behind Ernest Honerton's chair, and with a little bow leaned forward.

"I beg your pardon, sir," he said. "Middleton, the head keeper, is outside. He has just brought the plan of the beats up to the house. He wondered, sir, whether you had any further orders to give before he left."

The young man rose to his feet. There was perhaps a spice of vanity in the situation, but he was indeed keenly interested in the morrow's sport. He glanced towards his mother.

"Might I be excused for a moment or two?" he asked. "Middleton has brought up the plan of the beats for to-morrow, and I should like to have just a word or two with him. We lost a lot of birds at the park coverts last month, and as we finished there we didn't get them again."

The men of the party smiled approvingly, well-pleased at this reminder of the morrow's sport. The women were pleasantly indifferent, although Ernest's neighbour, who was a little minx, made a grimace at him and whispered something about not being long. But there were three people there who sat as though turned to stone. Lady Honerton's dark eyes, so much more brilliant in these later days, it had seemed, owing to the wasting of her skin, held for a moment a gleam of almost inhuman terror. From her husband's face, the patch of colour, heritage of his recent indulgences, faded into a streaky slur. His fat, pudgy fingers gripped the table on either side of him, his beady eyes seemed to have crept from underneath his eyelids till they were in danger of dropping out altogether. Further down the table, Samuel had leaned forward, his hands clasped on the top of his stout stick, his gaze wandering alternately from his brother to his sister-in-law. Ernest had walked several paces towards the door before he realised that anything was the matter. He stopped short at once as he caught sight of his father's face.

"Hullo, Dad!" he exclaimed. "Nothing wrong, is there? You wanted me to look after the shooting? It's all right for me to have a word with Middleton, isn't it? I'll be back directly."

"Quite all right," his father muttered.

"Don't be long," his mother begged.

"I feel like a naughty boy who has got down without permission," the young man laughed, as he continued his progress towards the door. "If Middleton keeps me more than a few minutes I'll join you all in the bridge room."

He passed out and the door was closed behind him. Very few people had realised the depths of the shock which for their host and hostess had brought, for a moment, an atmosphere of horrified reminiscence into the room. Conversation was resumed again almost directly. It was not until the Marchioness noticed the little beads of perspiration all over her host's forehead, that a sudden wave of memory assailed her.

"My dear Lord Honerton!" she exclaimed. "Do forgive us for not having recognised at once this most distressing coincidence. I was very young at the time — it must be thirty years ago, isn't it? — but I remember distinctly the shock we all felt, every one in the county felt, when they heard the terrible news. It was your brother, of course, who was murdered by that madman, wasn't it? And if I remember rightly he was fetched out of the room in precisely the same manner."

"The message was almost identical," Lord Honerton groaned, mopping his forehead.

"Most distressing," the Marchioness declared. "However, in this instance there need be no anxiety. Middleton is a most respectable man — Frederick thinks highly of him — and he has — er — no family.

It was the association, of course, which was so painful."

Lady Honerton rose a little abruptly, and the men,
after the departure of the women, drew closer together,
loud in their praises of their host's port, eager in their
discussion of the possible bag to-morrow. The Marquis
would have moved up to his host's left hand, but Samuel
Fernham had just anticipated him — Samuel, leaning
heavily upon his ivory-knobbed stick, had hobbled up
and sunk into the chair adjoining his brother's. He
leaned over and laid his shrivelled, yellow hand upon the
other's thick one.

" That was a shock, brother," he said quietly. " It
was like looking back into the past — that horrible
night! Never mind. That all lies thirty years behind.
That is finished."

Joseph looked at him gratefully, but with some of
the old terror still smouldering in his face.

" That is finished, Samuel," he acquiesced. " It is
the memory that never dies! "

CHAPTER III

Lord Honerton allowed his guests that evening far less time than usual for discussing his admirable port. He rose a little abruptly just as every one was settling down and led the way towards the door.

"They are waiting for some of us to play bridge," he vouchsafed by way of explanation. "The coffee and cigars will be in the card room."

There was something almost like consternation amongst those who had just filled their glasses. The Marquis declined to be hustled.

"We'll follow you in a minute, if we may, Honerton," he said. "Your port is too good to be treated in such a cavalier fashion."

Joseph mumbled something and hurried on. He was not usually a nervous man, but a queer little demon of unrest was sitting in his heart. He crossed the hall at a speed which left Samuel far behind, and looked eagerly around the bridge room. Most of the women were collected there, some already at the bridge table, one or two around the great log fire. There was no sign of Ernest, however. Through the half-closed portière he could hear the sound of billiard balls in the room beyond. He looked in there and found Judith playing another youthful member of the house party a game of pool.

"Seen anything of Ernest?" he enquired.

Judith paused in the act of chalking her cue.

"He hasn't been in here, Dad," she said. "I expect he's still with Middleton."

Joseph dropped the curtain, stepped back into the bridge room and made his way with somewhat greater deliberation towards the servants' quarters. He skirted these and, passing through a green baize door into a stone-flagged passage which led to the rear of the house, pushed open the door of the gun room. A little blue cigarette smoke was still hanging about, but the room was empty. Robinson, one of the under keepers, came out of an adjoining apartment, with the gun which he had been cleaning in his hand.

" Have you seen Mr. Ernest? " Joseph asked quickly.

" Not for the last ten minutes, my lord," the man replied. " He was in the gun room with Middleton then."

" Where is Middleton? "

" Gone home about ten minutes since, my lord."

Joseph nodded and turned away with the intention of rejoining his guests, continually telling himself he was a fool, and continually wondering at the damp on his forehead, the queer sense of impending disaster in his heart. He did his best to struggle against it, however, and exchanged casual greetings with the little stream of men whom he met crossing the hall. Arrived in the dining room, he summoned Martin.

" Martin," he enjoined, " I wish you would find Mr. Ernest for me. He has perhaps gone up to his room. If he isn't there search until you find him. I want him for bridge."

" Very good, my lord," the man replied.

Joseph returned to the bridge room. He looked around eagerly with some faint hope that he might have missed Ernest on his way to the back quarters. He was not anywhere in sight, however, nor was he in the billiard room, nor in the great lounge hall where there was another billiard table and where one or two men were playing pool. Joseph returned once more to the bridge

room, poured himself out a stiff glass of brandy and
drank it.

"Who's for bridge?" he asked, strolling towards his
guests. "We have enough for three tables, haven't we?
Will you play with me, Marchioness, and you, Lady
Levater, and you, Pownall? Good! Then you four
might play as you are," he added, with a wave of the
hand, "and Ernest can make you others up when he
comes."

"Where is Ernest?" Lady Honerton enquired, looking across at her husband. "I thought you went to
find him."

"He seems to have gone up to his room, my dear,"
the latter replied. "I've sent Martin to fetch him.
Will you come to this table, Lady Levater?"

There was a certain amount of hubbub for the next
few minutes whilst every one settled down; then com-
parative silence, broken only by the soft fall of the
cards, a subdued exclamation, and the occasional impact
of the billiard balls in the next room. Rachel, Lady
Honerton, who was not playing, sat in an easy-chair
pretending to read an evening paper, but with her eyes
fixed nearly all the time upon the door. Her husband,
who had fortified himself with another liqueur brandy,
had determined to conquer a fit of nervousness which
his sane self told him was little less than idiocy. He
puffed at a huge cigar and played his usual sound, if
somewhat aggressive, game. His skilful play of the
hand evoked his partner's heartfelt admiration.

"If I could only play like you, Lord Honerton!" she
murmured. "What I find so difficult is concentration.
I am all the time finding my mind wander off to something else when I particularly want to watch the dis-
cards or count how many trumps are in."

"Concentration," Joseph pronounced, keeping his eyes sedulously turned away from the door, "is one of the disciplines of life."

The Marchioness sighed.

"That sounds like a copy-book maxim," she declared, "but they never did help one a bit in real life, did they?"

The door was opened and Martin, followed by two footmen who had come in to remove the coffee equipage, entered the room. He made his way at once to his master's chair and stood there for a moment whilst a hand was being played, in respectful silence. As soon as the last card had fallen he made his report.

"I am sorry, my lord, but I have not been able to find Mr. Ernest," he announced. "I have been up to his suite of rooms, and I have tried the picture gallery, the ballroom and the squash racket court."

"Have you been in the library?" Joseph enquired.

"I went there first, my lord. There is nowhere in the house I have not tried."

Samuel came hobbling across the room, a queer look of concern in his gaunt face.

"What's become of the lad, Joseph?" he demanded. "What does Martin say?"

"It appears that he is not in the house anywhere," was the strained reply.

Major Pownall, who knew nothing of the family history, was impatient to get on with the game. He looked up from the cards which he had just sorted.

"Well, nothing can have happened to him here, can it?" he observed. "And after all it is not many minutes since he was with your keeper. He may have strolled out with him or gone to see what sort of a night it is."

"Anything in the nature of uneasiness is of course absurd," Joseph declared firmly, picking up his own cards. "It is simply irritating that he should have left three people waiting to play bridge."

"What is it, Dad?" Judith asked, coming through the portière. "Where's Ernest?"

"Hiding, apparently, because he doesn't want to play bridge with us," Joyce Cloughton, one of the three who were left out, observed. "I don't wonder. I let him down shockingly last week at home."

"He wouldn't mind about that," Judith laughed, "but it's too bad of him to keep you waiting. Shall I make you up until he comes? — All the same I wonder where on earth he can be," she added, as she took her place at the table.

"Martin can't find him anywhere," her father observed. "He'll probably turn up, though, in a few minutes."

"Is there anything more I can do, my lord?" the butler enquired.

"Telephone over to the garage and keep your eyes open," Joseph directed. "The lad has a new car he drove down from London in," he explained to the Marchioness. "He may have gone over to have a look at it."

Again the game proceeded; deal followed deal. Samuel sat in an easy-chair on one side of the great wood fire, thoughtful and absorbed. Rachel Honerton no longer made a pretence of reading the evening paper. She sat with her eyes steadfastly fixed upon the door. Half an hour, three quarters of an hour passed and with it the effects of Joseph's second liqueur brandy. At the end of a rubber he laid down his cards.

"I must ask you to excuse me for a few minutes," he

said. "This absurd escapade of Ernest's is getting on my nerves. I must make a few further enquiries."

"It does seem queer," Major Pownall acknowledged, glancing at the clock.

Joseph left his place and crossed the room towards his wife. The Marchioness leaned forward and in an undertone began to tell Major Pownall of the tragedy which had happened in the house thirty years ago. Joseph, as he approached his wife, tried hard to smile. It was rather a ghastly attempt. Her eyes watched his expression anxiously.

"My dear," he said soothingly, "it is ridiculous to be anxious about Ernest. At the same time I am very angry with him. He ought not to desert my guests in this fashion. I am going out to make a few more enquiries."

Rachel was only maintaining her self-control with an effort. Her long thin fingers were crushing the newspaper she held.

"Let me know, let me know quickly," she begged. "It seems absurd, of course, but if only Ernest had not sat in the same place, if Martin had not come round to him in the same way, given almost the same message! It was like a tragedy thrown back from hell!"

"Rubbish, my dear!" Joseph scoffed. "Sheer rubbish! These sort of things don't repeat themselves. It's just the setting. Damned unpleasant, but that's all! There'll be news of the lad directly."

Joseph bustled out of the room, found his way to his private study and sent for Martin. The latter appeared almost at once, ushering in Middleton, the keeper, a lanky weather-beaten man, a little disturbed at this unexpected summons, which had reached him just as he had been on the point of going to bed. In his haste he had forgotten to replace either his collar or tie, a fact of which he was nervously conscious.

"I sent for Mr. Middleton in case your lordship would care to have a word with him," Martin explained.

Joseph nodded. He was making a brave attempt to treat the affair lightly.

"We seem to have lost Mr. Ernest, Middleton," he said. "Have you any idea what became of him after he had finished with you?"

"I can't say, I am sure, my lord," was the doubtful reply. "I left him in the gun room."

"Did he seem much as usual?"

"I couldn't see no difference, my lord."

"He didn't give you any hint which might account for his absence at the present moment?"

The keeper shook his head, obviously mystified.

"All that I can call to mind about the young gentleman was that he seemed in a rare hurry to get back again. He did say something about having to play in a game called 'bridge' — I think it was, your lordship."

"Sorry to have fetched you up, Middleton," Joseph concluded, with a dismissing wave of the hand. "See that they give you a glass of wine in the servants' hall. — You have nothing more to say to me, Martin?"

"Nothing, my lord. Except that I should like to tell you that I have satisfied myself personally that Mr. Ernest is not in the house."

"And the cars were all in the garage?"

"Miles, the head chauffeur, has gone out himself to look them over, my lord. There were several visitors' cars the others weren't sure about."

Joseph looked at his watch.

"It is now five-and-twenty past eleven, Martin," he pointed out. "Just two hours since Mr. Ernest left the dining table to give a few simple orders to Middleton. What the devil can have become of him?"

"He can't be far away, your lordship," the man ventured.

His master brooded over the matter for a few moments, then turned towards the door. As he neared the threshold Martin spoke.

"I beg your lordship's pardon for making the suggestion, but would you care for me to ring up the police station at Norwich?"

Joseph was conscious of a little shiver. More than ever this strange affair of Ernest's disappearance was becoming full of hateful reminiscence.

"I don't think we need treat the thing quite so seriously as that, Martin," he declared, with an attempt at lightness in his tone. "After all, it's only a matter of two hours."

"If your lordship will excuse my saying so," the man observed respectfully, "Mr. Ernest isn't one of those harum-scarum young gentlemen. He's not likely to be in any trouble or anything of that sort."

"That's all right, Martin," his master acquiesced. "He's a good lad, as steady and level-headed as I am myself. That's what makes the whole damned thing so extraordinary."

"Just so, your lordship," Martin agreed.

Joseph, Lord Honerton, returned unwillingly to his guests. Except so far as regarded himself, his wife and Samuel, it was impossible for any one to fully appreciate the tragic note in this curious event. It was scarcely callousness, but the rank improbability of anything serious having happened to their host's son, which kept the rest of the party unconcerned. Half a dozen of them were playing "fives" on the billiard table and another four at bridge had been arranged. Rachel was knitting with fingers which seemed to fly faster than ever, but her eyes called wildly to her husband's across the space of the room. He shook his head with a cheerfulness which was half bravado.

"Anything been heard of the young man?" some one asked.

"Not yet," Joseph replied. "Miles is down looking over the cars. Thoughtless young idiot! I'll give him a talking to when he gets back!"

"Any poachers about, do you think? Could he have heard a gun?" another of the male guests suggested.

Joseph shook his head doubtfully.

"There are four keepers on duty to-night and no report has been made. Poachers wouldn't get much quarter here. I give most of the game away and employ half the neighbourhood. — Yes, my dear."

He crossed the room towards his wife. Her fingers were uncanny in their distortions and streams of light flashed from her stabbing needles.

"You have heard no news, Joseph?" she asked.

"None."

"You have met with no fresh cause for fear?"

"Pshaw! Of course not!" he answered with well-simulated impatience. "You and I are making idiots of ourselves over this business, Mother. Nothing can have happened to the boy. He was in no sort of trouble. He couldn't have had an enemy in the world, and he's as strong as a horse. We're making idiots of ourselves — positive idiots!"

Rachel made no remark. Her brain was a little weary, but the pall of apprehension remained. From the inner room Martin made a discreet reappearance.

"I thought you would like to know, my lord, that

Miles has just got back from the garage," he announced. "None of the cars is missing, nor is there any sign of any one of them having been tampered with."

"So that's that," Joseph murmured, a little aimlessly.

"Some of the under servants," the man continued, "have made up a little search party of their own and taken every room, back and front, including the cellars. It is absolutely certain that Mr. Ernest is not in the house. Two or three of the men have been through the outhouses and shrubberies and they have handed in a similar report. George, Mr. Ernest's own valet, has been through his master's things and assured me that not even a pair of shoes is missing. Mr. Ernest was wearing very thin slippers for dinner."

"Well, that settles one thing, anyway," Joseph declared. "He can't be far away. Let the servants retire at the usual time, Martin, and stop all gossip as much as you can."

"I shall discourage it as far as possible, my lord," was Martin's valedictory assurance.

From the billiard room came sounds of laughter and the shrieking of voices as the younger people played their unruly game, and from the bridge table in the corner the monotonous patter of the cards, the methodical calling over of the score. Joseph and his wife were in a little corner of the room alone. Rachel's fingers were still busy with their nervous task, but there were lines of anguish in her face.

"Can't you feel it, Ernest?" she whispered. "Somewhere in the background — not so far away — it seems to me that I can hear it all the time, and they laugh and deal! And in the billiard room — what a hubbub!"

"What do you mean?" he demanded. "What can you hear?"

The fingers slackened in their speed, the needles ceased to flash. There was all the throb and pain of actual tragedy in her mournful words.

"Ernest!" she whispered. "He's lost. He's gone into the darkness, and we don't know where to find him. We don't know!"

Joseph was half irritated, half apprehensive.

"What the devil are you talking about, Rachel?" he exclaimed. "Ernest's all right! He must be all right!"

His wife made no reply. She had recommenced her knitting.

CHAPTER IV

JUDITH, who had been a little restless in her movements during a morning of singular and tense unreality, finally pitched her shooting stick by Freddy Amberleys' side. He signalised the occasion by bringing down a very creditable right and left of high-flying cock pheasants. She decided to remain.

"I don't really enjoy watching shooting," she confessed, "but if I must I prefer to see it well done. I suppose you are a good shot, Freddy?"

"One of the best in the county," he assured her, with cheerful vaingloriousness.

She sighed gently.

"This confidence," she murmured, "is one of the most pleasing characteristics of extreme youth. Ignore me, please, and mark over on your left."

Again, her companion did his duty satisfactorily and Judith smiled approval upon him.

"Tell me," he enquired, a few minutes later, "what is that heap of ruins just outside the covert. I noticed them last time I was here."

A shade of rather sombre concern darkened Judith's beautiful face.

"Those stones," she explained, "are the remains of a tragedy which occurred here thirty years ago — long before I was born, and when you, I should think, were in your cradle."

"I've never heard about it," he observed curiously. "What was it?"

"It happened," she continued, "on the eve of a shooting party, just like this one. My father's youngest brother, Cecil, who was rather by way of being the family favourite, was murdered by the head keeper."

" I remember now," he acknowledged. " I heard the whole story in the smoking room last night."

" There was a girl, of course," she proceeded, " and the usual sordid business. You probably heard as much about it as I know. The tragedy, however, consisted in the fact that, without a doubt, the keeper never meant to kill my uncle, but was disturbed and threw him backwards so that he hit his head upon the stone floor."

" What happened to the keeper? " Amberleys asked.

" He was hung," was the quiet reply.

" The devil! It doesn't sound like anything more than manslaughter."

" The man was arraigned for murder and found guilty with a strong recommendation for mercy," Judith went on. " No one doubted but that he would get off with twenty years' penal servitude, but my grandfather — Israel Fernham, who was an old gentleman of singularly unforgiving temperament — had great influence with the Government at that time and he moved heaven and earth to prevent any reduction of the sentence. In the end he succeeded, although there was a terrible scandal, and the Home Secretary very soon afterwards resigned. Those ruins you were asking me about are the remains of the keeper's cottage. My grandfather had it razed to the ground on the day the man was hanged, and would never allow it to be rebuilt."

There was a brief interlude, whilst Judith's companion added to his bag. Then the beaters appeared at the end of the wood and the two young people strolled off together to the next stand.

" That old grandfather of yours must have been quite a character," Amberleys remarked.

"I suppose I'm wrong," she confessed, "but I admire him immensely. He was a strict Jew, a follower of the Mosaic law. He never smoked or touched wine or indulged in any of the modern luxuries. There were no rules in his household. Every one did as they chose, but he himself lived the most austere and simple life. He never failed a friend, and he never forgave an enemy. Cecil's death, however, broke his heart. He only lived for a very short time afterwards.

"It is curious," she continued, with a little tremor in her tone, "that you should have asked me about those ruins to-day. Do you know what my Uncle Samuel told me this morning? Cecil was fetched out from the dining table to see the keeper about the morrow's shooting exactly in the same way that Ernest was sent for last night. My mother and father and Uncle Samuel were there, of course. Can't you imagine how it must all have come back to them last night — the horror of it, the same message, the same hour, Ernest, again the youngest of our family — and now, this disappearance of his?"

"Most amazing coincidence I ever heard of in my life," the young man admitted. "Quite enough to upset any one!"

"Of course," she went on, "there couldn't be any possible connection between the two things. Middleton, this present keeper, as it happens, is a bachelor, and Ernest, I believe, is a remarkably moral young man. All the same there's something almost morbidly horrible ——"

"I think it's unspeakable," Amberleys interrupted. "Your father must be an awfully good sport to have gone on with to-day. I wonder he didn't send us all home till things were cleared up, anyhow."

She shook her head. There was a dreamy look in her velvety eyes.

"I think that we Jews are all fatalists," she said. "Father and Mother and Uncle Samuel are of course unbalanced by memories and associations. I cannot think it possible that anything could have happened to Ernest."

They were standing at the end of a glade and from some distance away came the sound of the tapping of trees, the shouts of the beaters, occasionally the keeper's whistle. They drew a few yards apart; Amberleys mechanically on the *qui vive*, Judith lost in a little sea of drifting impressions. It was a still day towards the end of October, fine and warm, but with the colours fading now from the clear sky. There was a queer smell of rotting undergrowth mingled with the odour of a recently kindled bonfire of weeds in the corner of an adjacent field. The air was becoming a little chilly, the trees beginning to take to themselves more definite shape. A promise of frost was in the air; the twigs broke crisply under the feet of the advancing beaters. The sound of firing all around was now much more frequent, and, her companion's attention being fully engaged, Judith found herself suddenly studying, with a curiously detached interest, the man whom she knew that she was expected to marry. Against his personal appearance there was not a word to be said. He was tall, inclined to sturdiness, but after all it was a man's figure. His features, without being regular, were good enough, his slightly red hair had a tendency to curl in a becoming fashion, his expression was frank and even amiable. He had sat in the House of Commons for two years and had made one or two speeches with moderate success. His politics were stereotyped but sincere. His outlook upon

the wider subjects of life, considering his upbringing and
characteristics, not intolerant.   Judith permitted her
thoughts to dwell deliberately upon the prospect of becoming Lady Frederick Amberleys, and afterwards
Marchioness of Holt.   There was a town house, and a
country estate, of course.   Her own great fortune
might provide also a flat in Paris, a palace at Venice
or a Villa on the Riviera.   She might count upon re-
taining a certain measure of the more intellectual life
to which she was already becoming accustomed, but a
measure which would have its limitations.   Nothing, for
instance, could interfere with the shooting.   The hunt-
ing would follow.   A grudging month in town for the
season, perhaps.   A month for a flying visit abroad.
Then the cubbing. — Supposing she decided to strike out
a line of her own?   She was the wrong woman to do
that, she thought, with a faint smile.   Life and heredity
had given her an amazing temperament; the fervid,
almost passionate imagination of the gifted of her race.
She was an unfaltering judge of herself and her weaknesses.   Venice with its traditions, Florence with its art,
Paris with its nameless sense of excitement, were no
places for her to visit as a wanderer alone.   Realising
this, was it wise for her to marry at all a man of Amberleys' type? — She found herself watching the rabbits
and an occasional hare as they rushed through the undergrowth, pausing for a moment at the sight of her, and
either dashing back again, or taking their chance of
safety — a poor one, as it happened, for both Amberleys and the gun on either side were shooting well.   One
hare in particular almost sat up and looked at her, ran
this way and that, dumb terror in its eyes, and finally
scurried by her, only to be sent head over heels in a
lifeless heap when it had reached the line of safety.   She

gave a little shiver. After all, it was death. She found
herself thinking of Ernest — an absurd connection, she
told herself, and yet there it was. The sense of fore-
boding, which she had carried with her all day, was
suddenly redoubled. As they walked homeward across
the park her feet scarcely seemed to touch the turf with
its little crackling hardness of frost. Amberleys, struggling to keep up with her, handed his gun at last to his
loader who was following behind.

"You say that you are no athlete," he remarked
good-humouredly. "I shouldn't like to take you on at
a walking match."

"I want to know if there is any news," she confided.
"Somehow or other I have managed so far to keep all
anxieties at the back of my mind, but the day has been
rather a nightmare, hasn't it? I hoped we should have
heard something by this time."

Her companion nodded sympathetically.

"It's one of those things which must be cleared up
before long," he observed. "A young fellow like Ernest
can't vanish into thin air, and he can't go far in a
dress suit and dancing pumps. There are no secret
wells or chambers at Honerton, are there?"

"None that I ever heard of," she replied.

"Then don't you worry," he begged. "Time enough,
if you've got to, when you hear something definite.
And — er — Lady Judith, you've got enough to think
about and worry about just now, but I don't like to go
away without telling you that there was something I
had it in my mind to say — that I wanted to say up in
town — but one gets so little chance to see you alone
there."

"As you aren't going to say it," she rejoined, with a
faint note of warning in her tone, "let us leave it alone

altogether, for the present, shall we? I feel that I have
more than enough to think about just now — that I
couldn't consider anything rationally until we at least
understand something about Ernest."

"That's all right," Amberleys assented with resigna-
tion. "I only thought that I'd give you an idea that it
had been in my mind, so that you knew what to expect,
eh?" he added a little nervously. "I see the family
omnibus is there waiting, with all the luggage, so I
expect that means we're booked to take our departure."

A sharp turn and a few minutes' climb had brought
them into sudden view of the house. To Judith's intense
sensibility there was something almost sinister in its
great unlit front with the smoke ascending straight from
many chimneys, and a faint mist rising in the park on
either side. Several cars were standing in the sweep
before the hall door. The shiver of a new and more
poignant anxiety chilled Judith.

"Evidently there is no news, then!" she exclaimed.

They hurried on, only to find that her surmise had
been correct. Incredible though it seemed to all of
them, not the slightest trace of Ernest had been found,
nor had any word come from him; a condition of affairs
which could no longer be regarded as anything but
gravely portentous. Most of the local guests had
slipped quietly away. Judith enquired for her father.

"His lordship is in the library with the gentlemen
from Scotland Yard," Martin told her. "Her ladyship is there, too."

Judith bade a few more adieux, and hastened to join
her parents. Two visitors of unmistakably professional
appearance were seated at the table, her father was
standing on the hearthrug, Rachel was seated in an
easy-chair, bolt upright, with her hands upon her lap.

"My daughter, Lady Judith," Joseph muttered, in a drab tone.

Both men rose at once to their feet.

"Is there really no news?" Judith asked almost incredulously. "Haven't you discovered anything at all?"

"We have had no success up to the present, Lady Judith," the detective who seemed to be in charge of the affair, confessed. "Your brother appears to have left the house last night immediately after his visitor, Middleton, the keeper. He walked down the back avenue, sometimes on the avenue itself and sometimes on the turf, as far as a gate which leads on to a very rough road, which Lord Honerton tells me is seldom used except for carting timber. From there we have lost all traces of him, but there are some indications of a car having been down the road. My men are searching it thoroughly now."

"And this is all you have discovered?" Judith exclaimed. "We still haven't the faintest idea where Ernest is?"

"Not the faintest," was the somewhat curt reply. "Disappearances as a rule," the detective went on, "are easily classified. They arise from loss of memory, fear of apprehension for some crime or misdeed, or an affair in which a woman is concerned. Loss of memory in this case seems scarcely feasible, as this would certainly not drive the young man out of the house. Your father insists upon it that the regularity of your brother's life renders the other two impossible. We seem, therefore, to be up against an entirely novel problem."

"This gentleman is Inspector Rodes," Joseph intervened, addressing Judith. "Mr. Rodes has had charge of most of the famous disappearance cases for the last ten years. There is not one of them, he tells me, which he has failed in the end to clear up."

"One may meet one's Waterloo at any time, of course," Rodes observed, "but I must admit that I do not look upon absolute disappearances as possible in these days. We have scarcely one record upon our books where we have failed to locate the missing person in time. And I am bound to say," he went on, with a slightly apologetic smile, "that we have invariably found the information given us by relatives entirely misleading. That is why I shall be forced, if I continue the conduct of this case, to make my own enquiries into your son's life and habits. Motiveless disappearances do not afford us a practical problem."

"You can do as you choose," Joseph declared brusquely. "All that I want is my boy."

The telephone bell commenced to ring. The instrument stood upon the table by the side of which Judith was seated. She picked up the receiver and listened indifferently. Suddenly her whole expression changed. Her eyes flashed. She threw out her arm.

"Ernest, Ernest!" she cried. "Go on, dear. Where are you? It is I, Judith!"

There was a moment's pause. Every one in the room was breathless with excitement. Rodes stole closer to the instrument.

"Ernest!" Judith pleaded. "Go on, go on! Tell me where you are."

Again she paused, and this time there was something like terror in her face. She handed the receiver to the detective.

"I heard his voice," she faltered. "He asked if this was Honerton Chase. Then he never spoke again. It seems all dead."

Rodes held the receiver to his ear.

" Hullo! " he shouted. " Hullo! "

There was no response. He rang up violently and held the receiver once more to his ear. The slightly cynical expression had left his face. He was genuinely interested. He turned to the little company.

" The line is dead," he announced. " Either the wire has been cut or there has been some accident! "

CHAPTER V

INSPECTOR RODES, one morning about a month after the disappearance of Ernest Fernham, looked at his notebook and found himself down for a consultation with the chief of his department. He made his way to the latter's office at the time appointed, and accepted the chair to which he was motioned. The two men sat facing one another on either side of a plain office table.

" I wanted to talk to you, Rodes, about this Fernham disappearance," Major Lorton, the Assistant Chief Commissioner, commenced.

The Inspector indulged in a slight grimace. There was no subject at the present time more utterly distasteful to him. He waited in silence to hear what his chief had to say.

" Of course I know," the latter continued, " that a case is a case to you, and that you'd work as hard on it for nothing as for the five thousand pounds reward which has just been offered. There's more than the matter of the reward to it, however. The efficiency of our whole department is being questioned. A young man in evening clothes, without an overcoat or hat, with apparently a blameless past, is spirited away from his family mansion in Norfolk and not even a trace of the message which summoned him has been discovered. On the face of it, the thing seems incredible! "

" It is incredible," Rodes admitted.

" What about his daily life? " the Assistant Commissioner asked. " You went into that thoroughly, of course. Was there no weak spot in it at all? "

" Not one," was the confident reply. " The young man — like so many of his race — seems to have been

exceptionally domesticated. His father had offered him
rooms of his own but he preferred to live at home. He
dined out often at the Ritz and Claridge's, but always
with his sister or friends in her circle. He had some
acquaintance with a few young ladies in the theatrical
profession, but they are quite the best of their type and
he was very seldom in their company. He had a large
allowance and a large income, and, although he seems
to have been fairly liberal, he was quite unable to spend
either. His private balance at his bank to-day stands
at over fifteen thousand pounds, and he owns a quarter
of a million pounds' worth of shares in the Fernham
business. He lived a pleasant, harmless life, and never
seems to have committed a single action which might
produce enmity on any one's part. He was rather
particular about his men friends and he has never been
seen with one of those whom we have upon our doubtful
list as probable blackmailers. You can rule out the
possibility of financial embarrassment, intrigue of any
sort with a woman, enmity on the part of any one whom
he may have wronged, or blackmailing threats."

"That," the Assistant Commissioner remarked, "does
not leave us much to go on."

"It leaves us nothing," the other assented.

Major Lorton frowned.

"We can't sit down under this, you know, Rodes,"
he said. "Let us leave the inner springs of the thing
for a minute or two and come to the few details we
have."

"I went over the whole of the ground myself," Rodes
declared, "starting from the gun room at the back of
the house where he was last seen. He must have left
the house by a certain back door, as otherwise he would
have met servants or passed the main kitchens. There

were slight indications in the drive of some one lightly shod having passed along as far as a gate about a hundred yards from the house, which leads on to a very rough road, chiefly used for carting timber. I found faint traces of a motor tyre in the ruts here, but I subsequently learned that both Lord Honerton's agent and the merchant who comes to buy the timber use that road in their cars. Naturally every possible enquiry as to strange automobiles in the vicinity has been pressed home — without the slightest result, however. Neither has a description of the young man himself produced any credible story."

"Then there was the telephone call," Major Lorton observed. "What about that?"

"I have visited the telephone exchange at Fakenham and the head office at Norwich," Rodes replied. "The young woman who took the call declares that it came from a call office, but she was very busy and made no note of its exact source. The company has made every effort to discover this for me, without result. The smashing of the line afterwards was without doubt an accident. They were felling timber in a plantation around which the wire comes, and one of the trees on which they had started had been left till the following morning half sawn through. It had been a perfectly still day and the tree itself seemed absolutely safe. A sudden wind sprang up that evening, however, and the tree fell, cutting the branch wire to Honerton Chase and another one to a house beyond. It was a cruel coincidence but nevertheless it was a coincidence."

"We learnt nothing, then, from the telephone call, except that the young man is still alive," Major Lorton remarked.

"Nothing."

" And there we are."

" And there we are," Rodes echoed gloomily.

" You will admit, I presume," the Commissioner went on, after a moment's silence, " that the situation is extremely unsatisfactory."

" I admit it most heartily," his subordinate agreed.

" Have you any theory on the subject whatsoever? "

" I have worn myself out with theories," Rodes acknowledged. " In the end only the shell of one remains, and that's too vague to be of any value or interest."

"All the same," Major Lorton urged gently ——

" It comes to this," Rodes interrupted. " I defy any one to explain the disappearance of this young man by any ordinary means. He hadn't an enemy in the world and he's one of the richest young men in the country. The one possibility left is that he has been abducted for the sake of a ransom — or possibly for the sake of the reward if his people can be induced to open their mouths wide enough. But when you come to ask me by what means he was induced to leave the house that night and to place himself in the power of any one, all I can say is that, considering the affair on the basis of everything that is known to us at present, it is absolutely inexplicable."

" I note your reservations," the other observed. " Continue, please."

" If I do," Rodes sighed, " I wander straight into the realms of nonsense. Science, however, is making fools of us every day, and I ask myself this question: is there any fresh discovery pending which might have been anticipated perhaps by some criminal brain before it has been announced to the world? If science won't help us here, what will? After all, why shouldn't a man be able to make himself invisible, for instance? Maskeleyne and Cook have done it, or produced the same effect."

" This is very interesting from the point of view of pure speculation," the Commissioner remarked drily, " but it isn't exactly the sort of thing the public are expecting from us."

" We haven't the goods the public want in this case, and they may as well know it," was the blunt reply. " I can't lay claim even to the possession of a clue. If the young man had gone as far as the back door to see his keeper off, one might build up an interesting hypothesis. He didn't, though. The keeper is very positive as to that. Get him as far as that back door and the possibilities have become more interesting. A flash of light in the lane. A call for help. A shadow in the drive. Anything might have tempted him out that little way."

"And when you have him at the gate, what then? " Major Lorton enquired. " He must have gone willingly. There were no signs of any struggle. It was market night and a good many carts were about. A young man in evening dress would have been a somewhat noticeable occupant of any vehicle."

" I am still presuming at the back of my mind," Rodes continued, " the existence of special ways and means for the transportation of this young man and a special influence to control his actions."

" You're harking back to the supernatural again? "

" Supernatural to the vulgar," Rodes objected. " Science to us."

The Commissioner sighed.

" I have to make a report to the Home Secretary on this case," he announced. " You don't suppose that this sort of stuff is any use to me? "

"I am not suggesting that it is," Rodes rejoined.
"I was talking to you as man to man, and I still say,
although I believe in the supernatural as little as you
do, that there are circumstances in connection with the
disappearance of Ernest Fernham which cannot be accounted for except by the admission of some new
agency."

"What a confession!" Major Lorton groaned.
"For heaven's sake, keep it to yourself!"

"You don't suppose I want to talk about it," was
the inspector's dogged response. "It's got on my
nerves already more than any case I've ever handled in
my life."

"You keep on earth sufficiently to admit that you
think it's blackmail that's intended — I mean a
ransom?"

"There isn't any other conceivable motive," the other
agreed. "If the Home Secretary wants sound advice
to hand on to Lord Honerton, I should advise him to
make the reward twenty thousand pounds, and no
questions asked."

"It's a humiliating position for us," the Commissioner
grumbled.

"It's worse for me than for any one," Rodes pointed
out. "It's my department, my responsibility. I can't
even talk intelligently about it, as you've realised.
Isn't it the most hopeless confession that an official in
my position could possibly make to his chief? — I can't
find the young man. I haven't a clue as to the perpe-
trators of his abduction. I am driven to recommend
the offering of a reward of twenty thousand pounds and
no questions asked!"

Rodes walked gloomily westward after his interview
with the Assistant Commissioner, apparently the same

as ever; keen-eyed, watchful, slightly pugnacious. His outward appearance, however, was no index to his feelings. The spirit had gone out of his work. He felt the humiliation of failure, the unspoken censure of his department, acutely. He was depressed and miserable. At the corner of St. James's Street, the most beautiful young woman he had ever seen in his life stepped out of her limousine, glanced at him with recognition in her eyes, and then paused.

"How do you do," she said. "It is Inspector Rodes, isn't it?"

"It is," he assented, "and of course you are Lady Judith Fernham. I have just come from a consultation at Scotland Yard on your brother's case."

"No news yet?" she asked, a little wistfully.

"None," he admitted.

He was prepared to pass on, but, although she did not immediately continue the conversation, she seemed anxious to detain him. Inspector Rodes, worried though he was, permitted himself for a moment or two the pleasure of watching her. She wore a chinchilla coat and hat, the latter a turban with a flash of unexpected colour. He knew very little of such things, but he realised that the geranium scarlet of her lips owed nothing to artifice, that her silky eyebrows, though their very perfection seemed to make them appear unnatural, were untouched by any pencil. The cold had brought a faint flush of colour into her usually ivory-tinted cheeks. Her eyes — almost black they were — fascinated him by their exquisite setting and softness. Her brows were a little knitted. She was evidently pursuing a thought which had crept into her mind.

"Mr. Rodes," she said, "don't think I agree with all those stupid criticisms in the papers, but isn't it rather an astonishing thing that a disappearance like my brother's should be possible nowadays? "

" If we don't clear it up soon, it will be the greatest humiliation of my professional career, Lady Judith," he acknowledged. " I cannot tell you how badly we all feel about it — I, worst of all, because it is my department."

" I am going to say something which may sound foolish, perhaps," she went on, " but you know I am a very imaginative person, and I sometimes think that where logic fails, imagination steps in and helps. Did you ever hear of the incident which happened thirty years ago in that very dining room under precisely similar circumstances? "

" I did, indeed, Lady Judith," the Inspector admitted. " That was even a greater tragedy."

" You've never thought of connecting the two, I suppose? " she asked abruptly.

" Connecting them? Not seriously," he assured her. " Stop a moment, though," he corrected himself. " I made the obvious enquiries, of course. I discovered that the family of Heggs had been extinct in Norfolk for twenty-five years and that your present keeper, Middleton, is a bachelor and a Dorset man."

" That sounds convincing enough," she murmured. "And yet ——"

"And yet? " he repeated, after waiting patiently for a few moments.

" Well, you see," she continued, " I have only the imagination to suppose things. I am like the water diviner who taps the ground where other people dig, but if I were you and had come to the end of all my resources, I should discard facts for a little time and try surmises. — Good-bye, Mr. Rodes! Let me hear from you, if you adopt my suggestion and anything comes of it."

She passed on across the pavement and entered a shop. Inspector Rodes continued thoughtfully on his way.

CHAPTER VI

WITH all his faults, and Joseph, second Baron Honerton, had many, it could never be said that he was ashamed of his origin or of the source of his wealth. He was never happier than when showing distinguished strangers over the marvellous Works from which his fortune flowed. Distinguished strangers were common enough, especially foreigners, for the Works themselves were in every way unique. Royalty, however, even in somewhat remote connection, was entirely a new departure, and Royalty introduced and accompanied by his daughter was an honour which made him for a moment forget his troubles and remember only the mighty organisation of which he was the head. The presence, too, of Frederick Amberleys was extremely gratifying. It was as well for his prospective son-in-law to realise the source of that vast wealth, a portion of which was to pass some day into his keeping.

" This warehouse, now," Joseph pointed out, standing in the midst of it and indicating an immense vista of counter and shelves, " is absolutely the largest room of its sort in the United Kingdom. There is an electric tramway, as you see, running its entire length. The stores are kept at this end, the packing is done at the other. The duty of all these people," he went on, directing his visitors' attention to forty or fifty young men and women in white overalls, " is to examine the products as they come up from the factory and pass them down to the packing room. These casks which are coming up, for instance, contain ' Maltby's Honey Milk '. They will be sent down to the other end, and packed in jars or tins according as it is for the home or the export market."

" So you make ' Maltby's Honey Milk ' ? " Amberleys exclaimed. " Tophole stuff! I had it when I was getting over the fever."

" We manufacture at the present moment," Joseph declared, " three hundred and thirteen different sorts of patent medicines and foods; including, I am sure, more than half the specifics you have ever heard of. ' Phillip's Lung Tonic ', for instance. ' Meadows' Beef Tea ', and dozens of others. We're the largest manufacturers of pills in the world, and though we have a plant going day and night we find it difficult to keep up with the demand."

" I am always interested in these advertisements of patent medicines," the Prince remarked. " One is warned against them, but I suppose some of them must be quite good."

" The drugs and foods that are turned out from this establishment," Joseph announced, " are absolutely and entirely pure. Patent medicines have an undeservedly bad name. Manufactured as we manufacture them you could not get purer stuff. The prescriptions are all the result of studied medical labour and no small chemist can command drugs of the quality we are able to buy. Our head chemist is a very wizard — the most celebrated young man in Europe."

" Do you ever take any of your medicines yourself, sir? " Frederick Amberleys asked.

" When I have anything the matter with me I never hesitate," was the prompt reply. " We make ' Donat ', the celebrated cure for indigestion. I take it whenever I have an attack and it never fails to relieve me. I have confidence in it because I know how it is made.

The prescription is there with the others in my safe. Come and I will show you some of the manufacturing processes."

The trio dutifully followed their guide and saw strange sights. They saw great vats of a famous " Nervine " being stirred by slowly turning wheels into the proper degree of consistency, pills flying from an amazing-looking machine at the rate of a hundred a minute, roots and hard knobbly nuts without shells being ground into a powder by yet another machine. They started from the basement, where the floor was of stone and huge vats full of liquid, some aromatic and some the reverse, were being warmed, tested and mixed, and mounted by slow stages to the fourth storey where the bottling was done. On the fifth floor, to which they finally ascended, there were long rows of men bending over fixed receptacles, which glistened like silver.

" This is where the more expensive remedies are prepared," Joseph explained. " There are two hundred men over on that side alone, mixing ' Mason's Cough Cure ', a medicine which has to be carefully handled. And here, in a sense," he added, passing on, " is the most important part of the whole building. I am myself responsible below for the commercial and financial side of the undertaking. This is the headquarters of the science and brain which direct it."

They had reached a solid mahogany door, set in a partition which extended the whole width of the building. Joseph knocked almost tentatively before entering, and ushered his companions into a large, handsomely furnished room, three walls of which were lined to the ceiling with bookcases, whilst the fourth was completely given up to a huge safe. A young man who had been writing at a desk rose to his feet at their entrance.

"Is Sir Lawrence in the laboratory?" Joseph enquired.

"I believe so, my lord," the young man answered doubtfully.

"Ask him to spare us five minutes. Tell him that Prince Edgar is here, looking over the Works."

The young man disappeared through an inner door. Joseph lowered his voice.

"You've probably heard of Sir Lawrence Paule," he said. "Quite a young man, but the most brilliant chemist in the world — taken every possible degree at London, Oxford and Leipzig, did marvellous things in the war and was the first scientist knighted. He is responsible now for the whole of our productions and we had a report from a committee of analysts only a few months ago, stating that they had never reached so high a standard. We pay him the salary of a Cabinet Minister, but he's worth it."

The messenger returned.

"If you will be seated, my lord," he invited, "Sir Lawrence will be here directly."

The little party accepted chairs and indulged in desultory conversation.

"Your safe looks formidable," the Prince observed.

"It needs to be," Joseph answered. "It holds all our secrets; the original prescriptions from which most of our products are made are in there, and a great many others, even more important — some there I wouldn't let a certain German firm see for fifty thousand pounds."

"I suppose the Germans are your greatest competitors?" Amberleys enquired.

"They used to be," Joseph replied. "Since the war, though, they can't buy the drugs."

"Tell us about this paragon of a scientist who is keeping us all waiting," Judith begged curiously.

Her father frowned warningly. The door opposite had opened and a man in a grey tweed suit, a flannel shirt and collar, and a tie the colours of a famous cricket club, entered. He paused for a moment to speak to the young man who had summoned him. Then he advanced to meet his visitors. Judith, who was seldom surprised, was staring at him in frank astonishment.

"Let me present you, Sir Lawrence," Joseph said, rising to his feet. "Sorry to disturb you but we are very much honoured this morning. Sir Lawrence Paule, our head chemist — His Highness Prince Edgar of Galwey — my daughter, Lady Judith — Lord Amberleys."

The newcomer acknowledged the introductions with composure. Judith's eyes had scarcely once left his face.

"Surely I have met you lately, haven't I?" she asked wonderingly.

"Indefinitely," he admitted. "We met in the Lawn Tennis Competition at Queen's last week. I was playing with Lady Ferber, if you remember."

"Of course I remember," she exclaimed. "You wiped the floor with us. Lady Ferber's introduction was almost inaudible, and I never caught your name."

"Your partner was very much off his game," Paule remarked. — "I am so sorry to have kept you waiting this morning. I was trying a slight experiment in the inner analyst's room, and was obliged to see it through. Would your visitors care to see the private laboratories, Lord Honerton?"

"We should like to very much," Judith declared promptly, without waiting for any one else to reply.

Sir Lawrence turned away for a moment, with a word of excuse, to give some instructions to the young man who was obviously his secretary. Judith's eyes continued to follow him. There was indeed in the light of her father's information some cause for her surprise. She had been expecting to see a studious if not grey-headed veteran of science, stooping and bespectacled, with all the aloofness of the savant. Lawrence Paule, on the contrary, although he was one of those men whose age would at any time have been difficult to determine, was obviously under middle age. He had the long, lean body of an athlete, a clean-shaven, thoughtful face, with a somewhat prominent forehead, grey eyes, hard and keen, a cynical twist to his mouth, black hair, glossy, yet slightly unkempt, and worn a trifle too long. He was wearing, over his clothes, a loose linen duster, and he carried in his hand a pair of thick magnifying spectacles. A single horn-rimmed eyeglass hung by a cord from his neck. Judith leaned across her companions.

"Dad," she asked, under her breath, "how old is this amazing scientist of yours?"

Her father grinned.

"Better ask him, my dear," he suggested. "He wouldn't tell me."

"I've heard of the fellow," Amberleys whispered. "Tell you something about him later."

Sir Lawrence finished his conversation with his secretary and at once rejoined them. He moved immediately to the inner door, opened it and motioned them to pass through.

"I am afraid," he said, "you will find very little here to interest you. This department is devoted to purely technical experiments. My assistants are busy this morning testing a shipment of suspected drugs from South America."

They all looked around; no one with very great enthusiasm. In front of a great uncurtained window, was a long marble table, on which were ranged a seemingly endless collection of glass vessels of various sizes and shapes, underneath some of which little electric fires were burning. From several of the others a faint brown vapour was being emitted, over which one of the four young assistants was holding some sort of a ball instrument enclosed in a silk mesh. On the farther side of the room a certain space was shut off by a solid mahogany rail, with iron lattice work beneath. In the centre of this space, overhung by powerful electric lights, was a marble table on which were several more glass retorts, and a large number of gleaming scientific implements.

" What exactly goes on here? " Judith enquired, curiously.

" Every parcel of drugs which comes into the place," Paule explained — " drugs, herbs or any component parts of our medicines — is tested and according to any divergence there may be in its strength or purity, from the recognised standard, so our mixer in chief varies his preparation. Sometimes, of course, we have to condemn parcels of drugs altogether. All our eucalyptus oil lately, for instance, has been most indifferent."

" And what goes on inside that jealously preserved space? " the Prince asked, pointing to the enclosure.

Paule strolled over to it and opened the iron gate with a Yale key attached to his watch chain.

" This is one of the places where I make experiments," he said. " Sometimes, for instance, it is possible to substitute a far less expensive drug for some of those we have been in the habit of using and procure exactly the same result. This is where I try to justify my existence as a commercial asset to the firm."

"And succeed too," Joseph declared heartily. "You'd be astonished, all of you, if I were to let you into the secret of how much money has been saved to the firm inside that little enclosure."

Paule remained impassive, watching a blue flame over some brown powder in one of the retorts. Judith found herself standing by his side.

"What on earth does that signify?" she asked, pointing to it.

"Just this," he replied.

He plunged into a highly technical exposition, winding up with a little movement of his hand towards the expiring flames.

"You understand?" he asked.

"Not a single word," she admitted frankly.

He smiled as the flame died out with a small report.

"No," he murmured. "Well, I didn't think you would."

"Why did you trouble to tell me about it, then?" she demanded.

"Because you asked," he rejoined.

She turned away. Joseph had himself been explaining the procedure of the room to his other two visitors.

"Well," she declared, "I am a little disappointed. Is there nothing more for us to see, Dad?"

Her father pointed to a solid mahogany door at the further end of the laboratory.

"Not unless you can persuade Paule to take you into his holy of holies," he replied.

"Has Sir Lawrence anything so exciting?" she queried. "Is there anything beyond that door, Sir

Lawrence, more interesting than a silly blue flame, a brown powder and a lot of stupid technical terms?"

"Vastly so," he assured her, without moving from his place.

"Then lead on," she begged. "I am in the humour to be thrilled."

He shook his head gently. Her father intervened.

"I ought to have warned you, Judith," he said, "that Sir Lawrence is rather by way of being a martinet about that Bluebeard's chamber of his. Can't quite make up my mind whether it's perpetual motion or something of the monkey's gland order he's after. Only been allowed to peep inside the door once myself."

"There's nothing going on there at the moment likely to interest any of you," Paule insisted coolly. "In fact, the whole of this department is a little technical for the ordinary visitor."

"Very interesting, all the same," Prince Edgar declared, stifling a slight yawn.

Judith leaned towards her guide and dropped her voice.

"Aren't we to be allowed just a glimpse inside that room?" she pleaded.

He shook his head. He had somehow the air of one addressing a child.

"To tell you the truth," he confided, "there are ghosts and evil spirits loose there. They recognise me as their master but they object to visitors. An evil spirit evolved from gasses is a terrible fellow to meet when he's not in the humour for amenities."

She made a little grimace to cover her anger.

"And a distinguished chemist when he is in the mood to be disagreeable can also be an unpleasant person," she observed.

Paule locked the gate through which they had issued and passed in front of them to the farther door of the laboratory.

" I am sorry not to have had more to show you," he remarked, with a bow of obvious dismissal. " Perhaps you may honour us on some future occasion when we are making some more interesting experiments. We have an idea, for instance, of a new cure for rheumatism, which if it succeeds will make England a brighter nation."

" Insufferable person! " Judith declared, as soon as the door was safely closed.

Her father shook his head deprecatingly.

" My dear," he confided, taking her arm, " he is sometimes very rude to me. I pretend not to notice it. I shall go on pretending not to notice it. Last year he increased the profits of his department two hundred thousand pounds. So long as he goes on doing that, he can be as irritating as he chooses."

CHAPTER VII

JUDITH, reclining on a *chaise-longue,* skilfully arranged in a corner of the rose garden at Honerton Chase, threw the volume of "Who's Who" which she had been studying on to the grass by her side and reflected for a few moments. An early heat wave had driven her with her parents out of London for the week-end, but already they were realising that the expedition was scarcely a success. Rachel had refused to leave the house, some invited guests had failed to arrive and in the absence even of tennis as well as other distractions, Judith was frankly bored. There was nothing to help her to forget the shadow that brooded over the place.

"Dad," she asked abruptly, "how did you come across Lawrence Paule?"

Her father laid down the *Times,* and mopped his forehead. He had a fancy for lying in the sun, but he was getting a little too much of it.

"Come across him?" he repeated irritably. "One doesn't 'come across' a man like that. I own the biggest drug business in the world and I wanted the best chemist, if money would buy him. As a matter of fact, I offered Sir James Lenton twenty thousand a year if he'd come to us, and he declined. At that time he was considered a better man than Paule — not to-day, though. Paule's easily the best man in the world, and I got him for ten thousand — and what I thought would be an ordinary bonus," Joseph concluded a little ruefully.

"What do you mean by 'an ordinary bonus'?" Judith enquired.

Her father laid aside his paper altogether. This was a subject upon which he felt that he needed sympathy.

"Well," he said, "I'll explain. It's this way. We put a lot of preparations on the market, as you know, but the bulk of our business is done in twelve of them, all household names, all bought up at odd times. It is the job of our chemist to buy the drugs for these — drugs or whatever else they may be made of — and turn 'em out at the price. We offered Paule — it was Samuel's idea and it seemed quite a sound one — twenty per cent. of any economy he could effect in the manufacture, provided that the preparation, of course, was turned out up to the standard. What do you think, Judith — the first twelve months he worked for us, he saved on the manufacture, in black and white, something just over a hundred thousand pounds."

"Jolly good for you," she murmured.

"Good for us, but what about him?" her father exclaimed in some excitement. "Who ever thought of him scooping up a bonus of nearly twenty thousand pounds apart from his salary? The man's a perfect wizard in drugs. He buys them from Botamia, and South America, India and Cochin-China, Japan and no end of out-of-the-way places. He seems to have correspondents everywhere, and he knows precisely what he wants. Not only that," Joseph went on solemnly, "but he's actually invented a cure for rheumatism which really does people good — we've tried it upon old cases. If I cared to spend the money on advertising it, there's another fortune waiting there."

"I suppose he would want a share of it," Judith observed.

"That's just it," her father assented. "We Fernhams have always made money for ourselves and the members of our family and we've kept the others out. Twenty thousand a year that young man is making from us in bonuses, beside his salary! And if I take up this new thing and give him a fifth of the profits, however we work it he'll make another ten. I can't bear to see money going out of the business like that."

Judith turned her head and looked at her father admiringly.

" No wonder you're a multimillionaire, Dad," she said. " What I was really going to ask you, though, was why don't you ask Sir Lawrence Paule to dinner some time? "

"Ask him to dinner!" Joseph repeated blankly.

" Yes," Judith went on. " He seems all right. I've been reading about him. He was born at Wormley in Surrey — no date given. His father appears to have been the headmaster of Wormley Grammar School. From there he went to Oxford, Leipzig and several other Universities. He seems to have accumulated all the letters of the alphabet, tacked on to his name in a sort of nightmare procession. He was knighted for valuable services during the war and his chief recreations are research, tennis and shooting. I think you might safely ask him to dinner."

" I thought you disliked the fellow? " her father remarked. " I've never seen you so nearly angry with any one in my life as when you came away from the Works."

Judith smiled faintly. It was a smile which her father knew well, and if his own feelings towards Lawrence Paule had been of a more friendly character, he would have been sorry for him.

" It is because I don't like him," she explained, " that I wish you to ask him to dinner."

Joseph stroked his chin.

"It isn't my job, anyway," he reflected. "He isn't the sort of man you can ask to come home and take potluck with you. You've got parties two nights next week. You'd better ask him to one of them."

"We will," Judith assented. "I'll write on Mother's behalf and invite him to dine on Thursday."

"He won't come," Joseph warned her. "He's often at the Works till nine o'clock at night and he sleeps there two or three times a week."

"Sleeps there?" she repeated.

Her father nodded.

"He has a slap-up suite of rooms — bathroom and all," he declared. "Holderness, who was his predecessor, had to have something of the sort, as, frequently, when they're experimenting, these things want watching for twenty-four hours on end. Paule's gone into the thing thoroughly though — spent some of his own money on fitting up the rooms and has his own servant."

"How interesting," Judith murmured. "Still, I think he'll come. — Dad, I've got the fidgets. I'm going to walk round."

Joseph suddenly dashed his *Times*, which he had picked up again, on to the ground, rolled over in his chair and reached his feet by a speedy but undignified method. The sun had brought the perspiration to his forehead, but his flabby cheeks were still colourless.

"Judith," he confided, "it's hell! I wish we'd never come. There's your mother there, under the cedar tree, with her back turned to us all, just knitting and knitting as hard as ever she can, and saying never a word."

"Poor Mother!" Judith sighed.

They were almost in the shadow of one of the most beautiful houses in England, softened with age, graceful and stately, its only note of modernity the flag which flew from behind one of the top chimneys. The rose garden through which they were passing was a dream of delight; beyond, the park sloped away for miles, a paradise of green verdure with carefully enclosed plantations and here and there a huge clump of rhododendrons. There were peacocks strutting about on the terrace, a noisy tumult of crows from the tall elm trees.

"It's a wonderful home," Joseph declared. " Your grandfather worked for it and I own it, and I think if I spend another day here I shall go crazy. And your mother's the same. I'm beat, Judith. We'll stick it out to-day but I shall motor back to-morrow. I wish I'd never brought your mother here. — It isn't like death, this. One gets over that, somehow — blunders along just the same. We've had our share of losses. It hurts and that's all there is to it. But, my God, there's madness at the end of this, Judith! I'd rather find Ernest's skeleton to-morrow than have this go on."

" You mustn't give up hope, Dad," she insisted. " I haven't."

Her father stopped in the middle of the narrow path.

" What in God's name is it that you hope for? " he demanded. " How can he come back? Where can he come from? Why did he go away? Can you answer me one of those questions? "

" I can't," she admitted. " I've left off thinking about it. I just have a feeling. I cling to that. And, Dad," she went on hurriedly, " you came down here for my sake, I know. I told you I wanted to come. I did. I told you I had no engagements. I had a dozen. I broke them all. I should have come down here whether you had come or not — and I can't tell you why."

Her father stared at her for a moment. Then he

felt in his waistcoat pocket, produced another cigar and lit it.

" Well," he said more calmly, " you've had your way. I wish I thought something would come of it. I'm going to talk to your mother. Perhaps I can get her to drive round the park with me."

Judith wandered into the house, across the great hall, cool and flower-scented, and made her way to the back premises. She walked with a little shiver down the stone-flagged passage past the gun room and through the heavy door at the end into the courtyard. A man in a grey knickerbocker suit was talking to one of the grooms. Something familiar in his tone attracted her notice and she listened.

" I was told I could see over the house at any time in May or June," the visitor complained.

" So you can in the ordinary way, sir," the groom answered. " The trouble is the family have come down unexpected like. If you care to go round to the front, though, and send your card in, very likely they'll give permission. There's no visitors."

Judith moved a step or two forwards.

" How do you do, Mr. Rodes? " she said. " Can I help you in any way? "

Rodes removed his cap. It struck Judith that he did not seem altogether pleased to see her.

" Very kind of you, Lady Judith," he replied. " I'm holiday making near, and I had a fancy for seeing over the house."

The groom touched his hat and departed.

" What do you want to see over the house for? " Judith asked, lowering her voice a little. " I should think you knew every inch of it."

The Inspector smiled.

"Well, your ladyship's not far off right," he admitted. "I'm like the moth, though. I can't keep away from the candle. All that I really wanted to do was to walk from the gun room once more along the passage and down the back drive as far as the gate."

"Great minds think together, Mr. Rodes," she observed. "I was just about to do the same thing myself. Come back with me and we'll start from the gun room."

She retraced her steps and Rodes followed her. The gun room was locked but the key was speedily forthcoming. It was a rude sort of apartment with few appointments, except a case at one end of the room in which were half a dozen guns and a couple of sporting rifles. Nearly the whole of one wall was taken up by a map of the estate, showing the different spinneys and coverts. There was nothing to look at, very little, it seemed, to think about, yet Rodes, for a few minutes, went into what was apparently a brown study as he stood on the stone flags in the centre of the room, leaning against the plain deal table, his eyes fixed reflectively upon the map, whilst Judith, standing upon the threshold, waited with carefully veiled impatience. In course of time Rodes, with a farewell glance around the room, moved towards the door, passed through it down the flagged passage, crossed the courtyard and turned deliberately in the direction of the back drive, Judith remaining by his side. Together they walked to the gate and stood looking along the narrow track, from the cleared space in the wood where great piles of timber were still heaped, to where it curved between its high hedges towards the main road.

"Rough road for a motor car," Rodes observed.

Judith laughed softly.

" What a blow for Watson," she murmured, " after waiting all this time for some elucidating word."

He produced a pipe from his pocket, and, with a glance at her as though asking permission, commenced to fill it.

" You are a Watson of intelligence," he declared. " I am, alas, a detective in real life and infallibility is not my heritage. You know just where I am — dazed, bewildered, at my wits' end if you like. I can't simply write this case down as one of my failures and go on with something else. They wouldn't tolerate it at the Yard, for one thing. So here I am, and you probably know why."

" I think I know," she admitted.

" I am trying to break away from the logic of facts," he announced, " to abandon the search for clues, to use what little imagination I have been granted, instead of such skill as I may have acquired. That is what you meant when I saw you at the corner of St. James's Street, wasn't it? "

" Precisely," she assented.

" Very well, then," he continued, " we must neglect facts and probabilities, ignore the young man's wealth and apparent content. We will say that he wilfully and deliberately chose to disappear. Don't say impossible, because according to all the facts of the case, everything else is also impossible."

" I am waiting," Judith said quietly.

" Middleton, the keeper, stopped for a few minutes, as was perfectly natural, in the butler's pantry — the butler's pantry or the housekeeper's room, I forget which — but he would naturally accept some slight hospitality and discuss the morrow's sport before he left. Ernest walks calmly down this passage, crosses the courtyard unseen and proceeds along this back drive. If he were in any way the subject of coercion, he would no doubt have been transported into a closed car which would have been waiting in this road, rough though it is. If on the other hand he was bent on a voluntary expedition, can't you see what he would do? He would cross the lane, cross that stile opposite, cross that single triangular meadow, and find himself on the main road — the main road, that is to say, from Norwich to London. The road into which the lane leads is, as of course you know, a good and a much travelled road from Fakenham to Holt, but it does not bisect the London road for another three miles. Having soared a little into fancy to bridge over a gap, I will now come down to realities. The great bulk of our police enquiries were directed towards the possible existence of a closed car upon the Fakenham road, or any sort of a vehicle which might conceal the results of an abduction. Now I am going on a different thesis. I have a little two-seater in the village and I am going to motor slowly up to London from the other side of that meadow, probably taking about a week on the journey. I shall make enquiries at every place I pass, but enquiries based upon a different idea. I shall enquire about a two-seated car, or at any rate an open one, containing a young man and probably an older one who were apparently in no hurry and who were on the best of terms. If I fail again I shall return here and work towards Norwich."

There was a long silence. Rodes, apparently, was occupied in watching the upward curl of the thin line of blue smoke from his pipe. Judith, her elbows upon the top of the gate, and her face resting between the palms of her hands, was gazing steadfastly across the meadow. Presently there came an interruption. A bell from the stable yard commenced to ring out its noisy summons.

"For me," she explained. "That means visitors. I must go."

"Well?" he asked a little anxiously, for he was beginning to have a curious feeling, almost a superstition with regard to this very beautiful young woman.

She hesitated.

"You have made a start," she admitted. "You have shown that you, too, have vision of a sort, but it seems to me — I don't know. I am terribly confused myself — but it seems to me that you'll have to wander even a little further from the usual ways before the light comes."

She turned away and hurried down the drive with swift footsteps. Rodes, with his pipe burning between his fingers, looked after her contemplatively. A rabbit came out of his hole and sat watching him a few yards away.

"What I should like to know," Rodes muttered, his eyes now fixed upon the rabbit, "is whether she suspects anything or whether she is just spooky."

The rabbit suddenly detected the odour of tobacco and with a whisk of his tail disappeared. Rodes was left to face the problem alone.

CHAPTER VIII

AFTER all the flag of proffered hospitality had not flown in vain from the parapets of Honerton Chase. Frederick Amberleys with his two sisters and a brother officer were waiting on the lawn when Judith returned. For the remainder of the day the atmosphere of horror which had chilled the household seemed lifted. There was tennis to the point of exhaustion, an adjournment to the swimming baths — one of the modern luxuries of the place — iced drinks, a car despatched to Holt for clothes and an improvised dinner party. Judith felt sincerely grateful to her suitor as they all sat outside under the cedar trees, drinking their coffee and watching the moon make its slow appearance over the dark fir spinneys.

" I am drifting into a mood," she warned him, as he passed her cup. " It is very dangerous."

" To you or to me? " he asked.

" To me directly, and to you indirectly," she replied. " I absolutely decline to be left alone with you this evening. See about some bridge at once, please."

" I shall do nothing of the sort," he declared. " You encourage me to hope that you will play up to your part as a heroine of romance and invite me to walk in the rose garden. What about it, Judith? "

" I certainly shall not," she assured him. " For one thing it is far too obvious. There is one corner where the path drops and there is a great clump of those moss roses, all mixed up with musk and verbena — a corner which you couldn't possibly pass without proposing to me."

"Please," he begged, holding out his hand.

She looked at him attentively, far too appraisingly for the moment and the circumstances. In the dim light he seemed to have lost something of that robustness, that almost animal vigour, only attractive at odd unworthy times, as a rule repellent to her more critical instincts. His face seemed even to have gained that touch of spirituality which she had often looked for in vain. His eyes were pleading, his manner anxious. There was no doubt that he was very much in earnest. Hesitatingly she placed her hand in his, and felt herself drawn to her feet by a gentle but invincible force.

"Frederick and I are going to have our usual half an hour's flirtation," she warned the others. "We shall be back for bridge directly. I don't know Captain Vanderson's tastes, but you girls must look after him."

They passed across the lawn, through a postern gate, through the square walled garden into a smaller and less rigidly kept enclosure where the walls were even older and more crumbling and the genius of a gardener, who was also something of an artist, had permitted a certain amount of riot. There were borders of old-fashioned flowers, whose perfume was pungent but sweet; a sort of heady background to the more exotic odour of the roses. Judith sighed as she laid her fingers upon her companion's coat sleeve.

"You don't know how grateful I am to you people for coming over this afternoon, Frederick," she confided. "It was an experiment coming down here, of course, and it was on the point of turning out a ghastly failure."

"I couldn't have kept away," he assured her. "It was so lucky we were at Holt for a week. The Governor was laid up with gout, and rather lonely, so we planned this visit late on Friday night. You must all come over and lunch with us to-morrow and we'll have some more tennis."

"It will be salvation," she murmured, "positively salvation!"

He stole a glance at her which was unwise of him, for her still, subtle beauty went at once to his head. He lost coherency.

"Judith," he said, "you'll have to marry me some day. Why not soon?"

"Why at all?" she asked him calmly. "I don't want to marry."

"But you must," he pleaded. "You can't go on living at home for ever. You told me once you were afraid of losing your individuality. You're more likely to lose it in Park Lane than in Mayfair with me. And Judith — I've never been fond of any one like I am of you. I shouldn't expect to play the old-fashioned sort of husband. You can develop in your own way, choose your own friends, strike out your own line in society or anywhere else — I sha'n't interfere. But I'm fonder of you, Judith, than I ever expected to be of any one in my life. Be kind to me, dear!"

She passed her arm through his.

"I want to be kind to you, Frederick," she said earnestly, "but think — oh, do think. We're ever so different in many ways. There is my race."

"Dear, what does it matter?" he interrupted. "Those sort of prejudices have gone long ago."

"Perhaps," she admitted. "And yet remember my people have their own peculiar characteristics. I have all the temperament, the mysticism, the moodiness of the Hebrew woman. Sometimes I think that if I had lived two thousand years ago I should have been a prophetess."

" I know," he acknowledged humbly. " Every one tells me that you have the makings of a great artist. Horthwaite says that you could be a painter, and Mayer that the world has lost a great musician because you are the daughter of a millionaire. But, dearest, you can look over the edge of the world as often and as long as you like, blow your bubbles and build your house of dreams wherever you will, but when your feet are on the earth, you must have a husband and I want to be he."

" You're almost irresistible," she murmured.

" The greatest thing in me is what comes from you," he declared. " My love for you."

She suddenly paused and looked at him. His expression as he gazed at her was almost adoring. A gleam of the moonlight shone in her smooth black hair. The marble whiteness of her cheeks, the soft fire in her eyes, the tender scarlet of her lips were all maddening. He took her suddenly into his arms and she lifted her head a little. Her eyes sought his, tenderly, yet with a curious wistfulness.

" Kiss me, Frederick, please," she whispered, " then I will tell you."

The glamour of the night, the unearthliness of her beauty were his salvation. All that even savoured of coarseness in his virility seemed to pass away. He held her to him with a strength restrained by an intense tenderness, the fire of an almost sublimated passion burning upon his lips. She lay in his arms, tense at first, but afterwards for a moment like a long-stemmed beautiful flower which had just been plucked. Then without any warning she broke away. He heard a little sob, caught a glimpse of her — a streak of white through the bushes — and still inspiration rested with him. He stayed where he was amongst the roses — happy, victorious, contented.

There were bridge and billiards, much laughter and the usual amount of chaff that evening, and it was midnight before the cars were brought round. Then Judith sought her opportunity. She kept Frederick back after the others had made their adieux and, with her arm through his, led him to her mother.

" Mother dear," she announced, " I'm going to marry Frederick. Dad, do you hear? Come and shake hands with him. Now that you both know, the others can come back if they like."

For a single moment Rachel seemed to return from the far-away world in which she had been living. She held out her hands, and Frederick stooped and kissed her forehead.

" Judith has made me very happy," he said.

" Well, well! " Joseph declared, pulling down his waistcoat vigorously. " Is that Martin out there? Martin, send me some champagne and glasses. Never mind about the whiskies and sodas. Damn the gout! Amberleys — Frederick — shake hands. My congratulations! "

The others came streaming in and Judith was surrounded. Her father stood on the outside of the little circle, his hands in his pockets, an air of immense satisfaction pervading his whole being.

" To tell you the truth, Mother," he confided to his wife, " I was beginning to get just a little nervous about Judith — a trifle too exotic, she seemed sometimes, what? Unnatural almost! You know what I mean. Seemed positively to dislike the idea of marriage. When a girl has a brain like Judith's and gets that notion into her head, she sometimes ends by being a spinster. There have been two in our family already, God help them! Amberleys is a fine fellow and with Judith's money — well, it will give you something to think about, Mother, eh? "

He looked anxiously down at her. It seemed to him that the pain was creeping once more into her pallid face. Nevertheless she took the glass of wine which Martin was handing and smiled bravely up at her husband.

"We should be very happy about this, Joseph," she said. "We will drink to their future, you and I together. God has brought this to pass. He may yet save my heart from breaking."

She drained her glass and set it down empty. Every one was talking very noisily about the plans for tomorrow, and Joseph himself was being dragged into the council. Rachel stretched out her hand and took up the knitting which was always close to her side. Soon her fingers began to flash and the needles to gleam. She listened, apparently, to the conversation, with a smile of sympathy upon her lips. Her eyes, however, saw beyond the room. In spirit she had already passed from it, wandering restlessly across the world in that eternal search.

CHAPTER IX

Judith, on the night of the dinner party in Park Lane, noticed her guest's slight hesitation after he had been announced, and, breaking off her conversation with Frederick Amberleys, stepped forward to meet him.

"You are looking for your hostess, I am sure, Sir Lawrence," she said. "My mother has given up entertaining for the present, and I am her deputy. We are very glad to see you."

Sir Lawrence made his bow and expressed his hope that Lady Honerton was not seriously indisposed.

"She is simply tired," Judith told him. "She finds the season a little long. Do you know everybody here?"

"Except Lord Amberleys, whom I think you brought with you to the Works, no one," he replied.

Amberleys heard his name and turned around. The two men exchanged greetings.

"I gather from an announcement in the *Times* the other day that I am to congratulate you, Lord Amberleys," the newcomer said. "May I at the same time take the opportunity of wishing you every happiness, Lady Judith," he added.

"Very nice of you," she replied, "but how can you expect me to be happy when I have a desire unsatisfied?"

"I can scarcely conceive such a possibility," he murmured.

"Not although you are responsible?" she reminded him, with a smile. "Don't you know that you are one of the few people in the world who have refused a request of mine?"

He looked for a moment blank, then he remembered.

" Is that still rankling? " he asked.

" Horribly," she admitted.

Joseph came up a little fussily.

" Glad to see you, Sir Lawrence," he said. " First time you've honoured us, I think, — not that we shouldn't have asked you often enough if I'd had any idea you were a diner out. Judith, as usual, was the clever one of the family."

" So I have you to thank for my invitation," he remarked, turning to her. " I call that returning good for evil."

" The episode is not yet closed," she warned him.

It was a dinner party of twelve — a smaller number than usual at Judith's express desire. Sir Lawrence sat on her left hand and Lord Clareton, an Irish peer and relative of Frederick's, on her right. Lady Clareton was on one side of her father — a most satisfactory dinner companion for him, as she never left off talking, hated even to pause for an answer to her stream of questions and was blessed with a marvellous appetite. Mrs. Lola Reistmann, on his other side, was the wife of a famous musician, dark, languishing, and entirely engrossed in a flirtation with Henry Fernham, who was over on a week's leave from Paris to make the acquaintance of his sister's fiancé. Then there was Reistmann himself, noisy, hungry and witty, continually seeking for opportunities to talk to Judith across the table, Joyce Cloughton, one of Judith's few intimate acquaintances, and Sir Phillip Dane, a very famous physician and medical adviser in ordinary to the family. It was a party of friends deliberately chosen by Judith after Paule's acceptance of her invitation, a party which was meant to give her considerable freedom with regard to the entertainment of this one particular guest. Everything had turned out as she had intended, but the enterprise had suddenly lost its savour. It was not that Paule had in any way disappointed her, nor that her almost passionate hope for the development of her affection for Frederick had been realised. She was conscious, for some unanalysable reason, of a marked indisposition to cross the boundary of the light outposts of conversation which had seen her and her neighbour through the opening courses. She had realised from the moment of their meeting that her ordinary weapons would be useless against this man, and for the first time in her life she was inclined to shirk a combat of personalities. There was something almost saturnine in his easy indifference to the demands which courtesy made upon him. The woman on his left — Lady Dane, carefully chosen as being a person who very much preferred her dinner to conversation — found him a most satisfactory companion. He paid her the attentions which civility demanded and afterwards left her alone. At Judith's silence he seemed a little puzzled. Indirectly he challenged it.

"I am still in disgrace, I fear," he suggested, "for preserving the secrets of my Bluebeard's chamber."

"If you realise the cause," she rejoined, "it is at least open to you to remove it."

"Ingenious," he murmured.

"Successful?" she queried.

He bowed.

"At any time," he assented, "when you come alone."

"Unchaperoned?" she exclaimed.

"Entirely."

"My fiancé?"

He shook his head.

"Inadmissible."

" The adventure is beginning to assume a new aspect," she declared. " Someone must have told you that I had a flair for doing improper things."

" I needed no gossip to assure me that you were in the habit of doing daring ones," he retorted.

" What risks shall I run if I come alone to your magic chamber? " she asked.

" If I were foolish enough to answer such a question," he pointed out, " the adventure would cease to be one."

" I am very strongly tempted," she admitted.

" You stand the least chance of being blown up on Wednesday or Thursday," he said. " My housekeeper makes tea about four o'clock."

" It all seems very easy," she remarked. " Really I needn't have taken the trouble to have you asked to dinner, need I? "

" Quite unnecessary," he assured her. " You might have spared me, too. I don't dine out twice a year like this."

" We are very flattered," she murmured.

He suddenly turned and looked at her, and she was conscious that she had never been looked at in the same fashion before.

" Well, in a sense you ought to be," he said. " You are the only woman in the world whose invitation I should have accepted."

His words were deliberate, spoken without enthusiasm or fervour of any sort. Yet Judith knew that they were the truth. She was aware of a sudden feeling of embarrassment, of a desire to withdraw from an unequal contest. She turned and began to talk restlessly to Lord Clareton. He brushed aside at once her tentative efforts towards conversation of a more conventional nature.

" I have just heard who your left-hand neighbour is," he confided in an undertone. " Do you know that he is one of the most remarkable men living? "

" Is he? " she replied, with an indifference which was perhaps a little overdone. " I know my father thinks very highly of his work."

" I am not a scientific man myself," Lord Clareton continued, " but my nephew Ronald was at College with this fellow Paule, and he's never tired of talking about him. I remember his telling us, for instance, that Paule, before he went down, after having carried off every possible honour, declared that before he was forty he would have solved the problem of the genesis of the world and the indefinite prolongation of life. Pretty good for a lad of twenty-two or twenty-three."

" He hasn't done it, has he? " she remarked drily.

" He isn't forty yet," Lord Clareton reminded her. " He's done some wonderful things, though."

Judith leaned across the table and exchanged amenities with Frederick. Then she turned once more to her left-hand neighbour.

" I have been told," she confided, " that you are pledged to discover before you are forty the secret of the genesis of the world and the elixir of life."

" I shall probably do both," he replied coolly. " I could prolong any reasonably healthy person's life about thirty years already, if it were worth while — it so seldom is."

" Could you prolong mine? " she asked.

" Easily," he assured her. " I could guarantee you a hundred years or so. You're much too sensible, though, to ask me to do it."

" Is that one of the problems you study in Bluebeard's chamber? " she enquired.

" Occasionally," he admitted. " Just now, however, I am engaged on something more interesting."

" I can't imagine anything more interesting than prolonging my life," she declared.

He smiled at her indulgently.

" You wouldn't really care for the aftermath of vital existence," he said.

" If your discovery was worth anything it ought not to be an aftermath," she objected strongly. " Why not devote your efforts also to keeping me young and beautiful? "

" You ask a great deal of science," he reminded her.

" I thought you were one of those," she rejoined, " who preached the doctrine that we are as yet only on the threshold of knowledge, that some of the planets are inhabited, for instance, by a race of beings infinitely more intelligent than we are, and that it is only because we are slothful that we have made so little progress."

" There is not the slightest doubt about that," he assured her. "As to the planets being inhabited, more than half the scientific men of the day have come to that conclusion."

" Then why don't we communicate with some of them? " she asked.

" We could easily," he replied. " It is simply a question of somebody with brains having time enough to spare to devise the instrument, or rather series of instruments. I'll give you the idea now, if you feel you'd like to devote yourself to it."

" Don't mock me," she reproved him. " If I am not a scientist, I at least have other qualities."

" So I understand," he acquiesced with a faint note of irony in his tone. "A great musician, an artist, a tragedienne and a poetess were all lost to the world thanks to your father's amazing facility for doctoring the human race at a cost of a few millions."

"You are pleased to be sarcastic," she observed. "I can assure you all the same that I really have brains."

"You have done one thing which makes me doubt it," he answered bluntly.

She felt his eyes rest for a moment upon the ring on her finger. A spasm of anger brought the quick colour to her cheeks, yet she never dreamed of resenting his speech in words. Already she recognised his domination, although she detested him for it. It was her environment, she told herself, and his position as a guest which handicapped her so completely. Next time they met the tables should be turned. He was after all one of the easiest victims the world offers to its beautiful women — a man of science engrossed in his work, a semi-recluse, deaf to the ordinary calls of humanity. There had been a long list of such who had been her faithful slaves. There was no reason why this one should survive. By degrees she recovered her confidence, talking round the table to her friends and acquaintances, ignoring for a time her immediate neighbours. The dinner went brightly on to its appointed end. Judith, however, was conscious of a little sense of relief as she gained the shelter of the drawing-room; she felt somehow that she had escaped from the proximity of danger.

"Tell me all about this wonderful guest of yours," Joyce Cloughton demanded, drawing her on one side. "You were rather a cat not to put me next him. He's good-looking too, in a forbidding sort of way."

"My dear, you can have him for the rest of the evening," Judith promised. "He's a little taciturn, but when he does speak it's to the point all right. He'll tell you how to live to a hundred if you like, and before he's forty years old he's going to tell us how the world started, and how long it's going on."

"If he's said he would, he'll do it," Joyce declared. "He looks that sort of man."

"Bad-tempered I should think and terribly domineering," Judith observed. "Half an hour of him makes one thankful for an ordinary person like Freddy."

"You're a lucky girl," Joyce sighed. "I've always thought that Freddy Amberleys was one of the nicest young men about town. I can see that I shall have to think seriously of your Cousin Sammy, after all. What are you going to do with us this evening, Judith?"

"Frederick and Sir Phillip Dane and Mrs. Reistmann and Dad are going to play bridge. You and the others are going to play poker."

"And what about you?"

"I am going to entertain Sir Lawrence," Judith announced. "He does not play cards."

Joyce whistled softly under her breath.

"Will Freddy quite approve?" she enquired.

"He won't be asked," Judith replied. "As a matter of fact, though, I arranged this party before it was settled between Freddy and myself. I can't back out of it now. I thought I wanted to talk to Sir Lawrence. I'm not quite so sure of it as I was."

"Better pass him on to me as you promised, dear," Joyce advised. "He's a dangerous type for an engaged girl. He wouldn't take me so seriously. No one does, for some reason or other. I should probably be able to lead him into the paths of a gentle flirtation. He would ask if he could give me a lift home — I suppose he has a car — and there ought to be at least a dinner and theatre in it."

Judith shook her head.

"It's my last fling, Joyce," she said. "I think I'll have to see it through."

"I warn you Freddy's inclined to be jealous," her friend confided. "I saw him watching you from across the table once or twice this evening. In his way the chemist man is very good-looking, you know."

Judith glanced warningly towards the door. The sound of men's voices was already to be heard in the hall.

"You go and rescue Henry from the wiles of that Reistmann woman," Judith enjoined. "Don't interfere with me, and don't let the others try and drag me into bridge."

"As much in earnest as all that?" Joyce exclaimed with uplifted eyebrows.

Judith smiled. She was looking across the room at the little phalanx of white-fronted men.

"I have a reason," she murmured.

CHAPTER X

AFFAIRS arranged themselves very much according to Judith's preconceived plan. She lingered until she saw the bridge party established and the chips being counted out for the poker, and then led Lawrence Paule across the white marble hall with its priceless rugs, through the little lounge into the billiard room beyond. One of the footmen who had been on duty in the hall hastened to turn up the lights and produce the balls.

" Will your ladyship require a marker? " he enquired, moving towards the board.

" Would you like some one to score? " she asked her prospective opponent.

" Score," he repeated vaguely. " Good heavens, no! "

She dismissed the man with a wave of the hand.

" You don't seriously propose to play this game, do you? " he demanded, with a glance of aversion towards the table.

" Why, it was your own idea," she reminded him.

" I mentioned the billiard room as a refuge," he explained. " How could one talk with that babel going on? I have never played a game of billiards in my life. I suggest that divan, the window open — I am right, am I not, in believing that this room overlooks the park? — and the privilege of your conversation."

" I accept your suggestion willingly," she replied, establishing herself on the divan. "As a matter of fact this is rather a favourite seat of mine. Can you manage the window? Thanks. Now we can sit here and try to imagine that the lights we see through the elm trees are will-o'-the-wisps and that those mysterious couples flitting about are in reality lovers."

" You forget that you are committed to probably an hour's conversation with a person who is supposed to be devoid of all imagination whatever," he rejoined, throwing on one side a cushion and settling himself in his corner. " I am a chemist and a scientist. Exactitude as to detail has to be my guiding principle in life."

" The man who obtained first-class honours in the mathematical tripos last year," she remarked, " told me that his only advantage over his rivals was that he had a more plastic imagination."

" Ingenious but of doubtful veracity," he declared. " In my work if I possessed imagination I should go mad."

" What do you do in your Bluebeard's chamber? " she asked bluntly.

" Seek for understanding," he answered. " We are woefully short of it in the world."

" Supposing I really wanted to live to be a hundred, would you help me? "

" No," he replied. " The aftermath of your life would be miserable. The more I preserved your vigour, the more you would regret the extinction of your beauty."

Her dark eyes were for a moment lifted to his.

" You think that I am beautiful, then? "

" I think that you are without exception the most beautiful woman I have ever seen," was the deliberate response.

" The last thing I expected to collect from you," she murmured, after a moment's rather startled pause, " was a compliment."

" You haven't collected one," he answered. " You are extraordinarily beautiful — extraordinarily beautiful and amazingly alluring. I can assure you that I am fully conscious of your charms."

"I sha'n't have to remind you that I am engaged to be married or anything of that sort, shall I?" she asked.

"You might, if you thought it worth while," he replied. "I am not in the least disposed to recognise the barbed wire."

She laughed very quietly with half-closed eyes.

"It seems to me that I am running great risks," she said.

"The woman who wasn't disposed to run them is yet to be born," he retorted.

"How do you know anything about women?"

"Instinct," was the uncompromising rejoinder. "The same instinct which sometimes brings me safely across an absolutely untrodden field of thought."

"Does it ever mislead you?" she asked.

His slight pause gave her an opportunity to study his profile. He was apparently watching those shadowy figures passing back and forth under the trees, his lips so closely set that there seemed to be but one thin dividing line where they met, his jaw massive yet shapely, the chin firm, his eyes deep-set behind his heavy eyebrows, even in this moment of abstraction, hard almost to steeliness. The prominent forehead and finely shaped head with its masses of clustering black hair seemed vaguely to remind her of some picture, something that came from the past. She found herself searching the recesses of her mind. It might have been in one of the smaller galleries at Madrid or Amsterdam that she had seen the original from which the likeness came.

"In life," he said, "I am one of those people who cannot afford to make mistakes. If I should make one at all — and I am, after all, only an ordinary human being — crash would go the foundations upon which my career is built. For instance," he went on, a note of irony creeping into his tone, " supposing I give out a wrong formula for next week's preparation of ' Fernham's Malted Milk '; twenty thousand people would have a pain in their insides, and there would very soon be a serious shrinking in your colossal dividends."

" What a pity," she sighed.

"A pity? "

" You have begun to talk nonsense. I was always afraid that you would."

" One has to seize every loophole," he observed. " I am in a unique position. I don't know how to govern it. I am compelled to drift."

"Now you're talking enigmas," she complained. " You are really most unmanageable."

" Enigmas with a ready solution at the tip of my tongue," he replied. " I am talking for the first time in my life with a woman who counts."

" I like that better," she said meditatively.

" Candour, I see, appeals to you," he went on. " You will make a hideous mistake if you marry Lord Amberleys."

" Isn't that going a little far? " she warned him.

" Not at all," he rejoined coolly. " It is so obviously the truth. The young man in question is one of a race and breed whom every one must admire. They are splendid young animals, gifted with a quite reasonable modicum of intelligence, and able to skirt round the outsides of most of the great subjects in life. Their inherited digestions allow them unlimited opportunities of indulging their appetites. They remain good-natured and equable to the end of their days and there are a precisely similar number of well-brought up Saxon young women who would make them excellent wives and produce at discretion wonderful counterparts for the next generation. You don't happen to be one of those young women. A union between you two would be ridiculous."

Anger was her only refuge from the strange disturbance which had flashed through all her being, a quivering vital shock.

"Considering the length of our acquaintance," she said icily, " you are being very impertinent."

She had only once seen him laugh before. It was not an effort which in any way suggested mirth. It brought into prominence more noticeably than ever the up-curved line of his mouth.

"That sort of speech isn't worth while," he assured her, "between you and me. You don't mean it, and I know that you don't mean it. You don't belong to these people. To the scientific man you represent a problem in heredity. You are not the daughter of your father, Joseph, second Baron Honerton. You are not the sister of that young Ernest who disappeared. You were born in mystery, the projection of generations. I can see your real mother, captive amongst the Philistines, eating her heart out perhaps in sorrow. Park Lane and Honerton Chase would seem as strange to those people from whom you came as the wilderness in which they sojourned and the moon under which they slept would seem to you. — Yours was once the greatest race on earth, you know, Lady Judith. The dross crept in and they became outcasts. Here and there the gold remains."

There was a little fluttering breeze amongst the elm trees outside; a warm June breeze scented with the perıume of the flowers in the many window boxes. It brought no touch of chill, yet Judith was conscious of a little shiver. The doors of the bridge and music rooms had been opened, and a babel of voices and peals of laughter came like an alien note to disturb the stillness of the room. Louder than any sounded Frederick's guffaw of amusement.

"I give in," Judith said quietly, rising to her feet. "I brought you out here to flirt with you and incidentally to find out all I could about your chamber of mystery. You are too masterful. I abandon the attempt."

"I thought that I recognised the atmosphere of temptation," he murmured. "I am afraid, though, that the state of my biceps would make the completion of the simile ridiculous."

"Come, and let us join the others," she proposed. "I am not going to stay here with you any longer."

"That seems to me," he complained, "a little ungracious. Do you know that you have not even offered me a cigarette since dinner," he added, stretching out his hand towards a box which lay open by his side. "Stay and smoke the pipe of peace with me. I will talk banalities until you are soothed out of all real feeling — since you prefer it."

She took a cigarette, lit it and leaned for a moment against the window frame. If her feelings were not entirely relieved, there was at least a lessening of the sense of strain in being a little farther away from him. It was, too, in a manner, the dawn of her own moment of triumph. He was watching her. His eyes had lost their steely gleam, the curve of his mouth was changed. In her gown of white brocaded silk, cleverly devised to seem but the cunning twist of a priceless shawl around her wonderfully lithe body, with her black eyes, narrowed now by the droop of her eyelids, her exquisite mouth, the gloss of her raven hair, she stood, as she very well knew, for no type of the present. She represented the lost mystery of womanhood, all the very soul of men's desire.

It was amazing insight on his part which guided him through those perilous moments overcharged with sensibility.

"We have talked unusually," he said, in level tones. "Why not? It is the better way towards understanding. — Tell me your plans. You are going to see the season out, I suppose?"

"I believe so," she answered a little wearily. "We have parties for Ascot and Goodwood. After that I think we shall go abroad, unless ———"

"Unless Lord Amberleys persuades you to get married instead," he interrupted. "Somehow I don't think he will. — I shall stay on until October and then, if your father gives me leave, I am going back to the West Coast of Africa. Exactly seventeen days' journey from the sea, in a particularly slimy and poisonous-looking wood, there is growing at the present moment a small shrub of which I must possess myself. And then again I may not go. I have a man out there working for me and he may have luck."

"There is no one in England with whom you spend your holidays," she asked; "no friends or relatives?"

"I have scarcely a relative in the world," he replied, "and life has been too exacting for me to make friends at any time. Some day I suppose I shall regret it. Just now I should resent any claims which interfered for a moment with my work."

"Any?"

"Some claims," he declared, "one, in particular, which the little world in which we live considers the greatest of all, could never interfere. What one would lose in actual moments, one would gain in incentive."

She threw away her cigarette restlessly and lit another. Even when, a few minutes later, she led the way towards the door, she paused as though loath to go, and played idly with the billiard balls.

"I looked you up in 'Who's Who' the other day," she remarked.

"Why?"

"I wanted to see whether it was true that your father was a schoolmaster."

"You doubted the scholastic strain?" he queried.

"On the contrary, I recognised it," she replied. "By the bye, your absorption of three quarters of the letters of the alphabet to tack on to your name seems a little grasping."

He sighed.

"Amongst my few gifts," he admitted, "I possess a special facility for passing examinations. I really had not to learn half the things I gained honours for. The knowledge of what I should be asked seemed to come without study. No wonder I am superstitious."

"Are you really superstitious?" she asked.

She was playing all the time with fire and she knew it. For a single moment she was in danger of meeting with her deserts. Then through those open doors came once more the babel of voices, mingled, this time, with the sound of approaching footsteps. Amberleys and Joyce came in side by side.

"My dear," the latter exclaimed, "I have brought you Freddy. He's in terrible disgrace. He's revoked twice and called 'diamonds' when he had seven 'spades' with four honours. The bridge people have washed their hands of him."

Amberleys was looking at the undisturbed billiard table and cue rack.

"You haven't been playing billiards, after all," he remarked, with a slight touch of asperity.

Judith crossed the room and selected a cue.

"Not yet, my dear Freddy," she said, "but I am about to. You shall give me fifteen in fifty and Sir Lawrence shall take your place at bridge or flirt with Joyce, whichever he likes."

"I am a humble amateur at both pursuits," Paule confessed, glancing dubiously across at Joyce.

"Joyce is an adept at one," Judith assured him. "Try and find out which. It's rather a stuffy table at bridge and I can see from here that they've seduced a poker player away. String for lead, Freddy."

CHAPTER XI

On the day after the dinner party in Park Lane, Samuel Fernham, having announced his intention by telephone, travelled up from Brighton and paid one of his rare visits to the Works. He was greeted warmly by his brother and affectionately by his son, Samuel Junior, who had just returned from a business visit to the States. At the latter's suggestion the three adjourned to what they called the " Board Room ", a very handsome apartment, richly carpeted and furnished, and hung with oil paintings of various members of the firm. There were twelve easy-chairs ranged around a long mahogany table. Samuel sighed a little as the three men seated themselves.

" There is no news, Joseph? " he asked.

" None," was the sad reply.

"At Scotland Yard, they have nothing to report? "

" Nothing whatever. They say they still work at it. Phew! In no other country in the world could such a thing happen. There has never been a disappearance like it which the police have not been able to account for. I tell them all this. I work myself into a fury. The only reply I get are those few starched words ' we are doing all that we can '."

" If they are," Samuel Junior declared pugnaciously, thrusting his hands into his trousers pockets and rattling his keys, " it's quite time they were all kicked out and a fresh lot given a chance. Why, dash it all, how can any one feel safe! It might be my turn to-morrow."

His father laid his hand affectionately upon his shoulder. Samuel Junior was not much to look at — a short, stout, young man, high-coloured, with a small fair moustache, and fair hair already a little thin at the top, a very indifferent replica of his mother, who had been an Andalusian Jewess. He was nevertheless his father's chief interest in life and the object of his constant solicitude.

"Joseph," the latter said earnestly, "and you, Samuel, I have had a bad week down in Brighton. I have had no sleep. I have been haunted with dreams. This morning I knew I could bear it no longer. I telephoned and here I am."

"You're alone too much, Dad," his son declared. "It's absurd! I'll come down and stay with you, if you like. I've got a lot of things on in town but I don't mind. I'll go back with you to-night."

Samuel patted his arm gently.

"You're a good lad," he sighed, "a very good lad. You shall come for a few days. I came up, though, to propose bigger changes. As I grow older it seems to me that I see some things more clearly. It seems to me that there is a hand of wrath stretched out over our house, because of Israel, our father, Joseph, and his one harsh deed."

"Grandfather Israel was right," Samuel Junior pronounced. "A life for a life. That's our doctrine, isn't it?"

"It was part of our creed before we wandered away from our belief," his father admitted, "but that man Heggs had been wronged, Joseph. He was beside himself with passion. The deed he did was evil, but it was not a deed which merited death. It was Israel who insisted. It was Israel who fought against the reprieve. It was Israel through whose efforts the man was hanged."

" These things are over and finished with," Joseph pointed out. " Thirty years have passed, Samuel. What has brought them into your mind now? "

" This calamity which has fallen upon our house," was the sombre reply. " It has come to me that it is the hand of the Lord, the judgment of the Lord God."

Joseph and his nephew exchanged wondering glances.

" There's nothing to be done about it now, you know, Dad," the latter reminded him soothingly.

" There is restitution which might be made," Samuel declared. " What became of the girl and the child, if there was one? I never heard. Whilst that cloud of horror hung around I closed my ears. I was a coward but now I suffer."

" The girl died in childbirth," Joseph announced solemnly. " The infant with her. It was perhaps merciful."

Samuel wrung his hands.

" The debt is greater than I thought," he groaned. " I believe it now more than ever. The sin of Israel our father will be visited upon us. Ernest has gone. It may next be the turn of my own son. It may be your turn, Joseph. The wrath of God is slow but sure. Have we listened to his voice? We have abandoned our religion, we have bared our heads to the despised race, we are outcasts. You have lost your son, Joseph. I shook and trembled all last week for fear I might lose mine."

" It is too late for us to weaken and hark back to the old ways," Joseph pronounced. " We have made our lives and we must live them through to an end. If further evil befall us it may be a judgment, as you say."

" It is our wealth," Samuel continued, " which has

been our undoing. It has bought your way, Joseph, into high places amongst the people who despise us yet whom we should despise. It has robbed me of two sons who ate of the fleshpots and died. I, too, am in my last days, and I am afraid for my youngest."

"All this morbid talk isn't healthy, Samuel," his brother protested, striking the table with his fist. " Where does it lead to? Nowhere! Besides ———"

" Stop! " Samuel interrupted. " It leads to this. I have come to make a proposition. We have great wealth, Joseph, you and I, and Samuel here and all the family. Let us cease to add to it. For ten years the public has been clamouring to buy our shares. Let them buy. We shall remain amongst the money princes of the world. That way we may attain to safety."

" It was not from here that Ernest was taken," his father muttered gloomily.

" Nevertheless," Samuel went on in rising excitement, " it has been shown to me that it is in this temple of wealth, which has grown under our hands till it has become a veritable paradise for the moneyseeker, that the danger lies. I dreamed last night that we were free men, that you had your boy back, Joseph, and that I had kept mine."

" Dad," young Samuel intervened, " as a practical proposition I don't think much of this sort of talk. The business is showing enormous profits. Why should we turn it over to any one else? Why should we stand by and see some one else get rich? We have more money than we can spend, perhaps, but who has more than he needs? Not Rothschild, not one of them. They stay till the end. This year will be wonderful. That fellow Paule is a wizard. Our profits are going to be larger than they ever have been before."

" The lad is right," Joseph assented, recovering himself a little. " You've been living too much alone, Samuel, brooding too much and worrying. If I had not this business to come to for an hour or two every day when I am in town, what should I do with myself? Nothing. I should have nothing to occupy my thoughts, nothing to interest me. If Ernest were here, I would say let us leave it to the lads. As it is, I agree with Samuel. We have money but there is no reason why we should not make more. Money is a very good thing, brother. You, too, thought so once."

" Samuel," his father pleaded, " you shall have half my share now. You will be worth more than you will ever need. Come away with me. We will find you a wife a little later. Two millions and nothing to do but enjoy yourself. I am an old man, but if Brighton is too dull for you I will drag myself to Paris."

" It isn't the money, Dad," the young man protested. " It's the making it that's the joy. I'll come home to Brighton with you to-night, stay with you, if you will, for the best part of the week, but I stick by the business."

Samuel leaned back in his chair. He seemed very frail and gaunt, and more than ever like a weak edition of Israel. He rubbed his hands slowly one over the other. He had the air of repeating a prayer. Vague memories of the past were in his brain. Joseph and Samuel Junior exchanged a quick glance of understanding. It was the beginning of the end.

" Come on, Dad," the latter begged. " I've got my car here and I'll take you along to get some lunch. Afterwards, if there's nothing much doing here, we'll call round at my rooms for a bag and we'll go home together by the early train."

"I eat but once a day," Samuel replied. "I need no lunch. I will wait for you here."

"Rubbish!" his son expostulated good-humouredly. "If you don't care about the Club or a restaurant, come with me to my rooms. My cook knows the sort of things you like — schnitsel and veal, eh? We shall be all by ourselves there."

Samuel Fernham rose unsteadily to his feet. He leaned on his stick and felt for his son's arm.

"It is early for lunch," he said. "Since I am here I should like to look round. It may be for the last time."

"Have a look round by all means," Joseph assented cheerfully, "but don't talk rubbish like that. Don't be so silly! We are a long-lived race, remember, and you have lived more carefully than any of us. — We will show you our new export department. — You see the marble tiles, Samuel? It is like a gigantic dairy. It is the cleanest factory in the world."

"You remember," Samuel asked, as he passed slowly on, "how proud we were when we built it? Proud and a little frightened. One of the directors of the bank came down. When he heard what it had cost us he was grave. Do you remember showing him the private ledger? I can see his face even now."

"I remember it quite well," his brother assented. "I remember what he said: 'I did not know that there were gold mines in London.' Those were his words."

They passed through the mixing rooms to the home packing department. Occasionally Samuel stopped to speak to an old employee. Presently they came to the laboratories.

"I should like to see our great chemist," Samuel declared.

"Paule doesn't care about being disturbed very much," his son observed doubtfully.

"I am not here often," his father persisted. "After all, I am one of his employers. I wish to shake hands with him before I go."

They passed into the office and word was sent to Paule. Presently he came out, still in his linen coat, with rubber gloves upon his hands and heavy spectacles.

"This is my brother, Mr. Samuel Fernham," Joseph explained, half apologetically. "He comes to see us very seldom now. He has been having a look round and thought he would like to shake hands with you before he goes."

Paule removed his gloves and glasses.

"I am very busy to-day," he warned them. "If there is anything you want to ask me, Mr. Fernham, I am at your service for three minutes."

Samuel shook his head. All the time his eyes never left the other's face.

"Paule," he murmured, "Sir Lawrence Paule. In what part of the country were you born, Sir Lawrence?"

"In Sussex, at a village called Wormley, if you happen to know it."

Samuel shook his head.

"They tell me that you are one of the cleverest chemists in the world," he said. "Can you make an old man young?"

Paule smiled.

"For an hour or two, perhaps," he answered. "Won't you sit down, Mr. Fernham? You have probably tired yourself."

"I am tired," Samuel admitted, "but mine is not the fatigue that passes. For an hour or two, you say. Well!"

" For an hour or two," Paule confided, " I could probably make you feel twenty years younger. At the end
of that time you would sleep. When you woke up, unless
you are a philosopher, you would curse me. You would
feel even more tired than you feel now."

" I am a philosopher," Samuel declared. " This is
probably my last visit to the business which was once
the joy of my life. Now I am going to lunch with my
son. Give me your drug, Mr. Chemist. Afterwards
matters nothing."

Paule disappeared and returned a minute or two
later, carrying an ordinary medicine glass in which was
some brown mixture.

" Not a dozen people in the world have ever tasted
this," he said. " Mind, it will only do what I say."

Samuel drained the glass and set it down empty.

" Now I will go," he announced. " I shall send you a
message by my son, sir. If you have done what you
promise, I thank you in advance."

He held out his thin, talonlike hand.

" You don't wish to see the outer laboratories? "
Paule suggested. " There is nothing special going on
except drug testing."

Samuel shook his head.

" I was never a chemist," he confessed. " It was
finance which interested me, the handling of money, the
teaching money to save money. I wish you good-bye,
Sir Lawrence. You shall have my message."

They left the office, Samuel in front, leaning upon his
son's arm, and Joseph behind. Paule watched them pass
through the door. Even after they had gone he remained motionless, as though listening to the receding
tap of Samuel's stick upon the hard floor.

" A wonderful man, that," the latter declared. " I

can feel the warmth of that drink in my veins. A great man, I am sure! Why has he come here as our chemist?"

"For the same reason that we others have spent the greater part of our lives toiling and bartering here," Joseph replied—"money!"

CHAPTER XII

JUDITH, on the afternoon of her visit to Paule, ensconced in a well-worn easy-chair of homely design, took stock of her surroundings with a curiosity which she made no attempt to conceal. She found herself in a large and lofty sitting room of absolutely ordinary appearance, except that the walls were lined with book shelves in every available space from the floor to the ceiling, and a table obviously pushed on one side was heaped with reviews and great piles of typewritten notes. On the mantelpiece were ranged a number of small bottles, each carefully labelled and sealed. The window, which was thrown wide open, looked out upon a wilderness of allotments and small houses, and beyond, the grey pall of the city. To enter the apartment Judith had descended three steps from the laboratory which she had been shown on her previous visit, and besides that door there were still three others leading into the room.

"I am afraid," her host remarked, "that you find my immediate environment a little disappointing. I don't know why, either. I am really not a person of mystery."

"Don't destroy the illusion which brought me here," she begged. "I fancied you in some unearthly garb, with blue fires burning all around you, snatching the secrets of the universe from some diabolically invoked genii. There is still hope, though. I see three more doors."

"Three more," he assented. "Through one my servant will presently appear carrying a tea tray. Such a revelation of domesticity I imagine will effectually crush romance in that direction."

"There are two more," she reminded him.

"There are two more," he admitted. "One, alas, must remain barred even against your curiosity. I am conducting an experiment there which would be imperilled by the slightest change of temperature. The other room is my chapel."

"Your what?"

"The place where I go to think," he explained.

"Where do you think, when you have to?"

"Wherever I happen to be," she replied. "Out of doors, if possible."

He shook his head.

"A mistake," he assured her. "Your visit after all shall not be made for nothing. Presently I will give you a new thought — if it is worth having."

The door opposite the one through which she had entered was quietly opened and a servant came in carrying a tea tray. He arranged it noiselessly upon a small table, Judith watching him all the time with fascinated eyes. He had the broad face, high cheek bones and yellow skin of a Chinese, but the correct dress of a European. His complexion, however, and the skin on his hands, though spotlessly clean, was yellow.

"A Siamese," Paule told her, as soon as he had left the room. "He was the head waiter at my hotel in Bangkok. I brought him home with me simply because of the absence in him of one disastrous trait so common to the British servant — curiosity. He does everything for me except cook — drives my car, looks after my clothes and keeps my tennis rackets in the press. If I told him to drive the car into a brick wall, he would do it. That humpbacked note of interrogation has been left out of his system."

"I am recovering my faith in you," she murmured.

"If it is necessary for you to go to Siam to get an incurious servant you must still be a man of mystery. — Am I to make the tea?"

"If you will," he begged. "It is the Chinese tea which used to go to Russia. Futoy gets it for me. Cakes I know nothing about. Rumpelmayer alone must take the responsibility for them."

"Rumpelmayer cakes at Acton Green!" she murmured. "I believe that in imagination, at any rate, you are a Sybarite."

Their conversation remained for a time upon the lightest of levels. When she had drunk her second cup of tea Judith helped herself to a cigarette from the box which her host had placed by her side. She looked up at him with a little smile. It was the only blend she ever smoked.

"How could you guess?" she asked.

"I noticed those in your case the other night," he confided.

"Even then I wonder how you knew that it makes so much difference," she remarked.

"Instinct," he explained. "You exist in my mind as a person entirely unique in your exquisite care for details. Whatever clothes you are wearing possess a certain directness of effect, as though they had been chosen without deliberation, yet every little trifle about your toilette seems to me to be selected with the scrupulous care of one to whom trifles are all important. Our limited vocabulary invites banalities. The perfection of those cream silk stockings, your speckless patent shoes with those buckles, which are of themselves a work of art, the droop of that lace about your throat, your ringless fingers, undermanicured perhaps, but soft and exquisite. You are like it not at this moment only, but always. From it I judge your apprehension of the value of detail. One wine, the finest of its sort, would attract you and no other. You discard as scrupulously as you select. This is the process of reasoning by means of which I arrived at the conviction that you would probably smoke only one brand of cigarettes."

" Is all this flattery? " she asked.

" You should know," he rejoined.

The telephone bell rang, and she listened to him whilst he gave a few brief instructions to the department which had rung him up — terse, final words, admitting of no argument and scarcely any comment. The strength of his face, dominated though it was by that massive forehead, was undoubted. Some of its other qualities puzzled her. She came to the conclusion that he was probably cruel. He certainly was not sparing the feelings of the foreman who had drawn his attention to some apparently trivial matter.

"And now," he said, as he turned back to her, " to pander as far as we can to this curiosity of yours. Except the architect and builders and Futoy no person has ever passed through that door into what I have termed my chapel. There is nothing whatever of interest there. I warn you that you will be vastly disappointed. Nevertheless you shall see it if you will."

" There is no pretence about me," she declared, rising to her feet. " Sheer, vulgar curiosity is what I am guilty of. Please lead the way."

He crossed the room, drew a chain from his pocket, the end of which was attached to his trouser button, and selected one of three delicate looking keys. With it he opened the door. She stepped forward after a moment's hesitation. He followed her. Almost immediately the door swung back and she heard the click of the lock.

Judith looked around her blankly.

" What does it mean? " she asked.

" Just what I told you," he answered.

They were in a room of the same size as the one which they had just left. The floor, composed of ordinary wood blocks, was perfectly bare, the walls of plain cement remained exactly as they had been left by the builders. The only window was in the roof — a great piece of stained orange-coloured glass — the only article of furniture, a wooden couch in the middle of the room, un-upholstered and with a single cushion of insignificant size. There was nothing here to kindle the imagination in any way, not even a cupboard or an aperture where anything might be concealed. She looked round the walls wonderingly, and suddenly she gave a little involuntary gasp. The door on the inside had been painted the same colour as the wall. To all appearance they were in a hermetically sealed chamber.

" Explain, please," she insisted.

" You disappoint me," he confessed. " To me my place of refuge has always seemed a trifle obvious. It is here I think. The room was built for no other purpose."

There was an unsatisfied expression in her eyes. After a moment he continued.

" Take my sitting room," he said. " You see for yourself that my walls are lined with books. I recline there to study one of the problems which I have occasionally to solve in connection with my work for your father. My eyes light on one of those volumes — a volume of philosophy, perhaps, or mental science, or speculative research. I am disturbed. My mind is at once in another channel of thought. I have to withdraw it. My thoughts will never move again with the same spontaneity. None of us ever realise," he went on, " the effect each person has upon another, the effect which even inanimate objects may have upon our brain when we need its best effort. Face a certain problem and your surest movement towards its solution will be the dawn of any speculative tendency concerning it. That is the one part of thought which is spontaneous. If that is interfered with it may not come again."

" You are upsetting many theories," she reminded him. " An artist would say that the best place for him to go and study a proposed picture would be a place where he could live amidst beautiful surroundings."

" I should join issue with him," Paule declared. " Under those conditions there would be a vein of re-production in his work. Any one who is ambitious to create should start from a state of negation, if he desires to give of his own brain, his own constructive force. — You are cold," he added quickly. " I am sorry. The atmosphere of this place is always a little chilly."

Her fit of shivering passed. It had come with the sight of that locked door, the feeling of being alone with him, cut off from the rest of the world. A sudden medley of desires seemed to give to the seconds an absurd significance. She wanted to rush to the door and beat against it, to stay where she was and look upwards again through that orange light. He was standing as he had done from the moment of his entrance, several feet away from her, his hands behind his back, his attitude towards her irreproachable, almost distant. She was suddenly quite sure that she hated him.

" Well," she observed slowly, " I've penetrated one of the mysteries."

" The only one," he assured her, as he led the way towards the door and swung it open.

They were back in the sitting room, back in that
atmosphere of roses and cigarette smoke and old calf
bindings, with its faint background of pungent drugs.
She breathed a deep sigh of something like relief. When
she sank into her chair once more she found that her
knees were trembling. She stretched out her hand for
another cigarette.

"Don't be afraid that I am going to outstay my
welcome," she said. "I give myself another five minutes. Can I take you anywhere?"

"Thank you, no," he answered. "I have my own
little car here which Futoy runs for me. I leave at all
manner of times."

She pointed towards the other door but he shook his
head.

"In there," he explained, "I study and pursue experiments, some of which are absolutely unconnected
with the business. I have a laboratory and beyond, a
bedroom and a bathroom, which I use when I have to
stay here all night."

"Tell me about your research work which is not for
the firm," she begged.

"It is too inconclusive," was the colourless reply.

"What is going on just now, in your laboratory?"
she persisted. "Blue flames and retorts and fizzing of
steam and that sort of thing?"

"Nothing of that kind at all," he assured her.

Futoy made his noiseless appearance and murmured a
few words to his master, who after a moment's hesitation
nodded.

"You will excuse me?" he asked, turning to Judith.
"I have to speak for a moment upon the private telephone in my bedroom. Your cousin Samuel, it appears,
has something urgent to say to me."

" Let me go," she suggested, half rising.

" I shall not be a moment," he replied. " If you do not mind waiting I will see you to your car."

He passed behind her chair towards the door which had excited her curiosity. She turned her head and followed his movements. He unfastened the door with another key from his bunch, opened it only just far enough to pass through, and closed it with a firm bang, almost a slam. Her eyes remained rivetted upon the panels. Scarcely knowing what she did, she rose to her feet. The very force with which he had closed the door had defeated his intention. The latch had not slipped back to its place. Meanwhile ——

She crossed the room, obeying simply a blind impulse. She had no sense of shame. She only realised that she was yielding to an ungovernable, unjustifiable curiosity, but a curiosity deeper than any mere desire to understand the why and wherefore of his reticence. She stood quite close to the door. Somewhere in the distance she could hear his voice at the telephone. She slipped her finger against the gleaming latch, pushed it back and swung the door a foot open. She gazed eagerly into the room, hugging her excitement, breathlessly eager to discover in that swift glance which she had decided must be all she could allow herself, something of the unusual. She had her glance and the world seemed suddenly to resolve itself into a place of sick and unmentionable horrors. Her self-control went with her failing senses. Her shriek rang through the rooms as she tottered backward, her hands pressed frantically over her eyes, asking only of life the forgetfulness which came with her swoon.

CHAPTER XIII

JUDITH opened her eyes to the pungent odour of restoratives and the stimulating consciousness of Paule's near presence. He rose from his knees and removed his fingers from the pulse which he had been feeling.

" You are all right now," he said quietly. " Even Fatima paid the price, you know. I must apologise for my carelessness. I must have left the door of my chamber of horrors open."

" You left it unlatched," she told him. " I pushed it open."

He felt her pulse again and, satisfied with her condition, moved away. Her eyes followed him.

" Well? " she faltered.

" Well? " he echoed.

" You will explain," she begged.

" Is it for Fatima to make terms? " he remarked grimly. " However, I will be generous. I was to blame, perhaps, for not securing the door. Do you think you could bear to look in again, leaning on my arm? "

" Yes," she assured him.

She struggled to her feet. He led the way, unlocked the door but kept her back until he had made the place brilliant with electric light.

" Now," he pointed out, " you will see that neither my skeletons nor my heads are so alarming as they seemed. Here is the explanation of this room, since you have forced it from me. Besides being a fairly capable chemist I am supposed to be something of an authority upon the nervous system. The skull which you see

grinning at you there with its background of black cloth
has been fitted with those imitation nerves — thin silver
wire you see they are — entirely by me. The skeleton
in the corner I consider rather a masterpiece. I have
left it in my will to Gabour, the Frenchman who is the
greatest living authority upon psychic disturbances of
the brain. There are three skulls there," he went on,
" one of them unfortunately with a small electric light
behind, which were probably responsible for your fainting fit. They are scarcely fit for lay eyes at present,"
he added, dropping a cloth over them. "I had to have
them in that condition to verify an hypothesis which I
have recently put forward with regard to the transmis-
sion of external influences to the cerebral nerves."

"What a chamber of horrors!" she cried. "What
is the chair there for and the dynamo and those strange
coils?"

"You must really excuse me," he said quietly, "if I
leave just a little mystery attached to my investigations. What I have explained to you, I have explained
for the sake of your peace of mind. It was not my
intention to divulge to you the hobby of which this room
is the outcome."

They were back in the sitting room. He closed the
door firmly behind him.

"I am sorry," he continued, "that your visit has
ended a little disastrously. You will absolve me from
blame, I am sure. I had no idea of obtruding this portion of my activities upon you."

"There is no need for you to be sarcastic," she complained. "I behaved very badly but I have certainly
suffered for it."

"It might have been worse," he remarked somewhat
cryptically.

"Worse," she repeated with a shudder. "I can't imagine it. I am not a nervous person, but I never had such a shock in my life."

"Worse for me, I mean, not for you," he explained. "My heads might have been covered up. They often are. As a matter of fact, they would have been to-day but that I have been readjusting the tension of Henry's nerves — Henry was the gentleman who gave you such a start."

"How would that have made it worse?" she demanded.

"You might have passed on to my holy of holies beyond. What I should have done with you then, I can't imagine."

"What an annoying reflection," she sighed. "I have really missed something, then?"

"What you will not miss," he remarked, with a glance at the clock, "is seeing your cousin Samuel, if you don't hurry. It was he who was telephoning. He is on his way here now."

"Then, please let me fly," she begged. "He is dining at home with us to-night, and I don't wish to see any one just now if I can help it."

"I can let you out through Futoy's quarters," he suggested.

"Anything to avoid Samuel," she assented.

He led the way down into the courtyard and despatched Futoy for her car. She was still a little pale and her manner had lost something of its poise.

"You're not in the habit of fainting, are you?" he asked, looking at her curiously.

"I have fainted once before in my life," she told him, "when I saw a man killed in a steeplechase. When you took me into that room the second time, of course it was nothing, but the first time I didn't know what to expect. The light was shining just behind that horrible skull and those others — they all seemed to be grinning at me. The setting is a little melodramatic, isn't it, — that black background?"

"Probably," he admitted. "It is there because I have to see them clearly myself. When you find your income increased by another hundred thousand a year or so and are told that it is due to the wonderful success of a new nerve food, you will perhaps forgive me."

The car turned the corner and drew up. He handed her in.

"Will you come and dine again soon?" she asked.

He shook his head.

"No, thanks," he answered. "I hate dinner parties. I would rather see you alone."

She hesitated.

"Well, you can telephone," she said, leaning back in her place.

Samuel Junior, who had been waiting in the reception room, presently made his appearance. He looked around him with frank interest. It had occurred to him more than once lately that every one in the firm treated Paule with rather too much respect. He determined to strike a different note.

"Hullo, hullo, hullo!" he exclaimed, glancing towards the tea table. "Snug little bachelor quarters you've got here, what? Tea for two, a bowl of yellow roses and cakes — damn good cakes too," he added, helping himself to one. "Nothing of this sort at the other end of the show, what?"

Paule made no reply. He took a cigarette and passed the box across to his visitor.

" Can you guess what I've come for? " the latter continued. " It's that draught you gave the governor. It made a new man of him. He enjoyed his luncheon and actually smoked a cigar afterwards — a thing he hasn't done for a year. He was as bright as possible all the afternoon, and then, as you warned him, he became sleepy. He wants to know whether he can have a prescription."

Paule shook his head.

" I am sorry," he said. " I can't give him one."

" I say! " Samuel protested. " Why not? No blooming etiquette or anything of that sort, is it? Surely you wouldn't consider that under the circumstances! "

" That is not the reason," was the curt reply. " I used an unknown drug which no ordinary chemist would be able to procure and I used it in conjunction with another which it is dangerous to take at any time except under special conditions."

" Make him just one more draught, then," the young man begged. " I must pacify him somehow."

" I would rather not do that," Paule confessed. " This unknown drug I spoke of can be used the first time upon any one with impunity. Every time afterwards, however, there is a risk, especially if the heart is at all weak."

" Well, I suppose you know best," Samuel conceded reluctantly. " I tell you what you could do if you would, though, Paule. My heart's as sound as a bull's, but — well, just feel my pulse."

Paule felt it for a moment and raised his eyebrows.

" I thought you were staying at Brighton with your father," he remarked.

" So I am," Samuel acknowledged, " but he goes to

bed at nine and I went round to the Metropole last night just to have a dance and a drink. I got back at five this morning, and I've got to dine to-night with his lord-ship, Uncle Joseph — a formal affair — no end of big-wigs going. You can see for yourself what sort of a state I'm in. I thought of going to my chemist chap, but if you'd give me something, I'd rather."

Paule nodded.

" Sleepy, aren't you? " he enquired.

" I wasn't conscious of it but perhaps I am," Samuel admitted. " I know I've had four aspirins and I've still got a foul headache."

" Sit down in that chair and I'll mix you something up in a moment. It wouldn't do you any harm," Paule continued thoughtfully, standing upon the hearthrug with his elbow upon the mantelpiece and looking down at his visitor, " if you went to sleep for a few minutes — just a very few minutes. Sleep would soothe your nerves."

Samuel held out his hand for the medicine glass and drained its contents. — He sat up in his chair.

" I say," he exclaimed, " I haven't been to sleep, have I? "

Paule shrugged his shoulders.

" You may have dropped off whilst I was putting my bottles away," he said. " How do you feel now? "

" Queer but different," the young man declared, standing up. " Jove, I was quite giddy at first! I'll be getting on, Paule. Thank you very much. I'm sorry you can't do anything for the governor. Good stuff, that! I'm beginning to feel brisker already. What a hell of a lot of books," he observed, pausing on the threshold for a backward glance around the room. — " So long, old chap! "

Paule listened to his visitor's receding footsteps. Then he touched the bell and Futoy appeared.

"Futoy," he announced, "to-night I work here, dine and sleep. You remain also."

The man bowed, picked up the tea tray and retired. Paule, with a sheaf of papers in his hand and a linen coat over his arm, passed out into the main laboratory.

CHAPTER XIV

THERE were three interests in life which were paramount with Joseph, second Baron Honerton. The first was bridge, which he played from four until seven every day and in the evening whenever it was possible; the second was his daughter Judith, whose triumphant progress into the innermost mazes of society and whose unspoilt personality were a constant source of wonder to him; and the third was the conference which was held once a month in the Board Room at the Works and attended by the directors and various heads of departments. The policy of these great pioneers of patent medicines was there decided upon. Occasionally a specific was dropped, or if any competing preparation had been successfully launched by a rival firm, the matter of its purchase was discussed. The advertising campaign was carefully planned. The matter of finance was dealt with but lightly; as a rule the profits were too stupendous to be spoken of freely before others than directors. These conferences, at which Joseph was in a sense supreme, occupied his thoughts for at least a week beforehand and a week afterwards, and were his surest resource against that dull sense of loss which plunged him some days into the deepest dejection.

One of these functions took place a few days after Judith's visit to Lawrence Paule. Joseph was in one of his most fussy moods, a state of mind which clearly indicated the existence of some unexpected business. Various minor items on the Agenda, such as a ten thousand pound advertising campaign for " Uneedum Charcoal Biscuits " and an alteration in the coating of a famous pill which had fallen a little into desuetude were decided upon and dismissed in a few sentences. When at last a pause in the proceedings arrived, Joseph pulled down his waistcoat portentously, straightened his tie and took the little company into his confidence.

"Gentlemen," he said, "I have now to invite your attention to an announcement which I am sure will be of interest to you. Ever since he joined us, a very distinguished chemist and savant, Sir Lawrence Paule has been at work upon a remedy for the greatest curse of these — er — overexuberant days — I refer to hyper-nervousness. Sir Lawrence has made many experiments and wandered into very distant fields to compile his formula. Within the last few days he has informed me of his complete success. We shall be in a position to put upon the market a preparation unique in the history of patent medicines. In a word, gentlemen, it will succeed in doing what our advertisements will guarantee it to do. — Sir Lawrence will very likely say a few words himself."

There was a little murmur of interest. Samuel Junior banged the table with his fist. Bearing always in mind his own brilliancy and confidence at his uncle's dinner table a few evenings before, he was a confirmed believer in Paule's gifts. The latter, who with rather a wearied expression had been studying the list of subjects for discussion labelled "Agenda" and distributed amongst the little company, looked up without changing his position.

"I haven't a great deal to add to what your chairman has told you," he said. "I have been experimenting for some time with a combination of known specifics and a drug which I think I may term of my own invention, my idea being to deaden the nerves without the penalty of a corresponding reaction. I am expressing myself of course in lay language but what I mean to say is this: In these days of high pressure there are naturally a variety of nervous ailments concerning which the physical condition of the body has very little to do. Claustrophobia is one of these. There are many men who simply cannot exist in enclosed spaces, who cannot sit in the middle of a row of stalls, who cannot walk near the edge of a precipice, who are subject to fits of giddiness at inconvenient periods — the symptoms, in fact, are too numerous and commonplace to be worth recapitulating. Of course, as you all know, no medicine in the world ever cures anything; it alleviates. I have perfected a mixture, of which if the most abject victim of Claustrophobia will take one draught, he is absolutely immune for twenty-four hours, at least, from any recurrence of his disorder. A man, for instance, who has been subject to fits of giddiness all his life under certain conditions, can take one dose of my specific, and face those conditions at any time within the next twenty-four hours without the slightest discomfort. In a hospital last week I found a man who for ten years had been unable to sit through a church service without such violent fits of trembling and giddiness that he was compelled to leave. I experimented upon him. He sat through the whole of the morning service at St. Paul's without a single second's uneasiness. He offered me, by-the-bye, a thousand pounds for the prescription. The mixture is only moderately costly, but it needs personal preparation. The doctors will attack it vigorously and there will be an immense demand for it. I should recommend, taking everything into consideration, that it be put on the market at a very high price. People will buy it just as readily and after it has once started it will scarcely need advertising at all. The share of the profits which I shall require I have already submitted to the accountants and to the company, who find them reasonable."

There was a little murmur of interest. Joseph cleared his throat.

"Gentlemen," he said, "I may add to what Sir Lawrence has told us, that I have given very close and personal attention to the figures which he has laid before me. I have consulted with various members of our executive staff now present and our decision is — subject to any suggestions — to entitle the preparation 'Neurota' and to sell it in bottles at one guinea only. On this basis I think I will have said enough if I tell you that the profits will be on the same scale as the rest of our productions."

For the remainder of the proceedings nobody talked about anything but "Neurota." Samuel Junior was one of its warmest advocates. The advertisement department went into a private session. Joseph laid his hand upon Paule's shoulder.

"This is an occasion, Sir Lawrence!" he declared. "I am lunching at home to-day. My car is waiting. Do us the honour. My wife, as you know, is, alas, half an invalid, but my daughter will be there. She will be delighted. Samuel, you must come along too."

Paule, rather to his prospective host's surprise, accepted after only a moment's hesitation. During the long drive to Park Lane, Samuel practically monopolised the conversation.

"Wish I could have got the Dad to have come up this morning," he said. "This would have interested him, although he would never have been a customer — not a nerve in his body, the governor! Weak as you like physically, but as brave as a lion! I suppose nerves are a form of cowardice, eh, Paule? "

" Lack of control," was the laconic reply.

Samuel babbled on, neither his uncle nor Paule taking very much heed. Arrived at their destination they were greeted with the usual ostentation, — too many flunkeys, too obsequious a major-domo, almost too urbane a welcome from the butler in the background. Guests before whom to display their magnificence were always welcomed by these denizens of Park Lane. The hall, however, was pleasantly cool and the perfume of the banks of flowers delightful.

" What about a cocktail in the winter garden? " Joseph suggested.

They found Judith lying in a long chair underneath two great palm trees before an open window. She scarcely turned her head at their coming, but as she recognised the unexpected guest, the listlessness seemed to leave her frame. She half rose and held out her hand.

" I never thought of you as a luncher out," she remarked.

" Nor am I," he assured her. " To-day is a sort of fête day at the Works. We are placing a new drug upon the market, for which I am responsible."

" The result of your study of nerves? "

" Only part of it. The results of science do not all lend themselves to interpretation by means of drugs."

" If you people will leave off talking above our heads," Samuel Junior intervened good-naturedly, " you will notice that Martin is offering you a very excellent cocktail."

Judith took one of the frosted glasses, held it for a moment between her fingers and looked up at Paule.

" Shall I drink to those other results? " she asked banteringly.

" Do," he begged. " ' Neurota ' will make a fortune, but immortality will remain with them."

"Any one lunching? " Joseph enquired abruptly; he hated to be left out of a conversation.

" No one," Judith replied, " unless anybody inflicts their uninvited presence upon us. We have persuaded Mother to lunch downstairs to-day on the understanding that we were practically a home party."

Rachel appeared just at that moment. In her thin black gown, with her snow-white hair, pallid cheeks and brilliant eyes, she had a look of exotic fragility, almost unnatural in its spirituality. Paule bowed a little stiffly over her wasted fingers.

" We have not met for some time, Lady Honerton," he remarked.

" I see no one these days," she answered. " Will you all come in. Martin has announced luncheon."

They passed across the hall in informal fashion. Paule found himself a little way behind with his hostess.

" They tell me, Sir Lawrence," she said, " that you are a wizard, that you have left the fields of science behind and entered the world of magic."

" There is a certain amount of exaggeration in the statement," he assured her, smiling.

" You have a great brain," she went on. " You see far into the heart of things. Why cannot you tell me what has become of my son? Why cannot you help them bring him back again? "

He looked at her with a gaze as steadfast and searching as her own.

" I am a chemist," he reminded her quietly, " not a detective."

" It will never be a detective who will restore Ernest to me," she replied. " It will be some one with other powers."

Conversation during the progress of the meal was almost entirely between Joseph and his nephew. The idea of another fortune had fired both their brains. Judith listened to them without sympathy, yet with some attention.

" I suppose, Samuel," she said, " you are now less than ever disposed to yield to your father's desire and give up business? "

Samuel's palms flew out — an often restrained but still occasional gesture.

" My dear Judith," he protested, " what should I do with myself? I am not what you call a sportsman; I can ride a little for exercise, shoot a little to pass the time at a country house, play tennis or golf, you know how badly, but these things are nothing to me. They fill in the odd moments, but they would never fill my mind. Business is my great pleasure. I am not ashamed to declare it. Fancy if you were to ask Sir Lawrence here to retire. He would laugh at you. Sport, travel — what are these things compared to the main interest in life? My main interest is business. Sir Lawrence's is science. We should neither of us be happy away from them."

" Yet you should obey your father," Rachel intervened unexpectedly. " He may see things which are hidden from you."

There was a brief spell of uneasy silence. The servants with whom the room was overfilled stood like mutes behind the chairs. Samuel was without doubt discomposed.

" There are some things the governor can't know more

about than any one else," he declared a little awkwardly.
" If you're thinking of the socialist blackmail theory,
they've been a pretty long time showing their hand,
what? Besides, forewarned is forearmed. I've nothing
to do with mysterious strangers nowadays, male or fe-
male. If you think I'm taking risks, what about this?
My servant sleeps in my dressing room and I have
bought another car for night work. I haven't been in
a taxi since I can remember and my runs in town are
pretty well constricted, I can assure you."

His aunt listened with unchanging expression.

" You are very clever in your own generation, Samuel," she acknowledged, " but you cannot believe that
you are so clever as the brain which plotted against my
boy, which removed him from us in the middle of the
country without a word of warning or without leaving
a trace behind. Can your intelligence prevail against
an intelligence which has foiled the whole of Scotland
Yard? If those who took Ernest desire it, you will go
too."

There was a further period of uneasy silence. The
domestics proceeded to the service of a new course.
Samuel and his uncle both looked startled, the former
almost scared. The corners of Paule's mouth seemed
to have crept a little higher up into a curve of faint
amusement. Samuel raised his glass to his lips and
drained its contents, fine Cabinet Hock of a famous
vintage. He felt the glow of it in his veins.

" I've no enemies," he declared obstinately. " I have
done no one any harm. I shall live as I choose."

For his aunt all interest in the subject appeared to
have passed. She had relapsed into her usual impassivity.

" The modern Ajax, defying the powers of evil,"

Judith murmured, with a gently derisive smile. " I wonder no one has worried about me. If there is any one in the family worth abducting, it seems to me that I should be the one to feel anxious."

CHAPTER XV

JUDITH had just returned from an early morning ride in the park a few weeks later when Rodes' card was brought to her. She interviewed him in one of the smaller and lesser-used reception rooms.

"Your ladyship will pardon the liberty, I hope," he begged, rising at her entrance, "but to tell you the truth, there was just a word you said to me one day in St. James's Street which I have never been able to get out of my mind."

"It hasn't apparently helped you much," she remarked.

"Not up to the present," he admitted.

"You are no nearer a solution?" she asked.

He shook his head.

"I fear not," he confessed. "Our blackmail theory seems to have become impossible. The twenty thousand pounds' reward has now been offered for all these months and nothing has come of it."

Judith glanced at the clock on the mantelpiece.

"I am willing to talk with you for hours," she said, "if it is likely to be of the slightest assistance. On the other hand, I am rather late as it is for an appointment."

"I will not keep you for long, Lady Judith," the detective promised. "Would you mind telling me, is that not a portrait of your grandfather Israel?" he went on, drawing her attention to a painting upon the wall.

She looked at it carelessly.

"It is," she replied.

"I wonder whether you have anywhere in the house

a photograph or picture of him when he was comparatively a young man — say thirty years old?" he continued.

Judith stared at him in surprise.

"I dare say. What do you want it for?"

The man hesitated. He seemed to make up his mind, however, to confide in his questioner.

"I have been making some enquiries," he explained, "about the child of your Uncle Cecil and the daughter of Heggs, the keeper. I have never been entirely satisfied as to the evidence of his death. Now, if he were alive, he might very well be a secret enemy of your family."

Judith considered the matter for a moment.

"It seems rather far-fetched, but of course it might be so," she admitted. "I have always understood that the child died at the same time as his mother."

"A child did die," he observed, "and was buried in the same grave as Heggs' daughter. The evidence that it was her child, however, is not to my mind absolutely conclusive. The Heggs family at that time were desperately anxious to have the whole thing forgotten."

"Let me see," Judith remarked, "if he had lived he would be about thirty years old, wouldn't he?"

"Just about that," the detective assented. "Your grandfather was a man of very strongly marked features and great personality. It is just possible that his grandson might resemble him. I have several photographs of your Uncle Cecil, but he seems to have been a young man of rather negative characterization."

"I'll go and see if I can find a photograph," she promised. "Do you mind waiting? I may be some little time."

"Not in the least," he assured her.

She left the room. The detective turned on the electric light which was fitted in the frame of the great oil painting and stood opposite it for some time. The artist — a very celebrated man — had painted a very striking picture but had shown his sitter little kindness. The harshness of Israel Fernham's large features, the firm, almost cruel lines of his mouth, the level gaze of his calculating eyes, were all reproduced here without flattery or toning down. It might well have been the portrait of a man of great ability but there was a lack of humanity, almost a rapacity about the face which made it absolutely forbidding and which accounted for its being hung in one of the smaller rooms of the house. Rodes studied it for a long time, with his hands in his pockets, whistling softly to himself. Then he turned out the light and when Judith returned was perusing a volume of *Punch* in a distant easy-chair.

"I have found a photograph," she told him. "It is a little faded. Otherwise I fancy it must have been a good likeness."

He examined it thoughtfully for a few minutes. Then, with it still in his hand, he turned up the light underneath the frame and studied the picture once again. Judith stood by his side.

"I prefer the photograph," she said decidedly. "We none of us like the painting."

He laid the former down without further reference to it.

"I don't think I need keep you any longer, Lady Judith," he remarked after a brief pause. "It has been very kind of you to spare me so much of your time."

"Has it helped you in any way, the photograph?" she enquired.

"It has helped me to this extent," he explained. "You must remember that I am in the very desperate — I am afraid I must add humiliating — situation of being without the slightest clue as to your brother's whereabouts or condition, if he is still alive. I am driven, therefore, to work according to your own advice, on theory only. If, by any chance, this son of Heggs' daughter and your Uncle Cecil should be still alive and should have inherited — forgive me — the somewhat fierce and unforgiving disposition of your grandfather, he might well be a secret enemy of your house. If heredity counts for anything, I know now what he should be like."

He took his departure, but Judith, although a few minutes before she had been in a hurry, lingered in the room. She took up the photograph and looked at it intently. It was a stern face even in youth, strong and without kindness, but it lacked the cruelty which the great artist had found in Israel and perpetuated upon his canvas.

A servant opened the door and made a respectful announcement.

"Lord Amberleys is here, your ladyship."

Amberleys entered close on his heels. Judith glanced from him to the clock.

"My dear Freddy!" she exclaimed, as the servant retired. "I am most frightfully sorry, but I had some one to see me and the time slipped away. I won't be more than a quarter of an hour changing."

"No hurry at all, dear," he assured her, raising her fingers to his lips with somewhat clumsy gallantry. "I say, what a ripping picture of your grandfather — bit of an autocrat, I should think!"

"I am sorry that he died before I was born," Judith

sighed. " I should like to have known him. He had some very fine qualities. This is a photograph of him in earlier life. I wonder does it remind you of any one."

He looked at it without much show of interest.

" No one particular," he remarked carelessly. " Strikes me as being a bit like that chemist chap, down at your Works."

Judith almost snatched the photograph back. For a few seconds she gazed at it with an absorption which was extraordinary. The fugitive idea which she had failed to grasp was suddenly materialised. It was there beyond a doubt — the inflexible mouth, the slight bulge of the forehead, the level eyes.

" No real likeness, of course," Amberleys continued with a stealthy glance towards the clock. " That chemist fellow's better-looking, I should say, than your grandfather was — more of the athlete about him, to judge from his shoulders. What about that change, Judith? We are due at Claridge's at one-fifteen."

" I'll be ready," she promised. " Wait for me in the winter garden, there's a dear! "

Judith hurried to her room, but before she commenced to change she telephoned to Scotland Yard and ascertained that Mr. Rodes had not yet returned. She left a message for him and just as she was ready to descend the bell rang. She took off the receiver.

" Is that Lady Judith? " a voice enquired.

" Yes," she replied.

" Rodes speaking. You asked for me."

" Yes. I hope you don't mind," Judith said. " It is really rather a ridiculous thing to ring you up about, but looking at that photograph again after you had left I suddenly realised who it reminded me of — some one you never heard of, I dare say, and whom I only met the other day."

" I should be interested to hear," was the measured rejoinder.

" It reminds me just a little," she confided, " of a man named Paule — Sir Lawrence Paule. He is the chief chemist down at our Works."

There was a moment's silence, then a deprecatory little cough from the other end of the wire.

" Very interesting, Lady Judith," Rodes admitted. " I am afraid, however, that Sir Lawrence Paule's antecedents are too well known for this to be anything more than a chance likeness. I shall take the liberty of seeing you again in a few days."

Judith replaced the receiver and joined her impatient cavalier. Even he noticed, in a few moments, that she was somewhat distrait.

" Nothing wrong? " he ventured.

She came down to earth.

" My dear man, no! " she exclaimed. " My visitor this morning was the detective who is working on Ernest's case. Talking about it always affects me just a little."

He laid his hand upon hers.

" Sorry I said a word," he apologised. " There is no news, I suppose? "

" None," she answered, with a little sigh. " I am beginning to believe that there never will be any."

CHAPTER XVI

THE issue of " Neurota " formed a new epoch in the commercial progress of the great house of Fernham and Company, Ltd. For the first time within their experience of launching a fresh specific, free samples became unnecessary and advertising superfluous. The preparation had scarcely been on the market a week when, in response to an urgent message of entreaty, Paule made his way to Joseph's private office. The latter was standing there in the midst of a maze of correspondence, his morning cigar as yet unsmoked, his manner excited but perplexed.

" We've gone and done a nice thing, Sir Lawrence," he exclaimed. " They had to telephone up to the house for me to come down at once, half an hour before my usual time. Do you know what our orders for ' Neurota ' amount to during the last four days? "

" I have heard no figures," was the calm reply. " I understood that it was going well."

" Our orders for the home trade alone," Joseph declared portentously, " amount to twenty-eight thousand bottles. The export trade hasn't commenced yet. Do you know you're making a fortune, young fellow? "

Paule raised his eyebrows at the familiarity, but Joseph was too agitated to heed him.

" The trade will have to be rationed," the former decided. " I cannot possibly guarantee more than five thousand bottles a week."

" There'll be a riot," Joseph protested. " There are telegrams coming in every few minutes from our travellers, and for the first time in our lives, we've had what we advertise — unsolicited testimonials — heaps of them. Grateful patients, and all sorts of slosh, but they're in earnest. I say, can't you squeeze the quantity a bit — lessen the proportion of that secret drug of yours?"

Paule shook his head.

"It couldn't be done," he pronounced. "Any variation in the prescription would be disastrous."

"Couldn't you find another market and get more of your drug, then?" Joseph pleaded. "I can't bear to read these letters. Good money going begging. Total cost to us, two and sevenpence halfpenny, two shillings royalty to you, and people on their knees begging for it at a guinea a bottle."

Paule considered the matter for a moment.

"So far from increasing the supply of my drug," he pointed out, "the supply itself may shortly come to an end. If I were you, Lord Honerton, I should ration these orders strictly, and in a month's time double the price."

Joseph's eyes glittered.

"It's an idea," he confessed. "We might do that sooner than lose the golden stream altogether. I'll consult with Samuel. He's coming up from Brighton today. My nephew would say we ought to get three guineas for it. He looks upon you as a wizard."

"It is the best advice I can give you," Paule said. "I can only complete the formula with the help of a vegetable drug which is almost as rare as radium. I came home through Silesia last week to try and get some, and had no luck."

"That idea of yours, though, about doubling the price, is beautiful," Joseph declared fervently. "They will pay it too; I am sure that they will pay it. We'll ration the orders and advertise the increased price. You didn't take much leave, Sir Lawrence."

"As much as I wanted," was the quiet reply.

"Look here," Joseph continued, "come down and shoot with us next week. Come down Saturday or Sunday and shoot Monday, Tuesday and Wednesday. Got some decent chaps coming, and if you're fond of partridge driving, we've scarcely touched the birds as yet. Lady Judith will be back on Saturday and you and she always seem to hit it off together."

"You're very kind," Paule said. "I think I can get away. I will go through my laboratory book, and if I can manage it I will motor down on Sunday."

"First rate!" Joseph exclaimed. "Middleton was begging me for another good gun. Samuel's about as much use at these driven birds as I am myself. We shall expect you then."

"Unless I let you know within an hour," Paule promised, "I will arrive in time for dinner on Sunday night."

On his way back to his own quarters Paule was accosted by a somewhat weedy-looking young man, apologetic, but persistent.

"If I could have just one word with you, if you please, Sir Lawrence," he begged.

"What about?" Paule asked shortly.

"I am writing a series," the young man continued, "entitled 'Notable Figures Amongst the Chemists of To-day', and we desire to include you."

"For what paper?" Paule demanded.

The young man hesitated.

"That is not as yet absolutely decided upon, sir," he admitted. "There are a few particulars I want from you, all the same. If you could tell me the exact place

and date of your birth, for instance. We understand
that you are a son of Doctor John Paule of Wormley
Grammar School. Is that so? "

"All the information you need about me can be found
in ' Who's Who '," was the curt reply. " I am not seeking publicity and do not desire it. I should prefer, as
a matter of fact, that your article remained unwritten.
Kindly excuse me. I have a busy morning."

He passed on but the young man fell into step.

" ' Who's Who ' is sometimes not altogether accu-
rate," he persisted. " My article aims at having all its
details perfect. Your age, for instance, is not in
' Who's Who ', and even the place of your birth has
been disputed."

Paule paused and for the first time looked closely at
his inquisitor.

" Have you a card? " he asked.

" I am sorry. I have just parted with my last," the
young man regretted.

" Exactly what paper do you represent? "

The young man hesitated again.

" I am by way of being a free lance in journalism,
Sir Lawrence," he confessed.

Paule called one of the packers to him.

" Show this person out," he directed, " and see that
he is never allowed to enter the Works again."

The packer was used to his task, for the premises,
especially in the vicinity of the laboratories, were always closely guarded, and the intruder had scarcely
time to protest. Paule turned towards his own quarters. On the way through the outer laboratories he
was stopped at least a dozen times, and asked varying
questions, to all of which he gave rapid answers. Arrived in his own domain, he loitered for some time with

one of his half-dozen assistants, examining some results which had just been given out. Finally he passed through the private door into his sitting room. Futoy was there dusting some books.

"There is one who waits for you in the office outside, sir," the latter announced. "His name is Rodes. He is a thin man with a hungry face and he refuses to go away."

"I seem to have heard the name," Paule reflected. "Very well, Futoy, I will go to him. Has any one telephoned?"

"Mr. Samuel Fernham, Junior, sir. He is coming up from Brighton and hopes to see you on his arrival."

Paule remained silent. Presently he made his way to the outer office of his department. Rodes, who was seated there waiting, rose at once to his feet.

"You wish to see me?" Paule asked, without undue cordiality.

"I was anxious to have a word or two with you alone, Sir Lawrence, if possible."

"You can speak before my secretary," Paule declared impatiently. "I have no secrets from him."

Rodes hesitated for a moment, and it occurred to Paule that he was being made the object of a great deal of scrutiny.

"You have my name, I think, sir — Rodes. I have been an inspector at Scotland Yard for many years. I am thinking of starting for myself."

"And — pardon me, but I am a very busy man — what concern is that of mine?"

"Just this," was the deliberate reply. "There is probably no one who needs the services of a private detective more than you do at the present moment."

Paule's manner up to now had betrayed a certain

amount of irritation. It suddenly changed. He became very still, but there was a note of menace in his quietude.

"I have never previously needed the services of any one in your profession," he said calmly. "Why should I now?"

"For the same reason that your firm paid two thousand pounds for their last safe, Sir Lawrence," Rodes rejoined. "You have at least six prescriptions, which would be worth a good many thousand pounds, and you have now added one — worth all the remainder put together, I should think. There are other thieves, you know, besides burglars."

"What is your proposition exactly?" Paule asked.

"To accept a watching brief over the place," Rodes explained. "I should watch your employees — especially any newcomers — trace out their daily lives and be sure that they had no connection with rival firms. I should also put in a little time on the premises, and examine the character of the safeguards which you have already established."

"What put this into your head?" Paule enquired.

"The fact that only last week," Rodes confided, "an Austrian chemist staying at a well-known hotel was visited two or three times by a man whom we know to be a high-class burglar. The same person applied for a job here last week."

"You have certainly justified your visit," Paule acknowledged, "but your suggestion requires consideration. As a matter of fact, the formula for 'Neurota' is not on paper at all."

"That of course eases the situation," was the ready admission. "It's 'Neurota' they're after."

"By-the-bye, wasn't it you who acted for Scotland

Yard in the matter of Ernest Fernham's disappearance? " Paule asked abruptly.

The detective was for a moment taken unawares. His start was noticeable.

" I did," he confessed. " To tell you the truth," he went on slowly, " that was the beginning of the trouble. Of course, it was very disappointing to all of us to have to admit failure, and in a good many people's opinion I suppose the Yard has lost prestige. What I kick at, however, is that the whole of the blame seems to have been laid on my shoulders."

" You must realise," Paule pointed out, " that your complete failure in a case apparently so simple is scarcely a recommendation here. If I were to employ you, I should have to explain to Lord Honerton exactly who you were. Frankly, I don't think that he would have the slightest confidence in you. Neither should I. Good-day, Mr. Rodes."

" But, Sir Lawrence ——"

Paule turned on his heel and the detective departed without further protest. Almost as he left the office, Samuel Junior presented himself. He was, as usual, dressed with meticulous care. Everything about him seemed spick and span and shiny. His complexion, however, was puffy, his eyes bloodshot, his jauntiness assumed.

" Can I see you in your room for a moment, Sir Lawrence? " he begged. " I have a message from the governor about ' Neurota '."

Paule glanced at him for a moment, searchingly and comprehensively. Then he turned towards the inner door.

" Come along," he invited. " I can spare you five minutes."

CHAPTER XVII

SAMUEL, when he found himself alone with Paule, in the latter's little sanctum, made a great show of being completely at his ease. He put his silk hat upon the table, threw his gloves into it and stretched himself out in a comfortable easy-chair. Paule watched him imperturbably. There were symptoms about his visitor's behaviour which were perfectly clear to him.

"You won't forget," he remarked, "that I can only offer you about five minutes. I have some important work to do in the mixing room before midday."

"Oh, hang it, don't be so unsociable, Paule!" the young man enjoined. "I don't often come in to bother you. I think we ought to find time now and then to shake hands with ourselves and each other. We're making a colossal fortune and you're in it now."

"Money is not the supreme concern of my life," was Paule's somewhat indifferent comment.

"Making money or seeing it made is my chief hobby," Samuel declared frankly. "However, that's neither here nor there. I've dropped in this morning as a pal. I want to ask your advice."

"Why trouble?" Paule observed. "You won't take it."

Samuel moved uneasily in his chair.

"You don't understand," he protested. "Why should you? I'm — well, I'm damned upset."

Samuel's bluff of easy confidence and bonhomie was deserting him. There was a strained look about the lines of his mouth, nearly hidden by his puffy, pendulous cheeks, a frightened expression in his bloodshot eyes. His lips twitched as he tried to speak.

"They're on to me all the time," he confided. "Just those two — Dad and Aunt Honerton. First it's Dad. He doesn't talk like he used to; like an ordinary, sensible human being. I take him out on the promenade or sit on the Pier with him at Brighton, and half the time he stares at me — stares as though he could see something that didn't exist. I ask him what's the matter. He just shakes his head. 'Samuel,' he begs, if it's in the morning, 'don't go to London to-day. There's trouble all around.' When I ask him what he means he just shakes his head. 'They've got Ernest,' he muttered only this morning, 'they'll get you.' I can stand a little of it, but it's getting on my nerves. Who'll get me? What for? What have I done?"

He paused. Paule said nothing. He sat quite still, waiting.

"Then, there's Aunt Honerton," Samuel went on. "I'm scared to go to the house. Even if she's upstairs she knows when I come. I gave Martin the office yesterday. I said, 'Don't tell her ladyship I'm here,' but in five minutes down came a message, and up I had to go. There she lies like a ghost, with her couch by the window all the time. I go in, try to be cheerful. She freezes the words on my lips. 'Still all right, Samuel?' she murmurs. 'All right!' Why the hell shouldn't I be all right?"

His voice had become almost a scream. He took out his handkerchief and mopped his forehead, on which little beads of perspiration had begun to show.

"She's just as vague as the governor," he continued, "full of silly advice. Wants me to go over to Sicily or somewhere quietly with him, and leave the firm. When I argue she looks at me with just that kind of gleam in her eyes that Dad has; as though she saw things around which no one else could. It sounds damned ridiculous, I know, Paule, but there you are! What about it? It's driving me mad!"

Still Paule was silent. In a moment or two Samuel, who had left his chair and had been walking restlessly up and down the room, began again.

"It isn't as though I did any particular harm in the world," he argued, "or had any enemies. I'm fond of my money but in a way I'm generous enough. I give my servants excellent wages, I always overtip the waiters — especially head waiters; they're important Johnnies in London nowadays, get you the best table and that sort of thing — and if I have a little affair I do the thing handsomely. I don't chuck my money about but there's no one who can call me mean. If we're making a heap of money, we're not robbing anybody."

"Do you, by any chance," Paule enquired, glancing at a pile of papers on the side of his desk, "contribute to any of these hospitals, or church army appeals, or help for invalid children, or any of these applications we get every day?"

"Never given a penny to a hospital in my life," the young man announced, with an air of satisfaction. "I've principles about that. Hospitals ought to be subsidised by the rates. As for the other so-called charities, I always think they're half swindles — can't be bothered, anyway, to sort 'em out — too much doing nowadays."

"I see," Paule murmured. "Have either your father or your aunt ever let drop any hint as to any reason they may have for this mysterious attitude towards you?"

"They haven't any real reason," Samuel declared

with almost feverish emphasis. "That's just it. It's all feeling. It's imagination. They're superstitious. They've nothing to go on, of course, but they look as though they see things and they're so damned gloomy — gets on one's nerves. Look at me this morning," he continued. "I'm not fit to do anything. I'm beginning to lie awake at nights. I'm beginning to fancy Ernest in all sorts of horrible places and myself dragged off and dumped down by the side of him. Ridiculous, Paule, of course," he concluded, nervously pulling at the corner of his stubbly little moustache. "But there you are!"

"Well, what do you want me to do?" Paule asked curiously.

"Look here," the young man pleaded, "you're the sort of chap one has confidence in — a strong, stout fellow, not a nerve in your body. It's all nonsense, isn't it? There can't be anything in it — the way Dad and Aunt Honerton look at me and talk, I mean? What could happen?"

"The only thing that seems likely to happen," Paule observed drily, "is that if you go on frightening yourself like this, you'll have a nervous collapse and be compelled to go into a nursing home. Why not try a complete change — a sea voyage or something of that sort?"

"I can't leave the governor," Samuel pointed out. "I was talking to his doctor yesterday. The old man might pop off at any moment."

"He would go with you," Paule suggested.

"I'm not brute enough for that. He wants to die at home amongst his own people. Nasty subject, isn't it?" he added, with a little shudder. — "Paule, would you mind feeling my pulse."

" I'm not a doctor," Paule replied, making no movement.

Samuel got up and held out his thick wrist.

" There's a good chap," he begged.

Paule acquiesced, took out his watch and replaced it
in less than a minute with a little curl of the lips.

" You're frightening yourself into a fever," he said.
" I should recommend a course of ' Neurota '."

" I'm taking it," Samuel declared eagerly. " I
pinched twelve bottles before the rush. What would do
me more good than anything is a few plain words from
a man like yourself. There's nothing could be going
on around us, sane, ordinary people, that's outside our
understanding, that we can't get hold of, is there? I'm
not a religious fellow, you know, Paule — ' Seeing's believing ' is my motto — but this disappearance of Ernest's has shaken us all up a bit, what? "

For the first time Paule's mouth relaxed. Nevertheless his smile was not pleasant.

" I am a clever man, Samuel Fernham," he said, " and
you are only gifted with a certain amount of cunning
— something which passes, I suppose, for intelligence
— yet let me tell you this. There are heaps of things
in the world which I don't begin to understand. It's
quite true that we find it difficult to believe things which
we cannot apprehend by our positive senses. On the
other hand, it's equally difficult, and for me impossible,
to disbelieve. I've an open mind towards many subjects, including even some branches of the art which a
thousand years ago passed as magic, and for which to-
day no adequate word has been coined."

" It's like a damned lecture! " Samuel grumbled.
" Doesn't do me any good, anyway."

" I'm sorry," Paule replied. " If I could help you I

would. I confess that your condition interests me. I don't think 'Neurota' will do you very much good. If you were capable of it, I should say that the best thing you could do would be to submit your mind to governance."

"You're a wonderful chap, Paule," Samuel admitted, "but you're always shooting off above one's head. Look here. I'm feeling like nothing on earth. Mix me up something, that's a good fellow — something that will really pull me together for an hour or two. — Is it true you're coming down to shoot?"

"Yes," Paule assented. "I'm coming down to Honerton on Sunday."

"That's great!" Samuel exclaimed. "Somehow or other, I feel safer when you're around. Stupid! I can't help that. I suppose you've got what they call a strong character. Give me that draught, there's a good chap."

Paule rose to his feet.

"I do not recommend this sort of thing," he warned his visitor. "It's the lazy man's escape from suffering."

He disappeared through his inner door for a moment — a door which this time closed behind him with a click. When he reappeared with a medicine glass, Samuel was watching him with a sly gleam of curiosity in his eyes.

"You don't half shut yourself up, Paule," he remarked. "You must have a perfect little suite of rooms behind there."

"If I have," Paule replied, "it is — to put it with that frankness which I am sure appeals to you — my own business. Drink this. You will feel much better for twenty-four hours at any rate."

Samuel swallowed the contents of the glass almost

feverishly. Paule remained standing, a note of dismissal in his attitude. The young man rose reluctantly to his feet.

"Twenty-four hours!" he muttered. "Well, that's something. I suppose you think I'm a pretty poor sort of chap, don't you, Paule?" he asked a little wistfully.

"You are like many others of your type and your style of living," was the indifferent reply. "You are a coward."

The young man spluttered. His dignity, at any rate — an artificial structure, but ministered to by heaps of sycophantic friends — was touched.

"Here, I say, you know, Paule!" he protested. "Don't come it too strong. They've made me nervy, these people, I admit it. I'm no coward when it comes to facing any ordinary danger. It's the things I don't and can't understand that terrify me."

"Those," Paule assured him, as he opened the door to expedite his departure, "are the real tests."

CHAPTER XVIII

AMBERLEYS, who had only one standard for men and only one judgment if they failed to come up to it, found it for that reason impossible to show ill humour towards a man who shot as Paule did. Nevertheless he very much resented Judith's complete desertion of himself during the first morning's sport.

" I had an idea that we were engaged," he managed to whisper to her on the way from one stand to another. " I don't expect to monopolise you, but I do expect to come in for my share."

She looked up at him with that faint note of insolence in her expression which he secretly admired. In her heather mixtured costume of rough tweeds, with tam-o'-shanter of the same material, she was extraordinarily attractive.

" Engaged to be married, yes," she admitted, " not to spend all our time together. Besides, even you, my dear Frederick, cannot shoot like Sir Lawrence."

" Can't think where he gets his practice," Amberleys grumbled. " I'm not saying a word against his shooting, Judith. I couldn't, if I would, but you might sit with me the next drive. I want to talk about that house in Curzon Street."

"An unpropitious occasion," she declared. " You always forget to whisper if you get interested. You'll turn the birds and then Middleton will be furious."

" I swear," he began ——

But Judith had already disappeared, swinging her shooting stick in her hand. Paule, turning round a moment or two later to survey his position, discovered her seated just behind his loader. The latter fell discreetly into the background. The beaters were not yet in sight.

" I'm annoying Freddy horribly," she confided. " I hope I'm not boring you, hanging about like this. I should hate to make enemies of every one."

" I am very much flattered," he assured her. " By the way, you're not looking well. No more fainting fits, I hope."

" Nothing of the sort," she replied, " yet I think that I am very ill. You wouldn't care to prescribe for me, I suppose."

" This open air sort of thing is the best cure for you," he declared.

" You prescribe for Samuel," she complained. " You give him wonderful specifics which make him feel as he expresses it ' like a two year old.' Surely I am more important than Samuel. Why won't you take me in hand, please? I should be such a grateful patient."

" There is nothing the matter with your cousin, except that he is a coward," Paule explained contemptuously. " I can easily give him Dutch courage. With you it would be a very different affair. You have two things which he lacks — courage and self-control. If you are ill it is your physician to whom you must go. I have no skill in the ordinary diseases of life."

" Mine is not an ordinary disease," she insisted softly. " I believe that physically I am strong enough. Mentally I think that I am losing hold of myself, drifting away so far that I am sometimes terrified as to whether I shall ever come back again. — I wonder whether there ever was insanity in our family. That might account for Ernest's disappearance. Some day I may be missing. Would you come and look for me, Sir Lawrence? "

" It would not be my privilege," he answered.

She was thoughtful for a moment.

" I think I shall break off my engagement with Freddy," she announced deliberately. " It seems to stand in the way of so many things. Now you won't even promise to come and look for me if I float away like Ophelia. — Do you think there is any chance of my going mad, Sir Lawrence? "

" One can never absolutely guarantee people of your temperament and your cousin's," he said.

" You couple me with Samuel! " she gasped.

He smiled.

" At the opposite poles," he explained. " Your cousin Samuel might very well drift into lunacy through sheer lack of intelligence. With you, on the other hand, it would be a superabundance of the same quality."

" As a matter of fact," she declared, " I think that I am mad now. I am beginning to be like Mother — to fancy that I see things. Mother thinks that she talked with Ernest only the other night."

" On earth — or in the other place? " he queried.

" Very much on earth. She is quite sure that she heard him calling her. Last night I woke up suddenly. There was no reason for it. I just woke up with a start. I found myself thinking intently of Ernest, and — you're not a creepy person, are you, Sir Lawrence? "

" Not particularly," he admitted.

" I, too, fancied that I saw him. This all must sound like balderdash to you, of course, but at any rate it has done one thing for me. I do not believe any longer that Ernest is dead."

Paule's loader, with a little gesture of apology, had resumed his place. From the far distance came the sound of a horn, the business of the drive commenced.

Paule shot as before with accuracy and skill, but perhaps this time with a little more restraint. Amberleys was on his left hand, and any bird concerning which there could be the slightest question he left alone. When they were again preparing to move off, Samuel appeared, swinging a shooting stick, but no longer carrying a gun.

"I've chucked it," he announced with an air of relief. "I'm not fit to shoot to-day. Never touched a feather in that last drive and they were streaming over my head. It makes a chap like me sick to watch you, Paule," he went on enviously. "'Nerves' again, I suppose, because you don't get nearly the practice that I do. I'm going to sit and see how you take 'em at this next drive. I may have a pop at the pheasants after lunch."

Samuel was obviously a fixture and disposed to be conversational. Judith lingered for a few moments and then turned listlessly away to rejoin Amberleys. Samuel, looking more pudgy than ever in his well-cut but ill-chosen shooting suit of the very roughest tweed and thick fleecy stockings, walked off by Paule's side.

"I wish you'd take Judith in hand," he said confidentially.

"Take Lady Judith in hand?" Paule repeated. "What the mischief do you mean?"

"Give her a little good advice and that sort of thing," Samuel explained. "She takes a lot of notice of what you say and I don't mind telling you that I am worried about her. She was never one of the stay-at-home kind — always ready for any beano that was going and that sort of thing — but she's overdoing it, Paule, overdoing it badly. She's in with a fast set, too. Smartest people in town, I'll admit, but wrong 'uns. 'A.D.G.'s' Freddy Amberleys christened 'em. Absinthe in the afternoon, drugs at night, and groans in the morning.   Not bad that, for Freddy!"

" I gather that Lord Amberleys does not approve," Paule observed, pausing to take a long but ineffectual shot at a pigeon.

"Approve!   My God, no!" Samuel exclaimed, as they continued their walk.   " He's a bear of the whole show — hates it like poison.   Thinks Judith's doing herself no end of harm getting mixed up with such a crowd.   You know some of 'em, I dare say — Dollie Bradshaw, Aggie Stuart, that Leperton woman — the best names and the worst morals in England.   Judith can take care of herself, of course, but a girl who's engaged to be married and to a fellow like Amberleys — a future Marquis, you know, and that sort of thing — doesn't need to get herself talked about.   Freddy's awfully sore about it."

"After all, it's no one's business except their own, is it? " Paule remarked, as he reached his stand and opened out his shooting stick.

" No one's actual business, of course," Samuel agreed, following his companion's example.   " What I thought, though, was that you might have a talk with Judith on the health side of the question.   It would be a knockdown blow for the old man, too, if this marriage didn't come off.   There isn't much money, of course, but that don't matter a damn to Uncle.   His father bought the title all right and it's ' Your Lordship ' wherever he goes, but he's no fool.   He knows the difference between the eleventh Marquis and the second Baron."

" Throw your cigarette away, there's a good fellow, and stop talking," Paule enjoined sharply.   " The horn's blown and there's a covey coming down on the right already."

They were on their way back to the house for luncheon when they met Rachel in a bath chair drawn by a
small pony. She was watching some builders at work
on the site of Heggs' old cottage. Paule stopped to
wish her good morning and she detained him.

" You see what we are doing there," she pointed out.
" You know the story? "

" I have heard it," he admitted.

" We are having Heggs' cottage rebuilt. My husband was very difficult about it. I was determined. I
always felt that Israel Fernham laid a curse upon this
place when he pulled down that cottage stone by stone
and swore that it should never be put up again. All
these years it has lain waste and the curse has fallen.
Now I am going to have it restored, and the garden
planted again with flowers. I am going to have some
homeless person live there — with children, if possible.
I want the birds to build in the trees again. Later on,
they are making a pigeon house. Only a few days ago
I read somewhere that curses flourish in the wilderness
and where weeds are, but they fade away where children's voices are heard."

She paused and Paule was conscious of her earnest,
almost strained regard. She was watching him as
though eager for his comment.

" I am a scientific man and a materialist, you know,
Lady Honerton," he said. " I do not believe in curses."

She shook her head slowly.

" You are too clever a man," she objected, " to be a
materialist. You could not live in so small a world.
You could not cramp your brain so far as that. You
know that Heggs the keeper was hanged and that Israel,
Joseph's father, could have saved him if he would? "

" I have heard that story," he admitted.

"It is the truth," she declared. "Heggs sat in his cell with his Bible in his hand, waiting for the reprieve that never came. When they went to take him to the scaffold he dashed the Bible he had been reading to the ground and he cursed Israel and his whole family in the words of the Old Testament. When they hanged him the words were still on his lips."

"It is a terrible story," Paule said coldly. "You dwell upon it too much, Lady Honerton. In any case, as I have told you, I do not believe in curses. I believe instead in retribution. I believe in the main that man reaps as he has sown."

She lay back in her chair. They were approaching the front door of the house, and the luncheon gong was sounding. She suddenly gripped his arm with long, feverish fingers whose clutch he felt through his thick shooting coat.

"Listen," she whispered. "The others would think I am mad. You know. In my dreams I have stepped over the edge of the world. I have seen Ernest. I have heard him speak. He is very different but he is alive."

Paule looked at her intently. He had not the air of one humouring an hysterical woman.

"Tell me something actual," he suggested. "Tell me what clothes he wore? What condition was he in?"

She fell back in her chair. She was on the point of exhaustion. Joseph came fussily down the steps.

"Come along, come along, Paule!" he called out. "Luncheon is being served quickly. Middleton wants us out again in three quarters of an hour. Rachel, you're overtired. I wish you'd keep away from that damned building."

Paule handed his gun to one of the keepers.

"I sha'n't keep you waiting," he promised.

CHAPTER XIX

DINNER on the concluding night of the shooting party at Honerton Chase was an unusually festive meal. Rachel had abandoned the effort to sit at the head of her table and remained in her room, and Judith, who took her place, was in one of her most brilliant and daring moods. She wore a gown of geranium-coloured chiffon, her hair shone like black ivory under a Russian headdress of wonderful pearls. Her complexion was so clear as to be almost unnatural. Her lips, her eyes, were never quiet for an instant. Prince Edgar sat on one side and Frederick Amberleys on the other, and she flirted with both indiscriminately and shamelessly. She found time, however, to play also the watchful hostess, to stimulate conversation in whatever direction it flagged. The only person to whom she did not once speak and from whom indeed she seemed to keep her attention as far removed as possible, was Paule.

"Dear Judith is at her very best this evening," the Marchioness murmured to Joseph. "What a hostess she will make. I am sure Freddy will be very proud of her."

Her host smiled graciously. The faint note of surprise, which so many people used in their amazed appreciation of Judith, was at times almost an irritation.

"Judith has certainly inherited the brains of the family," he admitted. "In appearance her mother was very like her at her age."

"I can quite believe it," the Marchioness assented, "a very sweet face even now. I am so sorry that Lady Honerton didn't feel well enough to come down this evening."

"My wife is not strong," Joseph confided. "She has had, of course, to bear such a shock as few people in the world have had to suffer and it has affected her nerves."

"The uncertainty of it all is so terrible," the Marchioness observed sympathetically. "That is the part I could not bear."

Martin, with a word of apology, presented a sheet of paper to his master on a silver salver. Joseph adjusted his pince-nez and glanced it through.

"This is the bag for the three days," he announced, raising his voice slightly. "I will read it out. Three thousand, two hundred and ninety-one pheasants, two hundred and thirty-three brace of partridges, forty-three woodcock, two hundred and ten hares, three hundred and seventy-two rabbits, twenty-seven various."

There was a little murmur of congratulation. Joseph beamed upon every one.

"I am very glad," he concluded, "that the sport has been so good. Much obliged to you all for helping to give us a record three days. Middleton assured me that the shooting had never been better — and Middleton is not an easy man to please."

"The Marquis has enjoyed it immensely," his wife confided. "He was saying, whilst he was changing for dinner, that there are no stands in the county to compare with yours."

"Like old Johnson, the trainer, who once shot here," Samuel Junior whispered under his breath to Joyce Cloughton, his neighbour; "used to say he preferred high birds and low women."

Joyce looked at him severely.

"Samuel Fernham," she said, "if you were not a millionaire and unmarried, I should be angry with you.

As it is, I suppose I must smile. It's terrible what we impecunious young women have to put up with nowadays in our frantic search for a husband."

Samuel Junior stroked his stubbly little bit of moustache. Joyce had been for years the object of his fervent admiration and he would have proposed to her long ago if he had had the faintest hope that she would have accepted him.

"You and Judith do nothing but chaff a fellow," he complained. "You know very well that you are responsible for my lonely state."

"I'm not so sure that it is altogether lonely," the young lady rejoined drily. "London's rather a congested area nowadays, you know."

"Well, I think you girls might keep away from Ciro's, at any rate," was Samuel's plaintive protest.

"Most amusing place I know," Joyce replied. "It's such fun seeing you poor dears trying to make up your minds whether you ought to be noticed or not."

"When I'm married there'll be nothing of that sort," he declared.

"No inducement at all," she retorted, shaking her head. "What on earth would your poor wife do when she wanted an evening off if you hadn't a little affair of your own to look after sometimes?"

The young man was nonplussed, as he generally was when either Judith or Joyce talked nonsense to him.

"I'm only anxious to please," he announced. "You girls seem to get everything upside down nowadays. If it's necessary for me to promise to be unfaithful, I'll make a bluff at it. I'm always for taking life as it comes along."

"Samuel's perfectly sweet this evening," Joyce confided to Judith. "I hope I don't get left alone with him in the winter garden or anything like that after dinner. I know I shall fall."

"My dear," Judith assured her, "I should love to have you in the family — even at a cousinly distance. Besides, I think Sammy ought to settle down. He's too sickeningly rich for a bachelor. He needs some one to spend his money on."

"It seems inevitable," Joyce sighed. "Nobody in the world needs some one to spend money on them like I do. Besides, I owe really quite a great deal. How should you feel, Mr. Fernham — or shall I call you ' Sammy ' — about debts contracted before marriage?"

"I'd pay 'em," Samuel Junior declared with enthusiasm, "pay 'em willingly."

"He really is wonderful," Joyce acknowledged. "Come and talk to me after dinner, Sammy. I might take you on at billiards. I owe so much money at bridge that I am afraid these people would look coldly at me if I sat down to play again to-night."

Prince Edgar glanced across at Joyce admiringly. With her piquante face and mass of chestnut hair she was undoubtedly attractive.

"Does Lady Joyce always talk nonsense so aptly?" he enquired.

"She's rather good at it," Judith admitted. "As a matter of fact, I wish she'd marry Sammy. It would be the making of him. Sammy wants training rather, but he's not a bad sort. Do you believe in the *marriage de convenance*, Prince?"

"I have more sympathy with the type of marriage to which you are committed, Lady Judith," he replied.

"Did you hear that, Freddy?" Judith exclaimed. "I call it a beautifully veiled compliment for both of us. I suppose we are in love with one another, aren't we?"

" I imagine that some feeling of that sort exists," was the somewhat stiff rejoinder.

" Freddy isn't really very fond of chaff," Judith confided in an undertone, " not about sacred subjects, you know, like our affection. — I am very happy here but I really think I ought to leave you. I believe your mother, Freddy, is trying to catch my eye. Here goes! I'm up! "

She rose, naturally enough, at precisely the right moment, and floated down the room, perfectly graceful, perfectly beautiful, with a curious air of intense living radiating from her. Paule, the one person whom she had ignored during the meal, watched her curiously, conscious of the slight effort with which she avoided catching his eye. He was not greatly disturbed at her attitude, but he was amazed at the warmth of his own admiration as he followed her slow progress towards the door; appreciating to the fullest extent the insolent little swing of her lithe body, the slight introspective curl of her lips which gave her an air almost of aloofness. All day long he had repelled her confidences, had kept her outside the armour of a reserve which no one yet had ever succeeded in penetrating. Yet he too, notwithstanding the gift of strength, was a man, a human being, very much as others, only stronger of will and purpose. His eyes were fixed upon the door some time after it was closed. Samuel Junior's voice broke in upon a medley of reflections, unusual, in a sense disquieting.

" I say, Paule, could I come along and talk to you to-night after the others have gone to bed? "

Paule dragged his thoughts back from their unwonted escapade.

" What about? Your health again? " he asked drily.

"Don't chaff, there's a good fellow," the young man begged. "I'm absolutely in earnest. I want to talk to you from a different angle. It may be very important."

"To you possibly, but not to me," was the somewhat unsympathetic reply, "especially if your idea is to knock me up somewhere about two o'clock in the morning."

"I won't be a moment later than twelve," the young man promised. "I know the girls won't sit up late and I'll come directly they've gone to bed."

"You can come if you want to, then," Paule acquiesced without enthusiasm, "but if you stay longer than a quarter of an hour, I shall turn you out. As a matter of fact, I am going to my room directly after dinner. I have some important work to do and, as I don't play bridge, Lady Judith has consented to excuse me."

Samuel indulged in a little grimace.

"Fancy work after a day in the open air like we've had!" he exclaimed. "Why, I should be asleep in ten minutes!"

"That is because you have little self-restraint and less inclination for work of any sort," Paule observed coolly. "If you'd follow out the programme of life which I could arrange for you, you wouldn't need any drugs."

Samuel filled his glass with port and passed the decanter to his neighbour.

"I'll take your programme on in the next world," he promised jocosely.

There was an enigmatic light for a moment in Paule's eyes, a mirthless smile upon his lips.

"One never knows," he murmured. "You may feel disposed to try it in this."

There were still sounds of revelry downstairs when Samuel presented himself in the small sitting room which was part of the suite allotted to Paule. It was a transformed and glorified Samuel. An amazing event had, for the moment, at any rate, lifted him from the level of his commonplace existence.

"Sha'n't bother you long to-night, Paule," he announced joyously. "I'm going down again. Great news! What do you think's happened?"

Paule shook his head without speech. The young man rattled on.

"Joyce has come up to the scratch. I never dreamed she would," he declared feelingly. "Never thought I should have the ghost of a look-in. She's all chaff, of course, but there are half a dozen fellows she could marry to-morrow. What about it, Paule? I say, what about it?"

"From the little I have seen of the young lady, I should say that you are very much to be congratulated," was the prompt reply.

"Congratulated? Well, I should say so!" the young man exclaimed, with a touch of his ordinary pomposity. "Of course, those sort of things don't matter so much nowadays, but after all she is the daughter of a Duke. I expect I'll have to spread myself with the Government a bit. Can't stand 'Mr. and Lady Joyce Fernham.' I couldn't believe my ears or my eyes, Paule, when she suddenly turned serious. We were playing billiards — quite her own idea — and she'd been chaffing along just as usual, when she suddenly stopped ——"

"Please spare me these details," Paule begged. "You're engaged to be married to a very charming girl. I have congratulated you, it is within a stroke of midnight and I haven't finished my work."

"Can't get rid of me like that, old chap," Samuel observed. "What an unsociable beggar you are, sitting up here all the evening!"

"I excused myself to Lady Judith as well as to your uncle," Paule explained. "I don't play bridge and I have some important work on hand."

Honerton was a house conducted on hospitable principles and Samuel mixed a whisky and soda from the decanter upon the sideboard and threw himself into an easy-chair.

"I say," he began, "you needn't look so alarmed. I'm not going to stay more than a few minutes, but I do want just a word or two of advice. I know I've knocked about a bit — got a bit soft and not taken care of myself as well as I might. That's all very well when a chap's got nobody else to think about, but it's all changed now. I've got to get rid of this nervousness, Paule, even if I go into training for it. I'm prepared to do anything reasonable — drink half as much, smoke half as much, and of course it's all finished with the little girlies and that sort of thing. You're the cleverest chap I know — better than any physician I ever went to. Help me to get back into line again, Paule. I'll never forget it. I promise you that. You think I'm a bit of a rotter, I know, because you're a serious-minded sort of a chap and I ain't, but I've got a bit of the family obstinacy in me. I can stick to a thing, when I mean to. What I want for the moment is something a little stiffer than 'Neurota'. I've got to go and stay with Joyce's people, and the very idea terrifies me. The old chap never moves out of Scotland, wears kilts and fancies himself as a politician and a religionist — writes long letters to the papers nobody ever reads, and never moves without a chap blowing into those bagpipes in front of him.   He won't like it, Paule, and he won't like me, but I've got to go through with it."

Paule had sunk a little lower into his chair and was watching his visitor with some accession of interest.

" No," he admitted slowly, " he probably won't like you.   You will probably even be a shock to him."

Samuel Junior crossed his legs and coughed.

" If I'm good enough for Joyce," he announced, " that's all that counts with me.   After all, there aren't many sons-in-law in this country who could settle half a million upon the woman they're going to marry — not that I've made up my mind to settle as much as that," he went on a little hastily, " but I could if I thought it advisable. — What I want to know, Paule, is are you going to help me? "

Paule rose to his feet.

" Wait," he directed.

He disappeared through the connecting door into his bedroom and returned in a few minutes shaking a small bottle in his hand.   He poured the contents into a tumbler and handed it to the young man.

" I'm all right now," the latter remarked, eyeing it a little dubiously, " full of beans and all that sort of thing, pulse as steady as a rock.   Can't I keep this until to-morrow? "

Paule shook his head.

" You must drink that now," he enjoined, " only one more whisky and soda to-night and you'd be better if you didn't smoke.   To-morrow I'll plan out an alto-gether new life for you.   If you follow my instructions, I may be able to do you some good, but I tell you frankly that I do not preserve the faintest interest in any one who does not do absolutely as he is told."

The young man drank off his draught and stood up.

" I don't care what you tell me," he declared, " cold baths, breathing exercises — I'll take 'em all. I feel as though I had something to live for now, if you understand me. One gets kind of selfish with no one special in the world to hang on to."

Paule moved towards the door and Samuel followed him reluctantly.

" I shall just have a prowl round downstairs," he confided, " although I expect the girls have gone to bed by now. What time are you off in the morning, Paule? "

"At nine o'clock or as soon after as I can. Close the door, there's a good fellow. Good-night! "

Samuel made his way downstairs, discovered, as he had feared, that Judith and Joyce had retired and turned away from the winter garden, where one or two of the male guests were still sitting up, with a little glow of conscious rectitude. He went to his room, where his servant — not expecting him for another hour or two, and having only just left a cheerful bridge party in the housekeeper's room — was engaged in a hurried execution of his belated duties. Samuel took off his coat and slipped on a smoking jacket.

" I'll look after myself to-night, Jenkins," he announced. " Is Martin still up? "

" He was up a few moments ago, sir," the man replied.

" Give him my compliments and ask him to let you have a few bottles of wine downstairs," Samuel enjoined. " I'll make it all right with his lordship to-morrow morning. You can drink my health and the health of Lady Joyce Cloughton."

" I'm sure I wish you every happiness, sir," the man declared, reflecting with satisfaction that a settled establishment was a great deal better than bachelor quarters. " I'll hurry down before Mr. Martin retires. Sure there's nothing more I can do for you, sir? The whisky and soda and some ice are on the side table."

" Nothing else, thanks, except make yourself scarce," Samuel replied. " I shall probably turn in almost at once. I am quite sleepy."

The man withdrew and Samuel helped himself to a whisky and soda and yawned. He strolled to the window and looked out across the moonlit park. Then he yawned again. He was really very drowsy, very sleepy indeed. Almost automatically he commenced to undress.

CHAPTER XX

Paule was finishing his breakfast on the following morning when Amberleys entered the dining room hurriedly. There was a look of trouble on his wholesome, good-humoured face.

" Have you heard what's happened, Sir Lawrence? " he exclaimed.

Paule shook his head.

" I haven't seen a soul this morning."

" They can't find young Samuel! "

" Can't find him? " Paule repeated. " I thought the trouble generally was to get him out of bed before ten o'clock."

" His bed hasn't been slept in," Amberleys went on. " His evening clothes are lying all over the place and his servant thinks from some things that are missing that he must have changed into a lounge suit. At any rate, he's not in his room and not a soul seems to have seen anything of him."

Paule rose to his feet, walked to the sideboard and helped himself to another cup of tea.

" He came to my room last night and talked about starting to lead a new life," he observed. " I expect he's gone out for an early morning walk and breathing exercises in the park. Better have some breakfast. He'll turn up."

" Well, I don't know much about the young man's habits," Amberleys admitted, " but from what I do know of him I cannot conceive a more unlikely person to start out for a tramp before breakfast on a wet morning. However, I suppose it's no use meeting trouble halfway. I shouldn't think anything of it except for the extraordinary episode of young Ernest's disappearance from this same house. Judith takes it pretty seriously. She rushed off somewhere at once — down to the garage, I think."

Paule stirred his tea thoughtfully.

"The garage?" he repeated. "Surely she could have telephoned to find out whether the young man had taken his car or not?"

"As a matter of fact, I happen to know that he has not," Amberleys remarked. "I telephoned down myself directly I was sure that he wasn't in his rooms, and his car is there and his chauffeur with orders to be ready at eleven o'clock. That was about Fernham's idea of a suitable time to commence the day."

"Lady Judith is very intelligent," Paule mused. "She probably has a theory of her own."

"She's over-intelligent," Amberleys agreed. "All nerves and brain and that sort of thing. I'm trying to persuade her to marry me this winter, and, if I can, I shall take her to Egypt right away from the whole show. Ernest was rather a cub, but she was genuinely fond of him, and if this young man has really hopped it too, it is getting a bit thick, isn't it? — Do you mind passing me the butter?"

Joseph made a somewhat abrupt appearance in the dining room. He forgot to be pompous, and was without a doubt seriously disturbed.

"Samuel's gone!" he exclaimed. "Not a sign of him anywhere! Left the house and no one can tell whether it was last night or this morning. There's one thing we do know this time, though. He left of his own accord and he left deliberately — even changed his clothes before he went."

"I've just been telling Lord Amberleys here that he

came to see me last night," Paule observed, " and that I gave him a talking to about his health and his manner of living. He has probably gone for an early morning walk."

" If he's done anything of that sort without leaving a message," Joseph declared viciously, " I'll wring the breath out of his body."

" I trust that Lady Honerton is not alarmed," Paule ventured.

" Her attitude is amazing," Joseph acknowledged, standing before the sideboard, his natural greediness struggling with a sense of incongruity as he studied his favourite dish of kidneys and bacon. " She takes the matter very seriously but she showed not the slightest surprise. Well, I suppose one must carry on," he added vaguely, lifting a spoon and fork. " The lad may be all right."

" Is there anything further I can do, sir? " Amberleys enquired, rising to his feet and pushing his chair back. " I'm not shooting anywhere to-day. Would you like me to motor over to Norwich and see the Chief Constable? "

" We telephoned there an hour ago," Joseph replied. " Telephoned up to Scotland Yard too. I don't think there is anything you can do, Amberleys. All the outdoor servants are spreading themselves over the place on bicycles. You might look after Judith for a bit, perhaps. These shocks are bad enough for us men, but they're the devil for highly strung women."

Amberleys left the room and Paule prepared to follow his example.

" There's nothing I can do, I'm afraid," he said. " You'll make my excuses to Lady Honerton and Lady Judith, if I don't see her. I'm very much obliged to you for an excellent shoot. Sorry this should have come to disturb you at the end of it."

Joseph set down his teacup noisily.

"That's all right, Paule," he rejoined. "Glad you could come, I'm sure. If there's no news I shall be up in town to-morrow, if it's only to go and tell them what I think of them at Scotland Yard. It's disgraceful, positively disgraceful!" he exclaimed, striking the table with his fist, suddenly overcome with a sense of personal injury. "Nearly twelve months ago my own son disappears from this house, walks out straight from this table in his evening clothes, and from that day to this nothing has been heard of him. And now his cousin, gone almost the same way. We've the worst police system in the world. I'd guarantee there isn't a country anywhere under the sun where two such disappearances could take place."

"Have you wired Samuel's father?" Paule enquired.

"Not yet," his host admitted. "He's in such a feeble state that I'm really afraid of the shock for him. I shall either send some one from here with a letter or go and see him myself to-night. A pleasant journey to you, Paule!"

Paule, making his preparations for departure, found much confusion in the household. The Marquis, who had just descended, insisted upon telephoning personally to the Chief Constable at Norwich, who was a protégé of his. The Marchioness, with a pencil in her hand, was making calculations, from an ordinance map which hung in the back hall, as to the distance to the nearest river. Several of the other guests were standing about talking in little groups, offering aimless suggestions. One young man had gone off in a two-seated car with a pronounced intention of "bringing the young cub home dead or alive." Joyce, thoroughly serious for once in her life, accosted Paule as he stood upon the broad steps of the entrance porch.

" Have you any theories, Sir Lawrence? " she asked.

" None whatever," he assured her. " My idea was that he had gone for an early morning walk."

" What about his bed not having been slept in? " she reminded him.

" I didn't know that till afterwards," Paule admitted. " Perhaps he slept half the night in an easy-chair, then decided it was too late to turn in, had a bath and went off for a walk. I've done such a thing myself before now."

She considered the idea for a moment.

" It isn't like Samuel," she pronounced.

" The young man was naturally unlike himself last night," was the thoughtful reply. " He came round to tell me his good news. I may be permitted, I hope, to wish you every happiness, Lady Joyce."

" Thank you very much," she murmured. " It's a queer start, isn't it? "

" It certainly is," Paule agreed. " However, I don't think you need be so greatly concerned. I cannot bring myself to look upon this disappearance very seriously."

" Well, it's comforting to hear you say so, anyway," the girl observed. " Perhaps it's the best thing that could have happened, so far as Samuel and I are concerned. I've been over a year making up my mind to marry him, and last night I couldn't sleep a wink for worrying about my promise, and now that he has been snatched away I feel that life has suddenly become a blank. Nonsense apart, Sir Lawrence, he's really not a bad sort and I should hate to think that anything had happened to him."

" Nothing serious has, I am convinced," Paule assured her. "I hope when we meet in town," he went on, watching the approach of his car, " we shall all be able to smile at this morning's disquietude."

Futoy, immaculate in his black livery, brought his long grey car round to the front entrance with a workmanlike sweep. Paule glanced back into the hall for a moment as he drew on his gloves.

" I am making rather an unceremonious departure," he confided. " I have not been able even to see Lady Judith to say good-bye."

" Judith went off to the garage half an hour ago and I haven't seen her since," Joyce told him. " I'll give her the usual messages, if you like."

" Thank you very much. Will you also say that I would have willingly stayed if I could have been of the slightest use."

" Which way are you going up? " she asked him, as he stepped into the driving seat.

" Newmarket and Royston, I think," he answered.

He raised his cap and swung off down the avenue. Judith, from the garage, saw him flash by. She turned to the man in keeper's clothes who was standing by her side, holding a motor bicycle.

" There goes the first of our departing guests," she pointed out.

" Who is it? "

" Sir Lawrence Paule."

Rodes touched the switch of his bicycle and pushed it clear of the door.

"Are you going to follow him?" Judith asked eagerly.

" Yes," was the terse reply.

" But why? " she demanded. " What can you possibly learn from his movements? "

Rodes started his engine.

"Lady Judith," he said, "I can only remind you of a time when you spoke to me at the top of St. James's Street. You advised me, I think, to discard facts and trust to instinct and imagination. We have alluded to the subject since, only a little more fully. I haven't the least idea why, but I have quite made up my mind to follow Sir Lawrence."

"You will never catch him. He confessed to having averaged fifty between Newmarket and here when he came down."

"I can do as much as that," Rodes declared, "and then accelerate a little if I want to. I haven't kept this bicycle here for some months for nothing, Lady Judith. Nor have I played at being an underkeeper for nothing," he added ruefully. "Every bone in my body aches this morning."

She smiled.

"Never mind, Mr. Rodes," she said, "you looked very nice, and I am sure all this time out of doors must have been very good for you."

"You're positive," he asked earnestly, "that no one else in this household or any one else amongst the guests knew anything about me?"

"Not a soul."

"Not Sir Lawrence, for instance? I have kept carefully out of his sight."

"I am convinced," she assured him, "that Sir Lawrence has not an idea that you were in the neighbourhood."

He mounted into the saddle and started off. Already miles ahead of him, Paule was gradually opening his throttle.

CHAPTER XXI

THE main entrance gates to Honerton Chase, through which Paule passed on leaving the park, opened upon a country byroad which, in about a couple of miles, led into the main road, on the left to Norwich, on the right to Fakenham town. Paule, who had driven slowly through the park, to avoid the deer, who were continually crossing the way, increased his speed in the lane, dividing his attention between the road in front and the mirror on his right. Once he spoke to Futoy.

" There is a motor bicycle crossing the park, Futoy," he said. " Look round and tell me which way it turns on leaving the lodge gates."

Futoy watched for a moment or two.

" It follows us, Master," he announced.

Paule slackened speed a little, until a small black object appeared in the centre of his mirror.

" Were there many motor bicycles in the garage, Futoy? " he asked.

" Only one, Master," the man replied. " His lordship dislikes them very much and has forbidden them in the park. This one belonged to one of the beaters, a stranger to the neighbourhood. Lady Judith was talking to him this morning."

They were nearing the spot where the lane merged into the high road and Paule had apparently been preparing to turn towards Norwich, his announced route. At Futoy's words, however, he slowed down still more, looked steadfastly ahead of him for a second or two as though deep in thought, and then swung round to the right.

" Is it a powerful motor bicycle, Futoy? " he enquired.

" It is the best I ever saw, Master," the man replied.

Paule glanced at the black speck in the glass. It was certainly drawing nearer. He touched his accelerator slightly. The road was good but winding. At Fakenham he had almost to pull up in the narrow street down to the railway, and from Raynham to Swaffham again speed was almost impossible. The small black speck was always there. Paule looked at it, frowning. He reduced his pace a little. The motor bicycle came no nearer. From Swaffham to Brandon he drove carefully, passing through Brandon so that even the policeman on duty gave scarcely a second glance at the car. Then he leaned forward with a faint smile. It was a still November morning with a promise of weak sunshine behind the clouds. The air was soft but a trifle damp, the roads dry for the time of the year. In the great open spaces across which they sped hundreds of rabbits were sitting at their holes; there were patches of gorse still in bloom and even thin streaks of heather. As they neared the village of Barton Mills, where the road merges into the main thoroughfare, Paule leaning forward, increased the speed of the car until the black speck in the mirror became almost invisible. He turned the corner and suddenly began a slow application of his brakes, bending over to Futoy and giving him brief directions. As they crossed the bridge to the road by the inn, Paule brought the car to a standstill, busied himself for a few seconds with the seat which he had vacated, and slipped into the yard of the hotel. Futoy, with the driving wheel in his hand, dashed off in second speed and was out of sight in a moment, whilst Paule entered the bar parlour and stood at the window. In less than two minutes the impatient hooting of a horn was heard and immediately afterwards Rodes on his

motor bicycle swung round into the road and headed
for Newmarket, following the car which was now little
more than a speck in the distance.   Paule watched both
until they were out of sight.

The twelve miles an hour warning through Newmarket brought the car and the motor bicycle within a
reasonable distance of each other, but outside the town
along by the race course and galloping ground, the car
once more drew away.   Rodes, who had owned a motor
bicycle for less than a year and hated it, groaned as he
leaned over his handles.   Nothing was happening as he
had expected, and yet he was loath to abandon the
chase.   The next twenty miles of perfect road he knew
would be all against him, notwithstanding which he set
his teeth and rode steadily on.   The wind had brought
the colour into his pallid cheeks, but his eyes, even
beneath his heavy spectacles, were watering.   Every bone
in his body seemed aching, every nerve on edge.   He
kept his mind fixed upon his task, however, and ignored
his discomfort.   People shouted abuse at him on the
main road; abuse to which he scarcely listened.   He
drew a sigh of relief when his quarry turned off towards
Royston — at least these narrower roads gave him some
advantage.   Nevertheless, for another half hour the car
kept its distance and nothing that he could do seemed
able to lessen it.   The railway gates stood open and the
car seemed to take the crossing in its stride, Rodes, with
clenched teeth, following.   The chase, so far as he was
concerned, was beginning to be a grim one.   The perspiration was streaming down his face, the hands which
gripped his handles felt numb.   Amongst the leaves of
the trees there seemed to be not a breath of wind, yet
his cheeks burned as though with the surge of a tempest.
There was a mist in front of his spectacles.   Every now

and then with care he had to remove them with one hand and make an effort at wiping them. At Royston the car passed through the bottle-neck contraction by the inn at such a pace that the policeman, whose back had been turned for a moment, shouted angrily after it. Rodes too, came in for his abuse but he gained a little on the hill towards the downs. For a few more miles the speed seemed to be ever increasing. They passed some race horses on the Common as though they were standing still; Baldock in a few minutes became only a memory — and then came, at last, relief. Halfway to Stevenage, Rodes, rocking in his seat, became conscious that the car in front was growing larger. He took off his spectacles for a moment and gave a little gasp. It had drawn to the side of the road and was stopping. He shut off his own engine and made a clumsy descent. Gripping one of the handles, he stood, leaning over the saddle in the middle of the road, gazing into Futoy's impassive face.

"The gentleman needs something?" Futoy asked courteously as he lit a cigarette.

"Where is your master?" Rodes demanded.

"Not with me to-day," Futoy replied cheerfully. "I drive the car alone."

"Your master started with you from Honerton Chase," Rodes declared, wheeling the bicycle up to the side of the car.

"It is quite true," was the grave assent. "My master he forgot something. He went back."

Rodes looked at the hat lying in the bottom of the car and the deep seats, and knew at once how he had been tricked. The very fact, however, that such deception had been indulged in, was like a tonic to him.

"When did your master leave the car?" he persisted.

Futoy blew out a little cloud of smoke.

" I am good English servant," he announced. " I do not answer questions about my master. He leave the car when he choose."

Rodes wiped the perspiration from his face and removed his cap. Great though the disappointment at the immediate result of his chase, it was ecstasy to be standing still, and to realise that at last he was on the track of unexplained things.

" Look here," he said, " you speak English quite well? "

" I speak English perfect," Futoy replied with dignity. " I understand too."

" Then listen," Rodes continued. " I am a policeman. I am from Scotland Yard. I have followed you in pursuit of my duties. If you would avoid trouble, tell me where your master left the car."

Futoy shook his head.

" That talk not very good," he objected. " My master is my master. I know nothing about the police. I do not know whether you tell me the truth. It does not matter. I do as my master orders and I do well. My master returned because he had forgot something."

" What are you doing here by the side of the road? " Rodes asked. "And why have you been driving so fast? "

" This car he is very powerful," Futoy explained. "And if you want to know, I stopped by the side of the road just because I enjoy a cigarette. My master told me ' no hurry '. I reach London now by half past one. That very good time."

" Are you fond of money? " Rodes asked bluntly.

" Good money I love," Futoy replied. " Bad money I spit upon."

"What do you call bad money?" Rodes demanded.

"Money which comes from those who ask me questions about my master," was the calm rejoinder.

"I don't mean a little money, I mean a great deal of money," Rodes continued desperately.

"I am not English," Futoy said. "There are many other things in life besides money. My master save my life in Bangkok. You offer me the money to buy that house we have been staying in, and my master shake his head, and I say no."

Rodes wiped his face again and lit a cigarette on his own account.

"You not very good with motor bicycle," Futoy remarked sympathetically. "You leave it somewhere. I drive you to London. My master not mind that."

"Thank you," Rodes answered. "I am not coming to London just yet."

Futoy nodded, settled himself down in his seat and touched his starting pedal.

"Very well," he acquiesced. "I wish you good morning, Mister. You ride carefully going back. You ride much too fast."

Rodes leaned on his bicycle and watched the car once more disappear. He was fatigued, yet dimly exultant. Somewhere in the distance loomed the shadow of new things.

CHAPTER XXII

THE morning papers were a little guarded in their references to this second mysterious disappearance in the great millionaire family. News so puzzling as to baffle even speculative propositions was exceedingly difficult to handle. Those papers who did attempt it at any length seized upon the only possible outcome and made a vigorous attack upon the police system of the country. It was left to the Sunday papers to let themselves go. Every one of these had a special article, written by a special correspondent. Every theory was explored, every incident in the lives of these young men recalled, their tendencies and weaknesses commented upon, their pictures freely reproduced. The fact of Samuel's engagement on the night before his disappearance somehow or other leaked out and added piquancy to the already sufficiently dramatic problem. Meanwhile Samuel Fernham, Senior, lay ill almost to death at Brighton, and Joseph, though he made an effort at complacent optimism, carried with him everywhere a new expression, half furtive, half anxious. He was forever seeking the sympathy of stronger men, asking for their advice, trying to borrow from their more equable poise. Paule was one of his victims, and Paule, when he could not escape, took it a little hardly.

"Speculation has become entirely unprofitable, Lord Honerton," he said, one afternoon, when the latter had sought him out in the laboratory, and interrupted him in the midst of an interesting experiment designed to materially cheapen one of the famous Fernham productions. "If any one can solve the mystery of the disappearance of these two young men it will have to be

the police, unless you care to employ some of these outside private detectives. We people who have our work
to get on with simply waste our time banging our heads
against a stone wall of improbabilities."

"Very true, my dear Paule, very true," Joseph acquiesced. "But just one word in your ear. We can
slip into your room for a moment?"

"For five minutes," Paule replied, his eyes fixed upon
the retort he was watching, "I cannot leave this place.
After that I am at your service for a minute or two.
They must have this formula in the main laboratory this
afternoon. We are days behind in the mixing department."

"Quite right, my dear sir," Joseph assented with a
touch of his old manner. "Business must be attended
to. I will wait."

He passed through the inner door and, in about ten
minutes, Paule joined him, wiping his hands carefully.
He threw the towel away into a corner of the room and,
without seating himself, waited coldly for his visitor to
announce the nature of his errand. Joseph had lost all
his pomposity of manner. He was almost cringing.

"I am sorry if I'm taking up your time," he began,
"but it seems to me that I have no one to speak to nowadays. Rachel lies perfectly still, her eyes wide open,
but she never speaks. I see her lips move often, and I
know what it means — she is praying. She eats and
drinks enough to keep herself alive, drives for an hour
in her pony carriage, always towards the rebuilding of
that cottage, and the rest of the time she knits — she
knits always, silently. When I speak she does not hear.
I have had to come away from Honerton or I think that
I should have gone mad."

"There is your daughter," Paule reminded him.

"It was of Judith that I wanted to speak to you," Joseph acknowledged. "In her way she is as uncommunicative as her mother, but it is in a different way. You spoke just now of private detectives. Well, Judith has one nearly always at her side. He was at Honerton all through the shooting. He was actually there the day Samuel disappeared. He and Judith spend hours going round the country together."

For a noticeable space of time Paule made no reply. His impassivity of expression was scarcely disturbed, but his lips seemed to have come more closely together and there was a steely gleam in his eyes.

"Do you know his name?" he enquired at last.

"Rodes he calls himself," Joseph answered, "Alan Rodes. He used to be a Scotland Yard man. I don't know whether he still is. I always understood that he had Ernest's matter in hand."

Paule followed his visitor's example and seated himself, although his manner was still far from hospitable.

"Do Lady Judith's investigations keep her in Norfolk?" he asked.

"They have done up till now," her father replied. "As a matter of fact, I think she is coming up this evening. There is a ball at Holt house — practically given for her — and Amberleys insists upon her presence. I don't blame him. After all, Samuel is only her cousin, and there is no certainty that anything has happened to him. Do you know what I am going to do, Paule? — Well, I'll tell you. I'm going to offer a reward of fifty thousand pounds for tidings of either of those two lads, dead or alive. What do you think of that?"

"I should strongly advise you to do nothing of the sort," Paule answered. "The twenty thousand pounds

you have already offered is ample. If you increase it
to such an absurd sum people will lose their heads and
you will probably find every minute of your time
throughout the day occupied by investigating impossible
clues, and interviewing impossible claimants."

" What does my time matter? " Joseph exclaimed bitterly. " I want my son, and there is my brother lying
near death. He wants his son. You're a strong man,
Paule — sometimes a little hard, eh? I've never heard
you even speak of a relative and there you are, young,
good-looking, wealthy, still without a wife. We Jews
are not like that. We have our faults. We love our
money overmuch, but we love our children too, our families and our womankind, our homes. There is nothing
to take their place. Now I've lost my son, and my wife
lies stricken, and my brother's heart is breaking because
his son, too, has gone. — I don't know why I come and
bother you, I'm sure. The lad Samuel always used to
say that to talk to you made him feel better — you gave
him strength. I suppose I drift in here with something
of the same feeling."

" Samuel, I am afraid, led a somewhat irregular life,"
Paule said, " and I used occasionally to prescribe for
him."

" He was like other young men," his uncle declared.
" He needed some one to steady him. That is the cruel
part of the business. This girl, Joyce Cloughton, whom
he's always set his heart on, made up her mind to marry
him just the night before he disappeared. She would
have made a different man of him, Paule. As it is, what
is going to become of the business, I cannot think. We
have no young men. Samuel is old and I am growing
old. We have young men at the heads of the departments but they have no claim. Why should they be

given a share in a gold mine? I would rather some one who had really helped stepped into a portion of the profits. Will you be a director of the Company, Sir Lawrence? "

" I am not qualified," Paule reminded him, after a moment's rather astonished pause.

Joseph's sigh was almost a groan.

" The business must have clever young men," he insisted. " Up till now not a single share has been held outside the family. Samuel and I have five thousand each, Samuel Junior has two thousand, there are two thousand held in trust for Ernest, my wife has four thousand, and Henry and Judith have two thousand. Do you know how much those shares are worth, Sir Lawrence? "

" I have not the slightest idea," Paule confessed.

" They are worth two hundred pounds each," Joseph confided portentously. " They have never been on the market. I do not think that they ever will be, but at two hundred pounds each they still pay a ten per cent. dividend. There has never been a business, Paule, like the business my father Israel founded here. I know that you gave up a brilliant professional future to come to us. You have made a great deal of money already compared with professional men. Now your chance comes to make more. We will appoint you a director. As for the shares, Samuel and I will each give you one hundred. That will qualify you."

" Give me! " Paule repeated.

" It is in the Articles," Joseph groaned, " we cannot sell. We need your services. We will give you these shares. It is a present of forty thousand pounds. No one has ever given me forty thousand pounds in my life. It is a terrible sum to give away."

"I am not sure that I am a good enough business man," Paule reflected.

"Of course you are not," Joseph acknowledged. "It is not for business we want you. That is for the counting house. It is for the drugs, for the medicines, to see that we make no mistakes, that we offer on the market the right things. 'Neurota' will travel to the four corners of the world. 'Neurota', handled and advertised as we shall handle and advertise it, will make a vast fortune. We must have you here to watch it, to analyse imitations and expose them, to conceive, perhaps, yet fresh preparations."

"It is an offer which I shall, of course, accept, Lord Honerton," Paule decided. "There is just this much I should say. I have no desire to be a millionaire. When I am worth a certain amount of money — not a large sum from your point of view — I shall retire and devote myself entirely to research work."

"You will enter into an agreement for five years?" Joseph suggested, with a little gleam in his eyes.

"I will consent to that," was the brief reply. "I should not engage myself for a longer period."

Paule's secretary presented himself at the door.

"His lordship is being urgently enquired for on the telephone," he announced. "I have switched him through here."

The young man took off the receiver and handed it to Joseph, who talked for a few moments whilst Paule gave some instructions to his secretary at the farther end of the room. As soon as he had finished, Joseph sank back in his chair.

"I shall have to go to that damned ball," he groaned. "Judith is going to stay at Park Lane. The Marchioness had invited her to stay in the house and Am-

berleys was keen on it too.   I thought it was all arranged, but now she insists upon coming to Park Lane
and having me take her."

He rose unwillingly to his feet.

"I say, Paule," he continued tentatively, as he made
his way to the door, "are you doing anything to-night?
You wouldn't care to come in and dine, would you —
just us three?   To tell you the truth," he added, his
tone half confidential, half wistful, "I don't altogether
understand Judith these days.   She's in one of her
queer moods."

"I am afraid I am not *persona grata* with Lady
Judith just for the moment," Paule observed.   "I
rather gathered that impression last time we met."

"Judith's been queer for weeks," her father confided.
"She and Amberleys have more than once been on the
brink of a serious disagreement.   I'm perfectly certain
she would be as glad as I am to avoid a *tête-à-tête*
dinner."

"I have a card for the dance," Paule observed doubtfully, "but that sort of thing is not much in my line."

"You're going to the dance!" Joseph exclaimed.
"Well, that settles it.   Come you must, and go on with
us.   Eight o'clock.   Glad I thought of it.   Capital!
Now I'll leave you to finish your work."

He bustled off and Paule prepared to return to the
laboratory.   His secretary, however, reappeared.

"The gentleman who was here the other day has
called again to see you, sir," he announced.   "Mr. Alan
Rodes, I think his name is."

Paule indulged in a very rare hesitation.   It was several moments before he arrived at a decision.   Then he
resumed his seat.

"You can show Mr. Rodes in," he directed.

CHAPTER XXIII

Rodes entered, silent and unobtrusive as ever, laid his dark Homburg hat on the table, slipped into a chair in response to Paule's gestured invitation, and, allegorically speaking, staked out his ground for the duel to come.

" Very kind of you to see me, Sir Lawrence," he began. " I was afraid, after our last interview, access to you might be a little more difficult."

" When was our last meeting? " Paule demanded.

Rodes hesitated.

" Well, well," he acknowledged, " I can't say that it was exactly a meeting, was it? I watched you kill some very high pheasants the first day and some very fast partridges the next."

"And afterwards? "

"Afterwards I made one of those mistakes to which you must by now have become accustomed," Rodes confessed. " I followed your car towards London and let you get out of sight. Still, a great question is opened up by the mere fact that you took so much trouble to avoid me. Why was that, Sir Lawrence? "

" I don't like you," was the cool rejoinder. " Surely that is sufficient reason."

" Not quite sufficient for leaving your car by a subterfuge and motoring off in a different direction. I made one bad mistake, I admit, in following your empty car. You surely made another when you told the man at the roadside garage your exact destination."

Paule smiled.

" I told him because there was no secret about it," he replied.

" No secret about it? " Rodes exclaimed. " Then why did you not drive direct to Norwich? "

" You are a very inquisitive person," Paule remarked. " However, since it seems to interest you, here is the truth. I left my car at Barton Mills and returned to Norwich as I realised that it was impossible for me to get to town, at the hour I desired, by car. I doubled back to Norwich and tried to catch the twelve-thirty train."

" You missed it, I think."

" If I did, what business is that of yours? I missed it by five minutes only."

" It still seems curious to me," Rodes persisted, after a brief pause, " that you should have left the car just as you did and returned to Norwich."

" Really? " was the indifferent reply. " Well, I trust you are willing to admit that I am not accountable to you for my movements."

" You are not accountable to me," Rodes acknowledged softly, " but however doubtful my position may be I still represent the law. I represent also Lady Judith Honerton."

" I see. You are the private detective Lord Honerton spoke of."

" I was not aware that his lordship knew of my existence. It was Lady Judith who engaged me and it is Lady Judith with whom I have been investigating."

" With success, I trust."

" With this much of success at any rate," Rodes declared, with a sudden access of vigour in his tone, " we have discovered that your movements on the day following Mr. Samuel Fernham's disappearance need a certain amount of explanation."

" If ever the time should arrive and a properly quali-

fied person should be the inquisitor," Paule assured him,
" that explanation would be readily forthcoming."

The detective sighed.

" I was afraid you might take it like that," he confessed. " We certainly are placing the cart before the
horse. Still, her ladyship showed a great deal of common sense. It was her suggestion that, rather than
spend a lot of further time upon the matter, I should
endeavour to discover from you personally whether you
had not some special reason for behaving in so unac-
countable a manner."

" Her ladyship is very kind," Paule observed, with
faint sarcasm. " You can go back and tell her that I
find your joint interest in my movements flattering but
absurd. If you wish to earn that twenty thousand
pounds, Mr. Rodes, you can use your time to better
purpose than in dogging the footsteps of a person of
my tastes and harmlessness. You cannot seriously suppose that I am concerned in the disappearance of either
of these two young men. Why, then, do you waste your
time taking note of my movements? "

The detective deliberated for some moments before he
replied.

" The problem of the disappearance of these two
young men, Sir Lawrence," he explained, " is one which
we are unfortunately obliged to tackle — in the way of
surmise, I mean — without the guiding light of motive.
We admit the sheer absurdity, on the surface, of your
being connected with the affair in the slightest degree.
Having admitted that, I must confess that but for Lady
Judith's intervention I should have settled down in Norwich for the next few weeks, to try and discover the
reason for your hurried visit there."

" It seems rather a pity that Lady Judith interfered,"

Paule remarked. " Norwich is a very interesting old city and you would doubtless have made some pleasant acquaintances. I should recommend ' The Maid's Head Hotel.' I lunched there after missing my train."

Rodes blinked several times. His eyes seemed sleepier than usual. He was working himself up now to a genuine effort at candour.

" Sir Lawrence Paule," he began at last, " I am as tired as you must be of these indecisive visits, these conversations in which we fence like third-rate diplomatists in Bayswater-written novels. This is my last visit to you unless I come with a warrant in my hand. My final words to you shall be at any rate frank ones. I am defeated and humiliated in my attempts to discover the fate, either of Ernest or of Samuel Fernham, but whether your knowledge be a guilty one or not, I believe that you have some knowledge which would help towards the solution of this mystery, and I appeal to you for the last time to assist the law and probably save the life of Lady Honerton."

" My reply to you," Paule rejoined coldly, " shall be equally frank. Except for that marvellous creation of Dickens, ' Mr. Bucket ', from whose methods I presume you gleaned the idea of doubling back on your tracks, I think you are without exception the most flamboyant and hopeless of all the detectives I ever met or heard of in real life or fiction."

Mr. Rodes rose to his feet and brushed his dark Homburg hat with his sleeve. His attitude was meek and Christian-like. He had not even the air of one who has received a rebuke.

" ' The Maid's Head ', I think you said, Sir Lawrence," he remarked gratefully. " I am very much obliged."

Paule was surprised, when, at a few minutes past eight, he presented himself at Park Lane, to find his host partaking of his second cocktail in the winter garden, wearing a dinner jacket and black tie.

" Is the dance postponed? " he asked.

Joseph made cryptic signs to Martin which resulted in the production of a fresh tray of cocktails.

" No, it isn't that," he explained, a little nervously, " but to tell you the truth I'm not much of a man at these starchy functions — you know what I mean, Paule, all formality and stilts — I — er — thought that as you were going, I might cry off, what? "

Paule shook his head.

" My dear Lord Honerton," he protested, " I am afraid you scarcely realise that this is an exceptional function, and that the Marquis, and the Marchioness especially, are people of old-fashioned ideas.   It would be entirely out of order for me to escort Lady Judith."

Joseph turned his head at the sound of light footsteps.   Judith in a gown of pale sea-green gauze, which floated around her almost like the foam from an upflung wave, came slowly across the room.   Both men were for a moment speechless.   She paused and dropped them a little curtsey.   Her eyes sought Paule's as though for his approval.

"A success, I hope? " she queried.   " Guy brought it over himself by aeroplane from Paris this afternoon. Why does Dad look as though he had had bad news? "

" Your father had a scheme for avoiding the dance to-night," Paule observed.   " He thought that mine would be sufficient escort.   I have had to point out to him that this is an exceptional occasion — that my escort could not possibly be in order."

" It is really wonderful how, with all your more serious activities, you pick up such a stock of miscellaneous knowledge," she declared satirically. " Sir Lawrence is quite right, Dad, but as it happens, my chaperonage is amply provided for. Joyce has just telephoned to say that she and her mother will call for me at ten o'clock."

Joseph's face cleared.

" In that case, my dear," he began ——

" Exactly," she interrupted ruthlessly. " You can go to the Club and play bridge."

Martin announced dinner. Judith at once laid her fingers on Paule's arm.

" Martin," she directed, " please see to the champagne yourself this evening. I want the best in the world and plenty of it. And, Dad, let's be as quick as we can over dinner. I want particularly to talk to Sir Lawrence afterwards before we start."

Joseph, freed from his responsibilities of the evening, was almost light-hearted.

" The quicker the better, my dear," he assented. " They begin bridge very early at the Club."

CHAPTER XXIV

JUDITH left the dinner table long before the conclusion of the meal and Paule had scarcely lit his first cigarette when Martin entered the room and approached him.

"Her ladyship would be obliged if you would come to her boudoir, sir," he announced. "Coffee will be served there."

"Got your orders, you see, Paule," his host declared good-naturedly. "Don't mind me. Judith's got it into her head that she wants to talk to you and you'll have to go through with it."

Paule laid down his cigarette and followed Martin from the room. They mounted the famous marble staircase, traversed a wide corridor, and finally, after a discreet knock, he was ushered into an apartment of which in those first few minutes he received a confused impression of smoke-coloured draperies, flashes of unexpected blue, and the odour of burning wood. Judith was half seated, half reclining upon a great divan near the fire. She motioned him to sit by her side and poured him out some coffee.

"Thank you for coming so soon," she said a little abruptly. "There are cigarettes on the table there. Cigars you don't smoke, I know. Don't neglect your coffee. It's really Turkish — orange flower and all. I'm glad you came early," she added, with a glance at the clock, "we have an hour and five minutes. I want to talk to you."

Paule murmured a word or two of polite acquiescence, helped himself to his coffee and lit a cigarette. The atmosphere of the room pleased him; chiefly be-

cause of the absence of that exotic note which would
have made it more commonplace.   The walls were almost
severe, panelled in white satinwood with faint gilt edg-
ings, and a thin inlay of blue damask.   The furniture
was French, but the upholstery was luxurious.   The
thick carpet was velvety and smoke-coloured.   There
were many flowers in wonderful bowls, but they were all
roses and carnations; none of the hothouse variety.
The only dominant colours in the room were a smokey-
grey, a delicious soft blue, and gilt.   The cigarettes
were of fine tobacco but unscented, the odour of the
burning wood faintly aromatic.

"You say that you want to talk to me," he observed.
"I know what about.   Your tame Sherlock Holmes
came to see me this afternoon."

"Do you ever make a mistake in life?" she asked.

"Infrequently," he admitted.

"Well, you have made one now," she declared.   "I
have not a single word to say to you on that subject."

"I confess myself surprised," he murmured.

She laughed softly and removed the cigarette from
between her white teeth.   It was a very pleasant sound,
even if its note of humour was scanty — a sort of long
croon, with a twang of provocativeness.   Little lines
showed for a moment at the corners of her eyes.

"I want to talk about myself," she confided.

"To me?"

"Why not?   Aren't you interested?"

There was a note almost of anxiety under the faint
insolence of her question.   The smile had left her lips;
she was looking straight into his eyes.   She had reck-
oned herself always something of a diviner of men's
thoughts and emotions.   Paule had baffled her more
than once, but after all he was a human being like the

others. There must be a way through the armour of
his imperturbability. Her moment must come.

"Every one," he said, "is interested in Lady Judith
Fernham."

His retort was trite enough, yet somehow or other it
brought her a certain measure of satisfaction. She
told herself that if she had not penetrated she had
grazed the surface of his defences.

"I am very unhappy," she confided. "You think
that extraordinary?"

"I do indeed," he admitted. "You seem to have
gathered in most of life's gifts. What is there more
for you to desire?"

"Better," she said calmly, "get over the obvious part
of our conversation as quickly as possible. I am young.
I have some good looks, a trifle of wit, a certain vogue
amongst people who count. I have all the money a
person could use or spend and I am engaged to marry
the eldest son of a Marquis. Therefore when I tell you
that I am unhappy you raise your eyebrows. Yet it is
to you that I have to turn for help — to you or no
one."

"Why?" he asked. "I imagined that you mis-
trusted me. I might even go so far as to say, after
that man's visit this morning, that I have reason to
imagine it. Apart from that, you have recently shown
a desire even to avoid me. What surety have you that
I would help you, even if I could?"

"No surety, only a conviction," she answered confidently. "In a way, I am afraid of you. In a way,
I suspect you of nameless things. Yet I know that you
are the only person who can help me. I know that you
are nearer to me than any of these others, that as I
speak, so you will understand."

He was on the point of interruption, but her arm flashed out, slim, white and beautiful.

"No," she insisted, "you fence with your tongue. You don't give me a chance. You shall remain silent. Afterwards you can say as much as you like. In the meantime this is my homily, and the text of it all is that I am unhappy. — You know what is to happen to me to-night, of course. I am to set the rivets upon my bondage. I am to be purred over by the Marchioness, my future mother-in-law, and to be treated with genial and affectionate courtesy by her hop pole of a husband. Consider them — they are to be my mother and father-in-law. I am to listen to the one without yawning, and mould my social life according to the tenets of the other. And then there is Freddy."

"Lord Amberleys will be your husband," he ventured to remind her.

"I told you not to interrupt," she objected. "Well, I am not a fool. I know very well that I can't go through life without a husband. I should much prefer a lover, but I have that much of my race in me. I am virtuous because I can't help it. I am virtuous in deeds and by the sheer selective instinct of my physical self; in my thoughts a wanton. Freddy doesn't help at all. Now can't you see? I don't want to marry Freddy. No, don't interrupt! I can see those very trite words hovering on your lips. I will say them for you. 'A little late to think of that, isn't it?' Well, I grant that it is, but what then? No human being is the same on Wednesday as they are on Thursday. I accepted Freddy and thought I could marry him on Wednesday. To-day is Thursday."

He threw his cigarette away. Was it his fancy, or was the atmosphere of the room losing its freshness?

The odour of the burning wood and the roses and the cigarettes seemed almost to have mounted to his head. He was conscious of an unwonted drowsiness, a languor only of the senses. His brain was working still, keeping pace with hers, — his brain which had never once played him false. All the time he knew his danger.

"Other women before me have done this thing," she continued, "have been qualified by their instincts to walk in the sacred groves, or have climbed the ladder and made their way there, only to follow the same will-o'-the-wisp and sink into the drab places. No one can ever really escape, you know. A lover might keep one's head up towards the skies for a few minutes; art or gambling, or any of the minor passions might walk like ghosts on either side and beat off despair, but of real escape there is none. Look at the clock. It is twenty minutes to ten. At ten o'clock the Duchess of Midlothian will be here with a little speech all ready upon her lips — 'So glad, my dear, to hear that it is really settled. How suitable! Freddy was always lucky!' — and so on."

"What do you want me to do?" he asked, not altogether steadily.

Her eyes swam with joy at the little break in his voice. She leaned towards him. One arm was around the back of the divan, the fingers of her other hand seemed creeping towards him.

"You know," she said. "You and I breathe the same atmosphere. Our eyes see the same things. You may be as wicked as hell but you are the only person to whom I could come for salvation. For some reason you have the will to hate me. Is it strong enough? Stoop down, Lawrence — nearer — nearer!"

After all his embrace was like nothing she had imagined. Every line in his face seemed to have softened. There was a tenderness in those stern eyes of which she had never dreamed. His arms went around her almost deliberately, his lips sought hers with something of the same studied care. There was nothing of the blindness of passion in that long, wonderful caress. She felt herself raised to her feet, her arms still round his neck. He held her throbbing body closely, whilst his lips sought her eyes, her hair, her lips again. She felt the sense of something overpowering, a passion born of other things than the strength of his arms and his softly whispered words. — Presently he let her go. Even then she feared to open her eyes. She heard his voice; a little stifled, curiously kind.

"It is ten o'clock, Judith," he reminded her. "In a moment your chaperon may be here."

She opened her eyes then and smiled at him.

"You are the only person who could have solved this for me," she murmured. "Do you mind going now? I am ringing for my maid — and, unless you care about it, don't come to the ball. Later on in life I'll make my curtsey of thanks to you."

"Later on in life?" he repeated a little vaguely.

She stood with her finger upon the bell, her eloquent smile one of dismissal.

"Why not? You have been wonderful. You alone could have saved me and I am very grateful. Later on I will tell you how grateful."

The maid entered and there were tidings of Joyce and the Duchess. Paule made his escape, haunted by an intangible but curious apprehension that some vital factor in the situation from which he had just emerged had eluded him.

CHAPTER XXV

For the first time in his life Paule, on the following morning, received without irritation a visit from the head of the firm. He kept him waiting for a few minutes whilst he finished a consultation with one of his chemists and then led the way to his private apartments. Joseph was obviously in a condition of great disquietude.

"A nice state of things!" he exclaimed, throwing himself into an easy-chair. "Have you heard anything?"

"I have no idea what you're talking about," Paule assured him.

His visitor handed him a slip of paper.

"Just as I was coming out this morning, if you please," he explained, "up comes her ladyship and presents me with this. 'Please see to it on your way down to the city, Dad,' was all she said. Read it, read it, man! It's for the *Morning Post*."

Paule read the single line in Judith's firm handwriting:

"The marriage arranged between Lady Judith Fernham and Lord Amberleys will not take place."

"Broken off!" he muttered under his breath.

"All done last night, it seems," Joseph continued. "Several other newspapers have been ringing up, as of course the announcement was to have been made publicly last night, although the engagement was pretty well known of beforehand. Changed her mind! That's all she'll say. The hussy! It isn't as though Amberleys wasn't the eldest son. From what I can hear of Holt, she'd have been a Marchioness in five years. I say, Paule," he went on curiously, " did Judith give you any idea of this yesterday evening? "

" Her conversation indicated that she was not altogether satisfied with the prospects of her engagement," Paule admitted. " I had no idea, however, that she was contemplating breaking it off so abruptly."

" I've never had anything against the young fellow," Joseph went on. "A bit stand-offish perhaps, but, after all, there never has been much for him and me to talk about. What the hell can the girl want? "

" Lady Judith is rather an exceptional character," Paule ventured to observe.

" Then if this is the result of her being exceptional," her father declared emphatically, " I wish that she were ordinary. With Ernest gone, and Henry with his career abroad, drifting away from our traditions, Judith was all her mother and I had to turn to. We Jews, you know, Paule — I ain't ashamed of being a Jew — have got just two weaknesses in life. The first you'd say was money — I wouldn't put it first, but let that go — the other is our family. We like large families. We like to see the younger generation of our own stock all around us. Judith was our last hope. We wanted her to marry and have children. It would have lengthened her mother's life by ten years. And she won't do it, Paule. I don't believe she's got it in her. She's thrown over this young fellow — a fine enough chap in his way — and gone off to Scotland this morning with Lady Joyce and her mother."

" From your point of view it is, I suppose, disappointing," Paule acknowledged. " On the other hand, Lady Judith will probably very soon marry some one else."

" Damned if I believe she'll marry at all," her father

groaned pessimistically. "She's all brain and fancies and temperament. That sort of a person finicks with the marriage question. She didn't give us a chance even to argue with her, Paule. Just hands me this slip of paper."

"Since she did hand it to you," Paule suggested, "perhaps you had better have it sent to the office of the *Morning Post.*"

"I had them copy it," Joseph explained. "I kept this to show you. It's so damned awkward for us too, down in Norfolk. We were just getting along nicely with the people, and now this will put the kibosh on the whole show."

Paule glanced at the clock.

"Well, I'm afraid there's nothing I can do for you, Lord Honerton," he regretted. "We're terribly busy here, and I've several appointments before twelve o'clock."

Joseph rose unsteadily to his feet. He had spoken the truth when he had declared that this had been a shock to him. He had indulged a little freely at the Club the night before, and his cheeks seemed more pendulous than ever, his colour more leaden.

"Well, I won't keep you, Paule," he said. "I've a busy morning myself — feeling cheap too. Rotten! What about giving me one of those pick-me-ups you used to give Samuel? I'm needing something of the sort if any one ever did."

For a moment it appeared as though Paule had not heard him, as though he had wandered off into some utterly different field of thought. Joseph moved on his feet impatiently and his companion seemed to become suddenly aware of his presence.

"Yes, I'll give you something," he assented, drawing

his keys from his pocket and moving across the room.
" Wait here a minute, will you? "

Joseph was smitten by a sudden and overpowering curiosity.

" What the devil do you keep in that Bluebeard's chamber of yours? " he exclaimed. " Let's have a look."

Paule swung round with his back to the door.

" The secrecy of these rooms is rather one of my hobbies, Lord Honerton," he observed. " If you remember it is part of our agreement."

" Stuff and nonsense! " Joseph scoffed. " No one wants to pry into your secrets, man. You know perfectly well that I'm not even a chemist. It's sheer curiosity with me, nothing else."

" It is because I realise the fact that I venture to advise you not to press your request," Paule said. " Investigations which I conduct here have a definite purpose, but they necessitate unpleasant accessories."

" Damn it all, what do I care? " was the irritable retort. " Come on! Let's have a look at the damned place! "

"Against my advice," Paule reminded him as he threw open the door.

Paule, alone once more, remained for some minutes gazing through the high, uncurtained window towards the murky horizon — to where the pall of London hung like a black smudge on the other side of a wilderness of small houses. When he turned away it was with a certain reluctance, as though he found the prospect of his morning's work distasteful. He gave a brief order to his secretary, through the telephone, crossed the room, and entered the little apartment with the orange light in the roof which he had once shown Judith. For an hour he lay stretched upon the hard couch, motionless, his wide-open eyes fixed upon one spot in the wall. He had the air of a man indulging in reflection so concentrated as to be almost trancelike. When at last he rose and made his way back, first to his private rooms and later to the laboratories, his face was a little drawn, there was an occasional twitch of the lips, more than once a slight wandering of his attention from the matter in hand. He completed a long morning's work, however, with his usual precise care as to detail, lunched alone in his quarters and sat afterwards smoking a cigarette and reading a review. Presently the telephone at his elbow rang. He took off the receiver and listened to the message.

"Will you tell Lady Honerton that I will call during the evening," was his response.

He rose to his feet, hesitated for a single moment, then passed through the door back again into his chamber of solitude.

CHAPTER XXVI

THE four young men who had been waiting in the library of the great house in Park Lane for over an hour rose with one accord to their feet, as the door was at last opened and Rachel entered. With her white hair and parchmentlike skin, her dress of unrelieved black and her dark, brilliant eyes, she presented an appearance which for a moment absorbed their interest to such an extent that the current of their thoughts was changed and not one of them asked the question which had been trembling on his lips for so long. Rachel was perfectly composed.

"I am Lady Honerton," she announced. "I understand that you gentlemen are from various newspapers and wish to see me."

The young man nearest to her constituted himself spokesman.

"We have been informed, Lady Honerton," he began, "there are some rumours going about, in fact — that Lord Honerton has — er — is not ——"

"My husband's prolonged absence from home is certainly causing us great anxiety," Rachel acknowledged calmly.

"May we ask for the exact particulars of his disappearance?" the journalist continued.

"They are very simple," Rachel replied. "He left home at the usual time this morning, spent an hour at the Works, called at his Bank in the city and sent the car back from there. Since then I have not received even a telephone message."

"You expected him here to luncheon?" one of the others asked.

"Not only did I expect him but he had invited some guests," she told her inquisitors. "They arrived at one o'clock, but we had to lunch without him."

"I take it," was the next query, "that all the usual enquiries have been made."

"Naturally," Rachel assented. "We telephoned to the Works and since then to all his Clubs, and every possible place we could think of."

"And the Bank," her first questioner suggested. "What about the Bank? Did he draw out a large sum of money?"

"He drew no money at all," was the unexpected reply. "His visit there apparently had reference to a quite unimportant matter. The cashier who attended to him declares that he was not in the place more than five minutes and the commissionaire on duty remembers his leaving the premises."

"Have you any idea why he sent his car home?" one of the visitors asked.

"None at all. It was a most unusual occurrence. He seldom walks a yard if he can help it."

The only member of the little company of journalists who had not yet spoken, ventured to intervene.

"Lady Honerton," he said, "you must forgive us for alluding to such a painful subject, but the successive disappearances of your son and nephew have been the most sensational items of news the Press has had to deal with during the last few years. The fact that Lord Honerton himself is now missing will, of course, come as a thunderbolt upon the public. May we ask whether you have any theory, any possible explanation as to this amazing sequence of events? Is there any vendetta, for instance, in your family, or — if you will pardon the suggestion — any trace of lunacy? "

" There is nothing of the sort," Rachel replied calmly.

The absence of all agitation in the woman who stood so patiently receiving their questions was almost disconcerting. The four men looked at one another.

" You have no theory, Lady Honerton, in your own mind? "

" I have no theory," she confessed. " I used to think and wonder — now I only suffer. If there is nothing more I can do for you, you will perhaps excuse me. I have a visitor waiting in another room."

No one ventured to detain her. The nearest held the door open, and she left the room with unseeing eyes. On the morrow the Press of the country could do little except announce without comment, in the baldest possible terms, the sudden and inexplicable disappearance of Joseph, second Baron Honerton.

Paule, who was waiting for Rachel in the room upon the ground floor which Joseph was accustomed to call his study, rose to his feet at her entrance and offered a murmured greeting. She brushed aside the commonplaces of conversation, however, with her first words.

" Sir Lawrence," she begged, " will you help me to find my husband? "

" I will help, of course, as every one would," he assured her, " but I fear that there is not the slightest chance of my being able to succeed where so many have failed."

" I think otherwise," she rejoined.

He looked at her curiously. Rachel, then, was the source of that suspicion, traces of which he had occasionally found in Judith's manner also.

"It is scarcely possible, Lady Honerton," he protested, "that you should suspect me of having any knowledge as to the nature of these disappearances."

She had chosen to seat herself by his side. She leaned over and laid her hand upon his. She was at all times a woman of reserved demeanour, undemonstrative and deliberate. Her action seemed to gain significance from the fact.

"I believe," she said, "that you could solve this mystery for us if you would, or, at any rate, put us in the way of solving it for ourselves."

"The idea is absurd," he replied curtly.

"I suppose it is," she admitted, "but then, all ideas or speculations on the subject seem absurd. Sir Lawrence," she went on, "I am an elderly woman and my strength is failing. I want to see my son before I die. Is a mother's appeal to you of any avail?"

He spoke to her very much as one would speak to a child of tender years.

"You must have some reason for this extraordinary suspicion," he insisted. "What on earth makes you connect me with the affair at all?"

She shook her head wearily.

"No reason," she acknowledged. "I just feel."

They sat in silence for a moment or two.

"I am too much interested in your attitude to resent it as I ought to," Paule finally spoke. "Can you tell me anything more about this feeling?"

"Not very much," she admitted. "It is there all the time, though. I am not a spiritualist," she continued, "but it has always been a belief of mine that there are many things going on around us to which at present we have no clue. An article of yours, which I read in the *National Review* — long before you came to the Works

— dealt with this same subject — 'Divination.' I believe you said that the mind could be trained into a receptive and apprehensive state."

" I remember something of the sort," he assented.

She leaned over again and looked at him, her great eyes filled with solemn purpose.

" You used guarded words," she went on — " you always do — but you must have meant that one can learn by training how to look, however hazily, over the edge of the world. Isn't that so? "

" This is, of course, pure speculation," he reminded her gently. " I do not see how you can connect my theories in any way with your husband's disappearance."

" Not definitely," she exclaimed eagerly. " I do not claim that. I only know that I detect a gift in you, a quality which I do not find in other people. You see farther and into a different world. I do not pretend to have your gifts, but my vision is attuned to yours."

He shook his head.

" This is all purely speculative," he warned her again. " You must put it out of your mind that I can be of any practical help to you in this matter."

She waited thoughtfully for some minutes. Then she asked him an abrupt question.

" Had you anything to do with Judith's breaking her engagement to marry Lord Amberleys? " she demanded.

" I? Certainly not! " he replied.

" Do you care for Judith? "

" I admire her as all the world does," he admitted coldly. " Beyond that women do not enter into my scheme of life."

" Precisely what is your scheme of life? " she asked him.

"Punctuality is a part of it," he observed, glancing at the clock and rising to his feet. "I have a committee meeting to attend at ten o'clock."

She caught him by the wrist and held him tightly.

"You are hard to move, Lawrence Paule," she declared. "I scarcely hoped that you would unbend, that you would speak to me as a human being. There is something about you aloof from us all. And yet you are a man — you must have a heart. I waste my time asking questions which you have not the will to answer, but remember what I have said — I am an old woman and I am suffering. If it comes within your power, let me see my son again before I die."

There was a little of the former toleration in his manner, a wintry note of kindliness in his tone.

"If your son should need my help and I should ever be able to give it," he promised, "I will remember what you have asked. For the rest," he concluded, after a moment's hesitation, "if I were you, I should think of him without a doubt as being still alive. The gift of life, the condition of living, is too amazing a thing to be trifled with or extinguished lightly. Fate may have dealt freakishly with him, but not to the last extent."

She dropped his hand.

"You have consoled me," she acknowledged, "because I believe that you know."

CHAPTER XXVII

PAULE, making rather a late appearance in the conference room at the Works, one afternoon, a few days later, was astonished to find Samuel Fernham in the chair and Judith by his side. He paused to shake hands before taking his seat at the table. Samuel was gaunt and hollow-eyed, but a touch of his old firmness of manner had returned. He had the air of a man stung by adversity into a new era of activity.

"You are surprised to find me here, Sir Lawrence?" he remarked, as he gripped his fingers. "It is my defiance to our hidden enemies. Ernest has gone, and Samuel has gone, and now Joseph. Yet we who are left are not afraid. I am here to work. I shall remain."

Paule's congratulations were vague and noncommittal. Judith leaned over as he looked around for a seat.

"I hope you don't object to a woman on the Board, Sir Lawrence?" she observed, making room for him by her side.

"Not in the least," he assured her. "I really have no place here myself yet, except in an advisory capacity."

The business of the day was being conducted by the managers of the departments and no reference whatever was made to the extraordinary conditions prevailing. Samuel Fernham had an agenda before him, which he occasionally consulted and which he folded up with an air of relief as soon as the last item had been dealt with. He rose to his feet as a signal that the conference was at an end, but laid his hand on Paule's shoulder when the latter prepared to leave the room with the others.

" Lady Judith and I would be glad if you could spare us a minute," he begged. " There is a little matter we desire to mention."

Paule nodded assent but did not resume his seat. Samuel waited until they were alone, then drew from his pocket a letter and tapped the envelope with his finger.

" This communication, Sir Lawrence," he said, " is from the secretary of the Board of Governors of St. Phillip's Hospital. It is addressed to you or to the Managing Director of the firm. My brother's secretary appears to have accepted the latter alternative and opened it."

He passed the letter across. Paule read it with un-moved face.

November 13th.

St. Phillip's Hospital.
Dear Sir:

I am directed by the Board to inform you that the number of bodies of patients acquired by the Hospital for research purposes is at present insufficient for our own needs and we are not, therefore, able to continue our arrangement with you.

Faithfully yours,

James Colbert,

Secretary.

" What does that mean? " Samuel demanded.

" It seems to me singularly plain," Paule replied. " The hospital authorities look upon my connection with the commercial side of medicine as debarring me for the future from my share of the — er — subjects with which they have been supplying me. It is annoying but, as it happens, my experiments are practically completed."

Outside there was a fog and the electric lights in the room were lit, although the curtains were still undrawn. In the somewhat ghastly illumination, Samuel appeared older and frailer than ever. Judith, in her rich furs, and with a touch of unusual colour in her cheeks, presented a strange contrast to both her companions — serenely beautiful, defiant of any adverse condition. Samuel suddenly lost control of himself.

" What the hell do you want with dead bodies? " he exclaimed.

" What does any scientist want with them? " Paule replied patiently. " I have, as you know quite well, made the human brain the study of my lifetime. ' Neurota ' has been one fruit of my investigations."

Samuel reflected for a moment.

" Sir Lawrence," he said, " I have been in the drug business since I was a lad. I have been at the back of a score of remedies, each one of which has brought us in a small fortune. We never bothered about employing a highly paid chemist or indulging in research work of any sort. We just took an ordinary physician's prescription for any of the ordinary ailments of life, altered it a little to our liking, found the cheapest drugs which corresponded with the original ones, bought them in the best markets, and turned the stuff out wholesale. That's how our business was built up."

" That sounds very unenterprising but it may be the case, so far as you are concerned," Paule replied. " On the other hand, it was an experimenting firm of wholesale druggists who discovered anti-toxin."

Samuel struck the table before him with his thin clenched fist. His eyes were bright and hard, although his voice lacked the vigour of his movements.

" I don't care a damn about anti-toxin," he declared.

" I hate your laboratories. This sort of thing doesn't go with our business. I told Joseph so years ago."

" I am sorry," was Paule's cold rejoinder. " Do you desire to give any practical effect to this conversation? "

Judith laid her hand soothingly upon her uncle's.

" Sir Lawrence," she said, " my uncle is naturally very much upset by all these strange happenings. I am sure he does not wish to be in any way offensive or to dispute the fact that your experiments have been of great service to the firm. At the same time, it is his wish that they should be conducted, not in private, but in the laboratories of the firm."

" My agreement," Paule reminded her, " gives me the use of my own laboratories with every facility for carrying on research work outside my duties as chemist to the firm. Do I understand from your uncle that it is his wish to alter the arrangement? "

" I can tell you exactly what it is he wants," Judith replied. " I am not sure that it is unreasonable. He desires to have access to your laboratories and to be informed precisely as to the nature of your research work."

" I see," Paule murmured. " Does he realise that Lord Honerton never expressed any such desire? "

" My father is no longer here," she pointed out, " and my uncle has assumed the responsibilities of control. You will remember," she went on, after a moment's hesitation, " that I myself, on a certain occasion, had a somewhat terrifying glimpse into your private laboratory."

" What is your own feeling in the matter? " he enquired.

" I think it would be as well if you acceded to my Uncle Samuel's wishes," she answered.

" Either that, or close the laboratories," Samuel intervened harshly.

" I am not compelled to adopt either course," Paule observed.   " My agreement ———"

" Damn your agreement!" Samuel interrupted, leaning forward.   " Is that plain enough?   I represent the Board of Directors who own this building and this business.   Your laboratories are part of it.   I desire to investigate their contents."

Paule for the first time smiled.

" Well," he said, " under some conditions I might feel disposed to resent this attitude.   As it is, I must, I suppose, make allowances for it.   I will conduct you over my laboratories.   I warn you, however, that you are going to be very disappointed.   You will discover nothing of my experiments.   Will you come with me now? "

" This instant, sir," Samuel assented, rising.

Judith caught the glimmer of Paule's smile, half challenging, half contemptuous, as he threw open the door of his private laboratory, and the sudden impulse of faintness passed.   She clutched her uncle's arm, however, as they stood side by side in the sinister-looking little room with its marble basins, marble slabs and shelves whose ghastly burden was fully exposed.   Samuel, apparently, felt nothing but blank amazement.

" I do not understand this," he declared.   " What have these skeletons and heads to do with our business of making drugs? "

" It is not necessary that there should be any connection," Paule answered coldly.   " I am perfectly at liberty to pursue here any independent research to which I am attracted.   As a matter of fact, however, as you may judge from these harmless objects," he added, pointing to a row of skulls, " I am greatly interested in the brain and the nervous system, and it was in this room that I conceived the idea of ' Neurota '."

" But these skeletons," Judith faltered.

" They are months old," he observed carelessly, " useless! I have had a human head here, though, not so long ago, practically still quivering with life. It is then that one has a chance. It is in the transition period between life and death that one may perhaps stumble upon some of the, as yet, undiscovered secrets of science."

" There is nothing left to discover," Samuel grumbled; " no new possibilities, I mean."

"A rash statement," Paule objected. " Now you are here you had better see everything. Here is my private library."

He led them through to an inner room, lined on all four sides with bookcases from floor to ceiling. There were volumes of every age and of every quality of binding. Judith read the titles of one or two of them.

" The mind, always the mind! " she exclaimed. " What has the mind to do with actual diseases, Sir Lawrence? "

" More than you or most people imagine," he answered. " I would even go so far as to suggest to you that if any startling discoveries are made during the next decade, they will be made in this field, rather than in the field of surgery. The will is a great force in the dissemination or the prevention of disease."

" Have you anything else to show us? " Judith asked a little abruptly.

" My rest chamber," he replied, throwing open the door of the third apartment. " There is nothing else."

They both glanced around the empty room with its

solitary hard couch, its atmosphere of chill negation. Samuel was becoming impatient.

"You are a man of strange tastes, Sir Lawrence," he said, looking at him from underneath his bushy eyebrows.

Paule shrugged his shoulders.

"Not so strange to any one who understands," he rejoined. "I do not pretend to explain everything to you. It is not necessary. You have asked to be allowed to inspect the apartments where I pursue my research investigations. I have granted your request. The private laboratory is also at your service. You will find nothing there but drugs in various stages of mixing and decomposition."

"Very well," Samuel said, "let us go."

"If your curiosity is now completely satisfied," Paule suggested, "would you mind telling me why you have insisted upon making this investigation into what I might term my private affairs? My discoveries, so far as they have gone, have been of immense service to the firm. Of what am I suspected?"

One of those sudden and entirely transforming changes, which seemed part of her versatile personality, swept over Judith. She passed her arm through his in friendly fashion; the cling of it was almost affectionate.

"Don't be foolish," she begged. "We are just beside ourselves, all of us. We are like a family smitten with madness. We scarcely know where to look or what to suspect, or whom."

A messenger from the cashier's department came in urgent haste for Samuel. Judith lingered in the large outside sitting room and moved to the uncurtained window. Below, the factory proper stretched out in two great wings. The fog had slightly increased, and lights flashed through a row of innumerable windows. In the distance was the dull throb of an enormously powerful engine. A fleet of drays were drawn up around the yard. There was everywhere a sense of movement, of tremendous pulsating energy. Judith's eyes were almost the eyes of a mystic as she looked downwards.

"It is like a great piece of machinery, this," she declared, "grinding out its millions and millions and millions. And who wants it all, what good is it? One by one — the men who built it up — Israel my grandfather, dead of grief; Joseph my father, Ernest his son, Samuel my cousin, all three gone. And still the gold making continues. Do you know what I should like to do?"

Paule shook his head but remained silent.

"I should like to destroy every brick and stone of these buildings," she cried passionately, "pour all these drugs into the sewers, pension the work people with those idle millions, wipe out this whole place from the face of the earth. Then go somewhere, as far away as possible and try to forget it all. These millions would crush any one. They're a yoke on any one's spirit. None of us know how or what it means, but we all believe that it is because of them this curse has come upon us."

Paule offered no sympathy, appeared wrapped still in an inviolable mantle of silence. She turned upon him suddenly. For a single moment she seemed to have lost something of her youth; lost it without the faintest detraction from her beauty. It was intense feeling alone which had brought the lines to her face and the shadows under her eyes.

"I don't know why it is to you I always turn when I feel at the limit of all my resources," she exclaimed. "In a vague sort of way I am afraid of you and yet you are strong — the strongest person I know — and I have all the time the thought that there is something behind your speechless lips. Why don't you behave sometimes like a human being? "

" Once," he began ——

" Once!" she repeated bitterly. " You kissed me once. I shall never know a greater humiliation in my life than the memory of it. And afterwards you could stay ——"

He crushed the words to death upon her lips. Her long, throbbing body lay vibrating in his arms. By degrees the strength seemed to pass from her. She clung to him still with her arms but the tension left her limbs. Then, without the slightest effort, he lifted and carried her to his easy-chair, kissed her hands and stood away.

" Rest for a few moments," he begged. " There is some one outside at the telephone."

She rested or dozed — she was scarcely conscious which. She heard him speak on the telephone, heard him give brisk, curt orders to the people who had disturbed him. Presently he came back to her side.

" Lady Judith," he began ——

She looked at him almost with terror.

" You're not going back? " she implored. " I won't be called anything but ' Judith '. I won't be treated any other way than as the woman who has given you the very breath of her body. Don't pretend that you don't understand," she pleaded. " I have been daring, people have gossiped about me, but you know as well as I do that no kiss has ever left my lips. And you — oh, I know about you! It's irrevocable, Lawrence Paule. I shall claim what belongs to me."

He raised her fingers to his lips. She watched the

change in his face with joy, met his embrace halfway. This time he held her with a new tenderness of which she was blissfully conscious. Without a single word from his lips she knew that victory was hers.

CHAPTER XXVIII

THEY dined together that night in a restaurant a little off the beaten track; a place more frequented by the élite of Bohemia than by Judith's own immediate circle of friends. The vogue of picture papers, however, and her own vivid characterisation made it as difficult as ever for Judith to avoid recognition. Her broken engagement, her great wealth, her reputation as a beauty and the amazing tragedy which had made her family the subject of universal discussion, had combined to render her notorious. People whispered about her and indulged in speculations as to her distinguished-looking but stern companion. To all this Judith was as blissfully unconscious as Paule himself. The thing which she desired more than anything else in the world was looming over her path; a little intangible still, it seemed, but increasingly desirable. It was amazing to repeat to herself that in all the emotions of her crowded life there had come to her nothing so wonderful as the joy of being alone with him, of knowing that she had broken through, to a great extent at any rate, the reserve and the mystery in which he had chosen to live. She was stimulated by her happiness into one of her most brilliant moods. She talked lightly but incessantly and her companion had little to do but listen with amused interest. She deliberately avoided all serious topics. It was not until the close of the meal that, with her elbows upon the table and with a cigarette between her fingers, she leaned across and brought the subject of conversation round to his work.

" Did you see the *Times* this morning? " she enquired.

" They are very curious indeed about the paper you are going to read at the Paris Congress."

A shadow rested upon his face as he answered her.

" I can't imagine how they know anything about it," he declared, almost irritably. " The president of the Congress dislikes all anticipations and we are not obliged even to disclose our subject."

" What is yours? " she asked him bluntly.

" I am going to give them the result of certain experiments I have made lately," he replied. " Most of my written work has been on chemistry but, after all, the inexact sciences become more attractive as one progresses."

" What do you mean by ' inexact sciences '? " she demanded.

" It is perhaps a foolish phrase," he admitted. " I mean the fields where our knowledge is obviously imperfect and where we can only work with theories. Astronomy is one, for instance. The fact that science has not yet enabled us to determine exactly whether the planets are inhabited or not and to devise some means of signalling to them, is sometimes almost humiliating. It just happens, I suppose, that the man with the right type of brain has never set his mind to it. The difficulties of the work are tremendous but there is no longer such a word as impossible where science is concerned."

" Has your paper anything to do with astronomy? " she enquired.

He laughed at her across the table; a laugh which delighted her from its very rarity. His whole expression seemed to change. She caught glimpses of suppressed youthfulness, a sense of humour, perhaps long and unduly restrained.

" No," he confessed, " I have wandered a little way

into another field of speculation but, in case you should feel tempted to go down to the office of the *Times* and set their minds at rest upon the subject, I shall spare you the burden of my confidence."

" I am not sure that I think that altogether nice of you," she declared. " Who has a better right to know than I? "

" No one," he admitted.

" Besides," she went on, with the faint beginning of a smile upon her lips, " a visit to the *Times* office would be opportune. I could hand them in an announcement of our engagement."

He looked at her with an expression in his face which she found it hard to fathom.

" Our engagement? " he repeated. " What do you mean? "

" You mean to marry me, don't you, Lawrence? " she asked. " You haven't been trifling with me or anything of that sort? "

He tried to fall into her vein.

" Do you think nature ever meant me for a trifler? " he protested.

" I wonder whether you are what nature meant you to be? " she demanded. " However, you haven't answered my question."

He called for the bill. She leaned a little farther across the table and laid her hand upon his.

" Must I repeat it, Lawrence? " she asked quietly.

He had relapsed into his old self, stony, aloof.

" If you knew what manner of man I was," he said, " and who I am —— "

" What have those things to do with it? " she interrupted. " Whatever you happen to be or whatever disagreeable things you may have done, you are the only man I have ever thought seriously of marrying. I do not press you, I am in no hurry, but if there is anything you feel you must tell me, let me hear it. I will be your judge. It will have to be very bad indeed if I let you slip away. You see, Lawrence — I am rather fond of you."

He paid the bill in silence and they left the restaurant a moment or two later. He handed her into the car and remained upon the pavement.

" Don't be absurd! " she exclaimed with quick impatience. " Get in at once. You are coming back with me."

He obeyed, and she linked her arm through his as their automobile plunged into the traffic.

" Whatever I am, or whatever crimes I may have committed," he told her sadly, " you have brought repentance into my soul."

" Presently," she threatened, " I will put you into the confessional."

" I will enter of my own accord," he promised, " in three weeks' time."

" Three weeks," she reflected. " Very well, I will wait until then if you remain what I wish you to be."

"Agreed," he murmured a little unsteadily.

In the hall of the house in Park Lane Martin hastened to receive them.

" We are going up to my room, Martin," Judith said. " Please have some Turkish coffee sent there, with some brandy and whisky and soda."

" Certainly, your ladyship," was the respectful reply. " There is a person here, however, who has been waiting to see you for an hour."

" Who is it? " she enquired.

" He gave the name of Rodes, your ladyship."

"Our mutual friend!" Judith laughed, turning to Lawrence. "We will go in and see him together."

Martin opened the door of a room on the further side of the hall and they entered, Judith with her arm through Paule's. Rodes, who had been reading a magazine, rose at their entrance. His words of greeting, however, remained unuttered. He was obviously very much surprised.

"Good evening, Mr. Rodes," Judith said. "Any news?"

"I have a communication to make to your ladyship, if you can spare me a minute or two in private," was the somewhat hesitating reply.

"Quite unnecessary," she assured him. "You can say anything you have to before Sir Lawrence."

Rodes's expression was half puzzled, half grave.

"Your ladyship," he announced, "what I have to say happens to concern Sir Lawrence."

"The more reason why he should be present, then," was Judith's cool rejoinder. "He may be able to confirm the truth of the information you have to impart, or deny it."

The detective was evidently dubious. He paused for a moment or two to consider the situation.

"Your ladyship," he decided, "I will obey your wishes. For many reasons, however, I am inclined to regret the presence of Sir Lawrence this evening."

"I am naturally curious," Paule intervened, "but if you would prefer me to leave you for a time, Lady Judith ——"

"I should hate it," she interrupted. "You can go on, Mr. Rodes. I can only hope that what you have to tell me will be helpful."

"I am hoping that it will prove so," Rodes acquiesced

gravely. " I have been working, Lady Judith, very
much on the lines you yourself once suggested. I have
been theorizing. I asked myself whether there was any
living person who might be capable of a great enmity
against your house. I turned back a page of your family history. I set myself to discover whether by any
chance the son of Margaret Heggs still lived."

Paule, who had been listening intently, had not moved
a muscle. Judith, whose interest at first had seemed
slight enough, was now absorbed.

" I discovered," the detective continued, " that the
tombstone to the memory of Margaret Heggs and her
infant son had not been erected until six years after her
death — a somewhat singular circumstance. I then
searched for the death certificates of the infant. The
entries as regards Margaret Heggs were all in order.
There was no record whatever as regards the infant.
The village was in a remote part of Surrey, the sexton
an octogenarian. The family who wished that child's
origin to remain unknown took a chance which succeeded. The boy was brought up under another name
and is alive to-day."

There was a moment's silence. Judith had moved a
little closer to Lawrence, who was listening with entirely
impassive expression. Her eyes wandered from his face
to the great painting which hung upon the wall.

" There is very little doubt," Rodes continued, " that
the gamekeeper Heggs was hanged mainly owing to the
malevolent influence exerted by Israel Fernham, — your
grandfather, Lady Judith, and the founder of your
house. In my search for some possible enemy of your
family I have discovered this grandson and I have in
my mind not the slightest doubt but that he is responsible for whatever may have happened to your brother,

your cousin, and your father. In plain words, Sir Lawrence, the truth is known. You are the grandson of John Heggs, the man who was hanged at Israel Fernham's instigation, and I charge you with being responsible for the disappearance of these three members of the Fernham family."

"Any warrant or anything of that sort?" Paule asked, almost carelessly.

The detective frowned.

"I am hoping that you will not drive me to that extreme," he said. "I have only just arrived at the end of my first series of investigations. The second I am hoping that you will render unnecessary."

"You seem to have interested yourself unwarrantably in my private affairs, merely upon an assumption," Paule observed, "and now that you have arrived at the difficult part of your task you expect me to help you. I do not contest the truth of what you say. It is true that I am the grandson of John Heggs, who was executed owing to the malice of that man whose picture hangs upon the wall. I admit the fact. As regards the disappearance of these three men, I have nothing to say. If you think that I am responsible, find them and prove it, or find the evidence that I have been guilty of any crime. I have no intention of doing your work for you."

The detective took up his hat.

"Very well, Sir Lawrence!" he exclaimed. "I accept the challenge. I tell you frankly that now I have arrived at a partial solution of the mystery, I do not think it will take me long to discover the rest."

"My best wishes," Paule said. "It scarcely seems possible that acumen such as you have displayed should remain unrewarded. I wish you luck."

"Is there anything you desire to say to me, Lady Judith?" the detective asked, as he prepared to take his leave.

"Nothing," Judith replied.

They were alone in the little room — Paule, more profoundly moved than ever before in his life; Judith, with a curious and overmastering reluctance to let her mind dwell for a single moment upon any of the material points of the story to which they had listened.

"Well," he said at last, "you have heard my pedigree. You must admit that I never forced myself upon you."

"All that that man Rodes has told me this evening, I guessed before," she replied.

"You guessed it?" he repeated incredulously.

She touched the light which hung above the frame of the picture, and Israel Fernham looked out at them.

"You forget," she said, "you are of my stock as well as those others."

"But if you guessed it," he persisted, "why — why am I here with you now?"

She passed her arm through his.

"You ought to know," she answered. "Now come up into my room, please. I want you to tell me what you have done to my people."

BOOK TWO

CHAPTER I

THERE was almost a swagger in the young man's attitude as he stood with his hands in his pockets, a homemade cigarette drooping from the corner of his lips, gazing at the crudely painted sign and other announcements displayed in the window of the cottage from which he had just issued. He had the air of one pleased with his handiwork and he looked up and down the hilly, cobbled street as though disappointed that there were no passers-by to share his interest and admiration. He read the announcement of his identity over slowly to himself:

REUBEN KLASK
DEALER IN HERB MEDICINES

Below were three bottles on the inner ledge of the window sill, with a small card behind, rudely printed in pen and ink, describing and enlarging upon their virtues. There was " Klask's Sarsaparilla, The Famous Blood Cleanser ", " Klask's Grey Pills ", which were pledged to remove biliousness from amongst the world's ills, and a third bottle containing a colourless liquid and labelled " Klask's Famous East Coast Tonic ". The only other adornments to the window were a pair of moderately clean muslin curtains, a canary in a wooden cage and a handful of dried leaves in a china bowl.

Reuben Klask, the manipulator of herbs, was obviously a young man on the lookout for business, and determined by some means or other to secure it. As there seemed to be no immediate prospect of customers he crossed the street with his hands still in his pockets, descended a stone step, raised the latch of a door and entered the premises of Eli Pank, cobbler. Mr. Pank, seated upon a bench, was hard at work at his proverbial occupation. He looked up over his steel-rimmed spectacles at his visitor's entrance.

"Shut that door, young man," he enjoined.

The newcomer, with a word of apology, obeyed.

"Just ran across to hear how the corns are, Mr. Pank," he said politely.

"They ain't troubling much," was the somewhat grudging admission.

"That stuff I made up for you," Reuben Klask continued, "is going to bring me in a fortune some day. There's no one else but me knows exactly how to mix it."

"It didn't do me no harm, anyway," the cobbler conceded.

"There's only one thing about it," the young man went on earnestly. "You got to apply it freely just at first. You want to rub plenty in and rub it in often, Mr. Pank. How are you getting on with the stuff?"

"Used about half of it — rather more perhaps."

"Then don't you wait until you're out," the vendor of drugs begged. "To-morrow or the next day I may be off at some of the markets. I might be closed up for days. Let me fetch you another bottle, Mr. Pank. I made one up all fresh not half an hour ago."

"I've got some left," the other pointed out.

"That don't matter. You'll use it all in time," the young man declared with emphasis. "It's good stuff, Mr. Pank. It's worth double what I am charging for it — treble they'd have for it at the shops. They're making it difficult for me to get the herbs. Let me bring you across that other bottle."

"Eighteen pence is eighteen pence these days," the cobbler sighed.

"Three shillings you'd have to pay in the shops," Reuben Klask reminded him.

The cobbler scrutinised his work for a moment and scratched his chin.

"Eighteen pence," he muttered. "Would there be a pint of beer to it, young man?"

"I don't drink nothing," was the eager reply, "but I like to do business. A pint of beer's thruppence. I'll take three ha'pence off the bottle and bring it right across."

The cobbler considered the matter.

"Three ha'pence," he explained, "don't do me no good. Make it tuppence for half a pint ——"

"I'll fetch it right away," the young man interrupted. "You stay there, Mr. Pank. It's a beautiful bottle. You won't have any corns no more!"

Reuben Klask crossed the street with great celerity, entered the little front room through the latched door, took a bottle from amongst half a dozen others in a deal cupboard, and hastened back. The cobbler counted out the money from a till and the young man, after a cordial farewell, sauntered once more out into the street. There was a well-pleased smile upon his lips. He had done business!

A noisy little crowd of work people from the clothing factory at the top of the hill came trooping down. They were a roughish lot, and for some reason or other the appearance of the young man loitering in the street seemed to annoy them. Reuben Klask, whose one idea was to be on friendly terms with every one in the world, especially any one likely to buy a bottle of his medicines, found himself, notwithstanding his polite protests, being hustled first to one side and then to the other of the narrow cobbled street.

" There's something about a Sheeny," one young man declared, spitting upon his hands, " always kinda riles me. That your shop, mister? "

" That's mine," Reuben assented anxiously; " my name's Reuben Klask. I make very good medicines. I cure corns. I got the best pills in Norwich."

An ugly-looking young man elbowed his way to the front.

" Got any sticking plaster, Reuben? " he demanded. "Anything that's good for a black eye? "

Reuben, intent upon business, was blind to the menace of the suggestion.

" I give you something to cure all those things," he promised. " I got a liniment, too, for bruises and cuts."

There was a peal of laughter. The young man who had spoken first spat once more upon his hands.

" Get 'em all ready, then. You're going to need 'em," he jeered.

Reuben Klask was suddenly pale. He realised his danger and glanced anxiously towards the door of the cottage, unhappily inaccessible by reason of the little ring of his tormentors.

" You don't want to hurt me, gentlemen," he cringed. " I haven't done you any harm. I just want to make a small living here. I ain't doing any one any harm."

" Makes me fair sick! " the arch bully observed. " What'll we do with him, lads? "

A girl, who had been watching the proceedings with disapproval, pushed her way through the crowd.

" You ain't going to do nothing with him," she declared resolutely. " Get along, all of you! Can't you see he ain't the sort a grown lad could knock about? The first of you boys who touches him has got to hear from me that he's a dirty coward. Get off home with you!"

They affected terror and fled. After all, Reuben Klask was a weak-looking little creature, already thoroughly terrified, and there was small chance of further sport with him. The girl lingered behind. Reuben, with his knees shaking, moved towards the door of his cottage. The girl watched him attentively and with growing interest. He represented a new type to her.

"You're a queer one to be about without your mammie!" she exclaimed.

"I'm not so bad as all that," he replied, gathering courage as the others turned the corner. "I don't see what they wanted to hurt me for. I ain't here to do any one any harm. I just want to make a living."

"They wouldn't have hurt you much," she observed. "They were just sky-larking."

"They were very rough," he objected. "I don't like rough people."

"I say, where do you come from?" the girl asked curiously.

He shook his head. There was an utterly blank expression in his eyes.

"I forget the name of the place," he admitted. "I got a good business here, though — good business if I can sell enough. Come in and see my drugs."

She hesitated. He opened the door and she passed in. She was a pleasant-looking girl, neatly dressed, pale through overwork and underfeeding, but with a mass of brown hair and a humorous turn to her lips. She looked round the little room into which he ushered her.

"I know this place," she remarked. "Old Mother Crurton used to live here — a bad lot she was, too."

"It was empty when I took it," he said. "You see," he went on, proudly opening the door of the deal cupboard, "I got over twenty bottles here. I made these all myself."

"Where do you mix 'em up?" she enquired.

"In the back kitchen," he answered, with his finger at the side of his nose. "I don't let any one see me do it. That's my secret. All of those bottles, very good. You try my famous 'East Coast Tonic'."

She laughed softly.

"Are you going to give me a bottle?" she demanded.

There was a look of positive pain in his face.

"Young lady," he said earnestly, "you were very kind to me, very kind indeed, but you get good wages at your work. I am very poor. What wages do you get?" he asked.

"Forty-five bob a week," she answered complacently. "I've just been made a forewoman."

His eyes glistened.

"Forty-five shillings a week is a great deal of money," he acknowledged. "You're very much richer than I am. I can't afford to give you a bottle of my tonic, but I tell you what I do. I charge you half price. It will do you good," he continued eagerly, "give you colour, make your eyes sparkle."

She looked at him wonderingly.

"You're a queer one," she murmured. "How much is half price?"

"Ninepence," he replied. "I won't deceive you, young lady. I might have said a shilling and it would have been very cheap, but ninepence is half price."

She counted out the money, accepted the bottle he gave her and slipped it into her pocket.

"Don't suppose I shall ever take any," she said.

"You take it," he begged. "You take it and tell the other girls in your factory that you're feeling better. You bring them here to buy more bottles and perhaps we do something, eh? I allow you a little or we go out together. If we sell enough bottles we might be able to go to the pictures."

"There's plenty of 'em anxious enough to take me to the pictures without me paying anything," she rejoined.

The young man sighed.

"Every one earns such good money," he complained, "and not enough people yet come to me for my medicines. When more people come I shall have more money. You tell all the people about me, miss."

"Bessie is my name," she told him. "Bessie Pank. That's my uncle, the bootmaker over the way. You're a queer sort, you are! What are you doing to-night?"

Reuben Klask considered the matter cautiously.

"I think I mix up two more bottles of corn lotion," he replied. "I just sold one to your uncle. Afterwards I sit in the Free Library for an hour, get a fried fish supper at the corner of the street and come home to bed."

"Pretty riotous evening!" the young woman observed. "Do you go on like that all the time?"

"If you haven't any money," Reuben pointed out, "you got to be careful until you've saved some."

"You go in and mix your medicines," she directed. "I'm off home to clean up. Afterwards I'll come and treat you to the pictures. How'll that do?"

Reuben hesitated.

"How much are the cheap seats?" he asked.

"I don't never go in the cheapest," she answered "I pay ninepence."

"Maybe I pay for my own," he decided slowly.

" We'll see about that," she replied. " You put on a clean collar and be ready when I come back. I ain't got no further to go than across the way. So long!"

Reuben Klask watched the disappearance of this modern Joan of Arc thoughtfully. Then he mixed his two bottles of medicine, washed, changed his collar for one a degree or two cleaner, fed the canary and with some scraps of tobacco, rolled himself another cigarette. All the time he was abstracted. Romance was finding its way into his life!

CHAPTER II

Bessie Pank listened to her escort's exceedingly half-hearted suggestion concerning refreshments, as they left the pictures, with some scorn. She placed her arm firmly in his.

"You just come along with me, young feller," she enjoined. "If you haven't got the money, I'll treat you. If you have, you ought to know that you can't take a lady out and send her home without offering her a glass of wine. Come right down this street and I'll show you one of the cosiest places in the city."

They turned down a narrow thoroughfare with office buildings and warehouses on either side, now closed for the night. A gleam of light came from a Public House at the first corner and was thrown across the pavement. Bessie stood on tiptoe and peered in at the window.

"It's all right," she told her escort. "Come along! This door!"

They stepped almost directly into a little sitting room leading off the bar. A stout lady, with many parcels in front of her, was seated before a small table with her feet upon the fender. Bessie and her companion seated themselves on the opposite side. The room was cheerful and a bright fire was burning. The host looked round from his place behind the bar and nodded.

"Good evening, Miss Pank," he said. "I'll be there directly. What'll it be?"

"Glass of port, glass of beer and two sandwiches," the girl replied promptly. "You can drink beer, I suppose," she added to her companion. "Don't tell me you're one of them lemonade chaps."

" Of course I can drink beer," he assured her quickly, " and I can pay for your port, too. I ain't mean, only you see there's not a great deal of money in selling herb medicines," he went on, " and one has to be careful."

" I'm not blaming you, not for a single second," the young lady declared benevolently. " I'm sick of these lads who go splothering their money about and expect a girl to be at their beck and call all the time, and at the end of the year they haven't a bob for the Savings' Bank. A girl needs to settle down and for settling down I'd rather choose some one who looked twice at their money. You haven't told me how you liked my fur coat, Mr. Klask. It's paid for — all out of my own earnings, too."

" It's beautiful," he acknowledged, as he drew his fingers almost reverently down her arm.

The landlord brought in their order on a battered pewter salver. The lady opposite, after a few cheery remarks, and a regretful glance into the bottom of her glass, picked up her parcels and took her leave.

" What I like about you," Bessie confided to her companion, " is that you ain't rough like most of the lads. I never saw such hands in my life. Where did you get them finger nails? "

" I don't know," he answered vaguely. " I suppose they were always like that."

" Haven't you never done any work? " she asked curiously.

" Not what you'd call work," he admitted. " I mix those medicines. If I could sell enough of them I should make money."

" And what would you do then? " she enquired.

" I should buy more drugs, more herbs, and make

more money," he replied.   " Maybe I get a larger shop. P'r'aps after a time I build a small factory."

" You're all for getting rich, ain't you? " she observed.   " What's the good of it? "

His eyes glowed.

" The good of it! " he repeated in a tone almost of awe.   " Why, money — money is just the best thing in life.   I should buy a beautiful house in one of those new roads just outside the city and have mahogany furniture and thick carpets and pictures in gilt frames, and maybe a servant.   But I shouldn't spend too much.   I like to save."

" How much money have you got? " she asked.

" Not much," he answered.   " Very little indeed."

" You'll get it, all right," she remarked, studying him thoughtfully.   " You've got the look of a money-maker about you.   Should you like to keep company with me, Mr. Reuben? "

He looked at her, a little startled.   She laid her hand against his cheek.   It was a soft caressing hand although the fingers were rough.   She had very nice eyes and a becoming hat.   The wine, too, had given her a pleasant flush.

" If you're quick about it," she whispered, " you can kiss me.   The old man don't like anything of that sort, but he knows I'm straight and he ain't looking."

Reuben leaned over and kissed her several times.   She rearranged her hat and smiled at him approvingly.

" You're a nice lad," she said.   " How much do you make a week with those bottles of yours? "

" Not much," he groaned.

" Two pound a week? "

" Some weeks," he admitted, " but I got to save. When I have more capital I buy the drugs cheaper."

" How much have you saved? " she persisted.

" Very little," he assured her hastily.

" I got a Savings' Bank account," she confided, after a moment's pause.

There was a marked increase of interest in his manner.

" Good girl," he declared approvingly.　" How much have you got, Bessie? "

" More than you, I bet," she answered carelessly. " You see my aunt left me a bit last Christmas.　Like to guess? "

" Fifty pounds," he ventured.

" More."

" A hundred."

" More than that."

Reuben moved a little nearer to her.　He was becoming conscious of a sense of excitement.

" Hundred and fifty? "

" Two hundred," she announced, in a tone of triumph. " Beside that, I got a bit of furniture left me at the same time."

He looked at her for a moment in awed silence.

" Bessie," he asked, " were you in earnest about keeping company? "

" Kind of," she admitted cautiously.　" I'd like to know a bit more about you — where you come from and who your folks are."

He sat quite still for a moment, gazing through the walls of the little apartment.

" I haven't got any folks," he said slowly.

" Well, I don't know as that matters," she acknowledged.　" I'm none too fond of ' in-laws '.　Where d'you come from — London? "

" Somewhere round there," he admitted.

"You've never been in trouble?" she asked, looking at him keenly.

"Trouble?" he repeated. "What sort?"

She laughed and patted his hand affectionately.

"Of course you haven't," she went on. "I could see you weren't that sort. Now listen here. Supposing instead of keeping company we were to get married?"

"Get married," he muttered vaguely.

"Yes, you booby, married," she repeated, laughing. "You talk about saving money. I'll show you how to do it. It must cost you something to live. Uncle and Aunt don't want me. They've got two other nieces and we're crowded out as it is. Supposing I move my bits of furniture into your cottage and keep on my job. What do you do in the daytime?"

"I go outside the city sometimes with my medicines," he told her. "Some of the villages round are fine. I sold eleven bottles in one small place yesterday."

"That'll do!" she exclaimed. "We'll get our dinner just as maybe and I'll be back in time to cook the supper. What with what you make and my forty-five shillings and me to look after you, we ought to get along all right."

"I'd like to think it over," the young man begged, a little nervously.

"I won't tell you no lies," Miss Bessie Pank continued. "I was going to keep a bit back in case you weren't so straight as you seemed, but I won't do it. It's two hundred and fifty pounds, and not a penny less. I can show you the savings book to-morrow. If you want fifty pounds of it to buy some of your herbs with it's yours right away."

There was for a moment an expression in his face almost of ecstasy.

" Fifty pounds! " he gasped. " I get all my things cheaper and cheaper and cheaper. I get better bottles if I pay cash. But, Bessie," he went on earnestly, " if we make a little money, you won't want to spend it — you're not that sort, eh? "

" Not to begin with," she assured him indulgently. " I was always one for saving myself. This fur coat is my only extravagance."

He passed his hand over it gently.

" Beautiful," he murmured. " Some day I buy you a diamond ring."

" A real diamond? " she demanded.

" Of course," he answered. " Them imitations are just waste of money. I like to buy something cheap that's always worth a little more than I gave for it. That's the way to do in life, Bessie."

The landlord, during a temporary lull of business in the front bar, turned and looked towards them.

" Closing time in ten minutes, Miss Pank," he announced. " Shall I fill 'em up? "

The two exchanged glances. It was a hard struggle for Reuben. He was spared the pain, however, of making an actual decision. The man took their silence for consent and, turning away, disappeared for a moment.

" That port was fourpence a glass," Reuben whispered a little anxiously.

She smiled at him approvingly.

" That's right, Reuben," she said. " Always think of what things cost. After to-night I'm going to drink beer."

The cloud passed from Reuben's face.

" That's a good business," he declared. " I know a place, too, where you can get good beer for three ha'pence a glass — maybe you might have to stand up, though."

The refreshments were brought and presently the two young people departed arm in arm. Outside, the night was frosty and a light powdery snow had been falling. The tops of the sombre houses were sharply defined against a clear sky. There was something snappy in the air which brought the colour into the girl's cheeks as they walked briskly along.

"I always wanted to be married, Reuben," she confided, "and to be married quickly, but the one thing I was determined about was I didn't want to marry any of these wasting louts who'd spend my money in the public house and make me work all the time with nothing to it. You may have your faults, Reuben, but you're not that sort."

"I don't waste money," he assured her truthfully.

They paused outside her house.

"Now kiss me," she directed.

His salute was a little hesitating. Bessie patted his arm as she turned away with a slight grimace.

"I suppose one can't have it all ways," she reflected resignedly.

A SHADE of anxiety clouded to some extent Bessie's welcoming smile as she watched her husband twelve months later, bent double over his bicycle, turn the corner of the street and make his somewhat painstaking way to where she was standing. To the bicycle was attached a light wicker trailer, covered over with a mackintosh. A few yards off he sprang to his feet and wheeled the machine for the rest of the distance.

"You come in and get your tea before you unload," she suggested. "Leave your bicycle in the entry. Tired, ain't you?"

Reuben admitted the fact. He wheeled his machine into the entry and followed his wife into the front room. It was scarcely changed during the ten months which had elapsed since their marriage. There were still rows of bottles in the window but a little more furniture in the room. A baby in a cot made strange noises as Reuben waved his hand.

"I'll have to think about one of those motor attachments," Reuben declared, taking his place at the table and sniffing appreciatively the atmosphere laden with the smell of fried fish. "Maybe I get one cheap from Mr. Goodess."

"I wish you would," Bessie agreed, as she finished laying the table and seated herself opposite to her husband. "The bicycle's bad enough without the trailer, and those bottles, they do weigh heavy! — Had a good day?"

He smiled ecstatically.

"Gets a little better every time," he confided. "It

was market day at Fakenham," he went on. " I paid a
sweet-stuff man two shillings to let me have a corner of
his stall, and I had 'em all around in less than ten minutes. That sweet-stuff man was sick. He wanted to
go into partnership. Do you hear that, Bessie —
partnership!"

They both laughed and appreciated the joke. Reuben began to eat with appetite. Every now and then
he waved his hand to the baby who was sucking contentedly at his rattle.

" That's a fine kid, Bessie," he declared proudly.

" Sometimes," Bessie rejoined, " he almost frightens
me, he's so clever. I'll swear he takes after you, Reuben. He'll be trading his toys before he's grown up.
Look at those eyes of his. He glances around all the
time as though he were trying to make up his mind how
much everything was worth."

" He'll be a money-maker," Reuben assented. " It's
in his blood all right."

" Why don't you ever talk about your folks, Reuben?" Bessie enquired as she poured him out his third
cup of tea.

A look came into his face which she had seen there
once or twice before — a look of vague trouble — less
trouble perhaps than uncertainty. He helped himself
plentifully to fish, frowning all the time.

" If you'll believe me, Bessie," he confided, " I can
scarcely remember a thing about my father, except that
he always seemed to be wearing new clothes and smoking
cigars. Lived in a big house too, only I can't remember
any of it clearly."

" Is he dead?" she persisted.

" I dun'no," Reuben confessed. " I sometimes think,
Bessie, I must have come here after some sort of an

illness. I remember bargaining for this cottage and buying the bits of furniture from old Mother Crurton, but how I came here and where the money came from I had in my pocket, I don't know."

" You don't suppose you've got a wife anywhere else, do you? " Bessie asked sharply.

" I'm jolly sure I haven't, and if I had she wouldn't count no more," Reuben assured her. " First of all there's that," he continued, pointing proudly to the bassinet, " and there's no one could fry fish like you, Bessie."

The young woman smiled contentedly. She was beginning to clear away now and she produced a packet of cigarettes from the mantelpiece.

" I pinched these from Uncle," she declared. " Better than buying them, eh? What about that motor attachment, Reuben? How would it be if we were to walk round and see them things at Miller's? "

" Presently," Reuben assented. " Only, listen, Bessie. We'll pretend we want to buy it by instalments — that we ain't got the money, eh? Then, when we've beaten him down as low as possible we'll try him for spot cash. It's a pity to have to part with any money, anyhow," he added, with a little sigh.

" You'd have more time to be selling and get over the ground quicker," she reminded him. " Time's everything with you. While the clock strikes, you're making money. You can't do it while you're pushing them pedals."

He nodded.

" I sha'n't be happy till I've made up what the thing will cost," he confessed. " You know what will happen to us in two years' time, Bessie? "

" What's that? " she demanded.

"Soon," he said, "I begin to look out for a good second-hand Ford car. Then I have it all painted on the back — 'Klask's Remedies' — and maybe sometimes you go out with me when I go to sell."

"A motor car!" she murmured rapturously.

"Why not?" he argued. "That don't cost much to run if one's careful, and it will do instead of a stall to sell from. The only trouble is," he went on, his face clouding a little, "people will begin to think we've got money."

"So we have," she declared.

He looked around anxiously.

"We don't want folk to know that," he confided. "They'll think we're making too much profit. Mr. Green was saying up at the Bank yesterday that I should have a motor car for my business. I don't like it that they think I'm making money."

She smiled.

"There isn't one of them would guess how much we've got," she said.

"Hush!" he begged anxiously. "We don't talk of that even to ourselves. We should have all these idle young men trying to make medicines and buying our herbs. Maybe I tell you what, though, Bessie, the old man Jarold that has the second-hand shop at the corner of the alley, he's got a diamond ring for sale — a very good stone, worth money. Every time I see him on the pavement outside I ask him how much, and laugh. Yesterday he ask me two pounds less. I seen his landlord in there twice the last few days and I guess he's behind with his rent. He's come down to eighteen pounds now. Maybe I offer him fifteen to-morrow."

"Honest!" Bessie exclaimed, in some excitement.

Reuben nodded.

" You say you bought it with some of the money your aunt left you," he warned her. " Don't you ever let any one know I gave it to you — to take care of," he added hastily. " It's kind of an investment all the time, you see, Bessie, only you wear it."

" How much is it worth? " she asked.

" In a London shop perhaps forty," he answered guardedly. " It's badly set and that don't matter to us. — Hullo! Come in! "

The front door was slowly opened and closed again. Reuben stared at his visitor with eyes into which an entirely new quality seemed suddenly to have stolen. The newcomer removed his hat and sniffed approvingly. The odour of the fried fish seemed to appeal to him.

" How are you, Ernest? " he enquired. " You remember me. I am your cousin, Samuel. Can I eat some fish? "

" Why, of course you can," was the cordial reply. " You take my seat. Bessie, this is my cousin Samuel."

Bessie, as soon as she had recovered from her first surprise, shook hands hospitably.

" Never told me you had one," she remarked, as she bustled around.

" I had forgotten," Reuben confessed. " Seems silly, don't it? I remembered as soon as he walked in. How's the folk, Samuel? "

" What folk? " the newcomer asked, settling down to his feast with appetite.

Reuben seemed puzzled.

" I dun'no," he confessed. " I just had an idea when you stepped in that I could see a whole crowd of them. Now I don't remember any more."

" Very good fish," Samuel declared. " How's business? "

" Pretty good," Reuben admitted grudgingly. " Not enough of it and profits might be bigger."

" I've come to help you," his cousin announced. " It takes two to run a business — one of us to make the drugs and the other to go out and sell them. You can't do both."

" He's managed to so far," Bessie pointed out a little sharply.

" That's because there hasn't been any one like me," Samuel insisted shrewdly. " Stands to sense that while he's at home making drugs, he can't be out selling them."

" I've thought of that more than once," Reuben acknowledged.

" You leave them with some one else to sell," Samuel continued. " You give him a commission — not the profit. What does he care about selling? The man what sells best is the man what's making the profit."

Reuben nodded approvingly and glanced towards Bessie.

" My cousin speaks good," he said. " I don't believe in no travellers or agents."

" You won't need any," Samuel assured him. " You and I are going to make money. — That your baby, Reuben? "

" That's mine," was the proud reply. " He'll make money too, when he grows up. How much money have you got, Samuel? "

Samuel thrust his hand into his pocket and laid a bundle of notes upon the table.

" I got a hundred pounds," he announced.

Reuben shook his head disparagingly.

"A hundred pounds is not very much money," he pronounced. " I had two when I started."

Samuel hesitated for a moment and finally thrust his hand with some reluctance into his other pocket.

"There!" he exclaimed, laying another roll down in triumph. "I got two hundred. I put that with yours, Reuben."

Reuben's attitude still lacked enthusiasm.

"I want you to know, Samuel," he confided, "that my two hundred isn't two hundred any more. I can't take you as equal partner."

"How much have you got?" Samuel demanded, somewhat anxiously.

Reuben whispered in his cousin's ear. The latter was obviously impressed.

"Not only that," Reuben went on, raising his voice to its normal pitch, "but I got the business, I got the connection. I know how to mix these medicines so people like them."

Samuel winked solemnly.

"I can mix them all right," he declared, "and I bet I sell them as well as you, Reuben. We take it in turns, eh? One day you buy herbs and make medicines and I sell; another day we do it different."

"That's all right," Reuben assented, "but you don't get no equal profits, Samuel."

"Very well," the latter agreed. "I take one third. When my capital is as big as yours I take a half. I think I save money quicker than you," he added, with a glance at the bassinet.

"Maybe we find you some nice girl here," Reuben suggested.

Samuel shook his head. For a moment there was a look of trouble in his face.

"I got a girl somewhere," he confided. "I wait for her. Give me a cigarette, Reuben."

" You've got some in your pocket," his cousin pointed out.

Samuel coughed.

" I forgot," he said. " I'll smoke one of my own. Have you got a match, Cousin Bessie? "

She rolled a spill from an old piece of newspaper and handed it to him. He smiled.

" You're a good wife for Reuben," he declared. " We shall all make money together."

CHAPTER IV

IT was Samuel who, one morning some months later, undid the padlock and threw open the door of the small factory. Reuben stood a few yards back, his hands in his pockets, studying with eager interest his new acquisition.

"A neat little place, Samuel," he pronounced, "and cheap. Just what we were looking for. Twenty pounds a year and rates and taxes nothing to speak of. We should make money here, Samuel."

They wandered over the two-storeyed building, planning how to make the best use of it at the least expense. It had once been a small shoe factory and the wholesome smell of leather still haunted the place. They discussed eagerly the most economical way to make the necessary repairs. The painting of a wooden sign outside was a matter for serious consideration. Presently they locked up, passed down the entry and into the street. A somewhat dilapidated-looking Ford car, with "Klask's Remedies" painted in white on either side of the bonnet, stood by the kerb-stone. They mounted and drove off. Samuel took the wheel and Reuben leaned back with an air of enjoyment.

"Wonderful," he murmured, "just wonderful! When I think how my back ached with pushing that old bicycle. Samuel!"

"Yes, Reuben."

"Push back the throttle a little, so! We use less petrol then in the city. We don't need to go fast, Samuel. Bessie ain't expecting us till seven o'clock."

They made their way along the narrow crowded

streets, past the cobbled byways down to the river, and on to an outlying part of the city, a suburb marked down by the speculative builder for defilement and abuse. There were rows of houses in process of construction, each with a small patch of garden; houses all exactly the same, with white plaster walls and rustic porches, a tribute to the artistic yearnings of the garden suburb fanatic. The roads themselves were unfinished; barrels of mortar stood about and piles of bricks. In front of the house where Samuel presently brought the car to a standstill, however, everything was neat and clean. Grass seed had already been sown by the side of the tiled path, and in the window facing the street was a row of bottles, each bearing the name of one of " Klask's Remedies ". There was a name plate upon the gate, another in the window. It was impossible for any one to go by without knowing that this was the home of Mr. Reuben Klask. — No ordinary home, either; a carpet even in the hall, a carpet in the front room, a carpet in the back one. There was a gramophone, framed oleographs upon the wall, a case of stuffed canaries upon the sideboard, and a suite of furniture fresh from the factory, very new and shiny, the padded seats of which, without the closest inspection, might well have passed for leather. It was all highly polished to the point of stickiness, without a speck of dust anywhere. Reuben looked around with an air of delight, almost of reverence. Then he closed the door and the two young men made their way into the back room where Bessie was laying the cloth.

" If you two didn't give me a start! " she exclaimed. " What's the news, Reuben? "

" They've accepted," he declared. " We've got the factory. We've been to order some drugs in first thing in the morning, and maybe Samuel and I will spend a day manufacturing instead of selling."

"If you two aren't the lads!" Bessie cried admiringly. "Why, we're wholesale now!"

"Wholesale and retail manufacturers of drugs," Samuel interposed. "'Klask's Famous Remedies' will soon be known the world over. Maybe we make them Fernhams in London take notice of us by and by."

"Where's the kid?" Reuben demanded.

"Upstairs and listening for you," his wife replied. "Go and fetch him down if you like while I dish up the supper. Samuel, your room ain't straight yet. If you want to wash you'd better go in the back kitchen."

The young men separated. Reuben, after an incoherent conversation with the fat and wholesome replica of himself, descended the stairs in triumph with the infant crowing upon his shoulder. Bessie, better-looking now than in the days when she had worked at the clothing factory, took her place behind the tea tray, and, Reuben's attention still being distracted by his young charge, Samuel seated himself at the other end of the table and served the fish. They all talked a great deal and very fast, and they were all in a state of high good humour.

"Samuel," his cousin declared, "you'll have to get a girl. Maybe there ain't another like Bessie but we'll try and find you one as near as can be."

"There's Dolly Higgins," Bessie murmured reflectively. "Her father's in the coal and greengrocery halfway down the hill. She's crazy to get married and I don't think she's a bad manager."

Reuben shook his head doubtfully.

"I don't think she's saving enough for Samuel," he said. "She'd want to be going to the pictures all day long. What a man wants," he went on earnestly, " is a wife who understands what money means. The worst of women as a rule is that they love to spend money. I hate to spend it even when I got to."

" So do I," Samuel echoed.

" Money was meant to keep and make more money," Reuben continued. " When you have to buy anything, then you ought to buy it so cheap that you can always get the money back for it when you want to. Hold up your finger a minute, Bessie."

Bessie obeyed and Reuben looked ecstatically at the gem which glistened upon her finger.

" Fourteen pounds five I gave for that," he announced with manifest satisfaction. " Fourteen pounds five, a hot brandy and water and glass of beer is just what it cost. It's worth forty pounds if it's worth a penny. That's the way to spend money, Samuel, if you must spend it."

" It isn't all of us has your opportunities," Samuel complained.

" You can all make them," Reuben insisted. " To buy cheap is as easy as to buy dear."

" I wonder whether Mollie Bentley would do for Samuel? " Bessie suggested. " Her father, maybe, hasn't got as much money as Mr. Higgins, but she's real careful and she's looking for a steady chap to keep company with."

Samuel laid down his knife and fork. Up to then he had been too busy to join whole-heartedly in the conversation.

" I don't want a girl at all," he pronounced. " They're nothing but an expense to take round and I'm not for marrying."

" That don't seem natural to me," Bessie objected.

"A young fellow like you, Samuel, ought to be thinking about it."

"You want a family, don't you?" Reuben put in. "There ain't anything in life like seeing plenty of them round the table. That's what I tell Bessie and get my ears boxed for it."

"And serve you right too," the young woman retorted, "with your brazen talk."

Samuel was looking thoughtful. There was an expression in his face which had more than once puzzled his cousin's wife.

"It seems to me," he said slowly, "I've a kind of feeling as though I'd got a girl somewhere."

"For lord's sake!" Bessie exclaimed. "Perhaps you're married."

"No, I ain't married," Samuel replied confidently. "All the same, I got a girl somewhere. Seems to have passed out of my memory where she is just now, but I got the feeling just the same. I shall just wait. She'll come along some day."

"It do seem to me as though you two were crazy sometimes," Bessie declared, replenishing the teapot. "It's a good thing for you both I ain't a curious person, for two more mystical young men about your early days I never met with. Why, we've been married now goodness knows how long, and Reuben hasn't as much as told me where he was brought up! Might have dropped from the skies into Norwich, or been let down in one of them aeroplanes. And now there's you, Samuel, very nearly the same. It's a skeery business!"

Reuben leaned over and patted her hand. There was a quality of earnestness in his face which made him almost good-looking.

"That doesn't need to worry you, Bess, old girl," he

assured her. " The great thing is that you and me are husband and wife. We've got the youngster to start with, and if I'm a bit hazy about my folk we'll soon have a family of our own. Aye and a fortune too! "

" If he isn't off again! " Bessie laughed. — " Why, who's this? " she went on. " That don't seem right for any one to be walking in on us so casual."

The front door had been opened and closed. There were steps in the passage. The door of the room was opened. Joseph stood on the threshold, looking in upon them.

" Good evening, Ernest, good evening, Samuel," he said bowing slightly to each. " I thought I should find you here."

There was a moment's awed and rather wonderful silence. Both Reuben and Samuel had risen to their feet and were staring at the newcomer. There was no surprise in their faces, only a curious anticipatory interest. Bessie, on the other hand, was frankly bewildered.

" It's Dad," Reuben exclaimed softly.

" It's Uncle Joseph," Samuel echoed.

" Your child, Ernest? " Joseph asked eagerly, making his way round to the other side of the room and bending over the bassinet.

" Mine," Reuben assented. " My wife Bessie, Dad — the best in the world."

Joseph handled the baby for a moment affectionately and the child responded to his advances with spirit. Then he replaced it gently in its bassinet, turned to Bessie and kissed her on the forehead.

" Well, well," he murmured. " I'll take a cup of tea, my dear, and a plate of fish, Ernest, if you've got it to spare."

" His name's ' Reuben '," Bessie protested wonder-

ingly. " Why do you all call him ' Ernest '?   Samuel
did when he first came."

" ' Reuben Ernest ' he was christened, my dear," his
father explained. " We didn't care so much for
' Reuben ' as he grew up, so we generally called him
' Ernest '. ' Klask ' was my name a long time ago — a
very long time. I changed it. I really don't remember
why. This is good fish, Reuben, and well cooked,
daughter-in-law."

She was trembling a little — as well she might. This
middle-aged man, with his quiet manners and general air
of having slipped so naturally into the place, baffled her
completely. Reuben had sometimes seemed to her a
mystery; Samuel and his coming had often perplexed
her; but this was the most amazing happening of all.
Nevertheless, she remembered her first duties. She made
his tea carefully, and cut him bread and butter.

" Have you come far? " she asked.

" My dear," he confided, " I don't know. To tell you
the truth, I'm in a very curious position. I was somewhere — perhaps it was in London — when I suddenly
felt that I must find Ernest. Now we're all three here
together — Samuel too. Capital! We might start
some business. I've brought money with me, Ernest."

" Thank Heavens you all bring a bit! " Bessie gasped.
" But I wonder how many more there are of you? "

" Yes, quite a little money," Joseph continued, eating
his fish all the time with appetite.

" Dad," Reuben intervened abruptly, " there's some
one I want to ask about. It doesn't quite come back to
me. It hurts because I want to know."

" Your mother, of course," Joseph declared, skilfully
filleting his last piece of fish. " Your mother and
Judith. Your mother has been ill, Reuben. She trou-

bles a great deal for you. Judith too is troubled. But what can one do? There they are and here we are."

" Why can't they come and see Reuben, or why can't he go and see them? " Bessie demanded. " Of all the mystical creatures! "

Joseph looked at her with a blank expression. Reuben shook his head as though she had asked an absurd question.

" They're over on the other side, my dear," Joseph explained kindly. " Perhaps we shall be able to let them know some day. It doesn't depend upon us. Or they may come too. We never know."

Bessie glanced from one to the other of them.

" You talk of yourselves as though you were ghosts! " she exclaimed. " I should be properly scared, only I don't reckon that ghosts could eat fried fish."

" Ghosts? " Reuben repeated vaguely.

" Now, what does she mean by that? " Samuel asked.

Joseph who had finished his fish helped himself to another piece of bread and butter. He stirred his tea noisily and drank it. Then he leaned over and patted Bessie's hand.

" You're a very nice girl, Bessie," he said. " I like it that my son should have married you and you have brought him a beautiful baby. I think we shall all be very happy together."

Bessie returned the grasp of his fingers a little tremulously.

" I like you too," she confided. " I have always been ready to welcome Reuben's father. I should like to know his mother too. Why doesn't she come? "

Joseph smiled at her quite kindly. Then he pointed out of the window. Below, in the valley, the lights of the city spread up the hillside. Above was an early star.

"You know what keeps that star in its place?" he asked.

Bessie shook her head. Her father-in-law smiled triumphantly.

"We none of us know," he declared, with the air of one who has finished the argument.

CHAPTER V

THE vagueness had entirely departed from Joseph's manner on the following morning when he had studied the list of " Klask's Remedies ", admired the Ford motor car, been conducted to the newly acquired factory, and been allowed a cursory examination of Reuben's much prized ledger.

" We make a little business together, what? " he suggested; " me and you two boys? "

They were seated on cases in the, as yet, unfinished office. Reuben coughed. Samuel stroked his stubbly moustache.

" That's all right, Dad," Reuben declared. " We'll make use of you, very likely. Samuel and I, we've got some money in this."

"And why not, indeed? " Joseph exclaimed. " You two boys don't think I'd propose coming in with you unless I brought my share, do you? I've got money too," he went on, tapping the place where his pocketbook obviously reposed, " a little money, that is to say," he added hastily. "As much as you lads, very likely."

" That makes it easier," Reuben acknowledged.

" Makes the thing sound better to me," Samuel echoed.

" You see, Dad," Reuben continued, " relatives are relatives and all that, but business is business. I started this first — made up small bottles in a four-roomed cottage down in the city, and took them out to sell on a bicycle with a wicker trailer behind. Then I married Bessie and she had money. We spread a little, made more money. Then Samuel arrives. He brings money. Samuel has worked very hard. We make good profits. The business is good."

" I can make it better," Joseph assured them. " There was never any one knew how to sell medicines better than I did — and as for money — well, let's hear about it. What have you boys got? "

" Samuel brought two hundred pounds," Reuben confided, " and I reckon that his share of the profits up to date comes to close on another hundred. You might put Samuel down at three hundred."

Joseph stroked his chin meditatively.

" What's his share of the profits and how much does he draw a week? " he asked.

" He gets a third and he draws two pounds a week, out of which he pays Bessie thirty shillings for board and lodging," was the prompt reply.

" And what about you, Reuben? " his father enquired.

" My own capital was two hundred," Reuben explained, " but as well as that I put two hundred of Bessie's in. That's four hundred, and I got my two thirds of the profits to add to that. How much money have you got, Dad? "

Joseph smiled confidently.

" I got five hundred pounds," he announced. " I'll put that in with you other boys and we all go together, eh? You keep me at home, Reuben, and I draw one pound a week."

"And me ten shillings! " Samuel protested loudly. " Not likely! "

Reuben shook his head.

" You've forgotten the good will, Dad," he pointed out. " I worked like a slave to start this business. After me comes Samuel, and he works too. He got a small share in the good will, but I got a bigger. You haven't any."

Joseph was a little staggered.

" Ain't I to stand in a third? " he asked.

" Not likely," Samuel objected once more.

" Seems to me a quarter would be fairer," Reuben propounded.

Joseph looked thoughtfully out of the dust-begrimed window into the untidy yard. There was something wrong about this somewhere, some things he ought to be able to say, some things from the past of which he ought to be able to remind Reuben, but they were gone. There was that black pool which remained just behind, and a lot of things down at the bottom of it. Reuben was a little hard. Had he been like that when he was young? Still, it was the principle he had taught them. Every man must look after himself. It was the principle upon which even he had been acting. He patted the roll of notes in his breast coat pocket.

" Maybe I make it six hundred and fifty," he announced with a sigh.

" What, you got more than that five hundred, Dad? " Reuben exclaimed.

" Cheese it, Uncle! " Samuel cried. " Trying to come it over us! "

Reuben glanced at his cousin who coughed in an embarrassed manner and looked away.

" How much have you got, Dad? " Reuben asked suavely.

Joseph produced his roll of notes.

" I got eight hundred pounds, less the price of a cup of coffee, a bun and a fourpenny cigar," he confessed, spreading it upon the table. " You don't want to be too hard on me, you boys. I'm not so young as I was

and I like to keep a five-pound note tucked away in case
of a doctor being needed. You lads have got health.
Seems to me I've seen you when you didn't look near so
well, somewhere. I get giddy fits, and I have an empty
feeling at the back of my head."

Reuben considered these statements cautiously.

" Sure you want to work at all, Dad? " he asked.
" With that bit of money you could stay with us quite
a long time. There's a strip of garden to look after
and Bessie'd be glad of some one to take the baby for
a walk now and then."

Joseph was silent for quite a long time. Reuben laid
his hand upon his shoulder.

" Sorry, Dad," he apologised. " What's the good of
your talking sick? You're as strong and well as we
are."

" I'm agreeable to let the old man have his third,"
Samuel conceded. "After all, it's in the family."

"A third it shall be," Reuben pronounced. " We'll
go down to the Bank now and afterwards we'll buy some
wood cheap — I know where there's a factory being
broken up, and we'll get this place into shape ourselves.
Then we'll plan our rounds. We'll make some money
here, Dad. You watch our banking account. We none
of us ain't going to spend. You watch."

Joseph passed his hand across his forehead. He was
smiling amiably but he seemed worried.

"All the while," he murmured, " I keep thinking it's
the second time. Ain't that queer, lads? "

It was a little later than the usual hour when the
evening meal was served at the house of Klask. Nevertheless, at the newcomer's desire, the youngest member
of the family reclined in his bassinet and contemplated
the proceedings with a slightly tempered interest. The

three men were tired but cheerful. Bessie, flushed with leaning over the fire, was still as neat and attractive as ever. She smoothed back her abundant hair and drew the teapot towards her. Joseph stretched out his hand.

"Wait," he enjoined. "You got any wine glasses?"

"There's five belonged to my aunt in that cupboard there," Bessie replied.

Joseph stooped down and from between his feet lifted up a black bottle which he placed upon the table.

"Port," he announced reverently. "Bought it at the best wine shop in the city. Fetch the glasses, Bessie."

His daughter-in-law obeyed promptly, and Reuben produced a corkscrew whilst Samuel eyed the bottle with an air of keen anticipation. There was nevertheless a slight atmosphere of gravity engendered by this reckless proceeding.

"You boys don't need to worry," Joseph assured them as he filled the glasses. "I bought this out of that five-pound note you let me keep. I ain't going to be sick and this day when we all start in business together, I got a new daughter and a new grandchild there — why, it's a great day! You don't need to fear, Reuben, that I'm extravagant. This is the first and last time, and I got a gold watch and a diamond ring we ain't said anything about yet — maybe the ring will be Bessie's some day — until the kid grows up."

Reuben's face cleared.

"That's all right, Dad," he assented, as he stretched out his hand for his glass of wine. "I tell you what, Bessie, if you just put that tea into a bottle and cork it up tight it will do for breakfast just as though it had never been made."

Bessie accepted the suggestion good-humouredly.

" You don't suppose I was going to waste that, Reuben Klask, I hope," she observed.

" Not you, my dear," Reuben rejoined.   " Anyway, I feel more comfortable about it now."

Joseph raised his glass.   He looked at them all, but longest at the infant, who had turned over in his cradle and was apparently taking an absorbed interest in the proceedings.

" To ' Klask's Remedies '," he proposed.   " May we make money ! "

CHAPTER VI

Joseph, appointed orator for the day, paused for breath, to remove his hat, and wipe the perspiration from his forehead. As usual the stall holders were almost in a state of revolt. Practically every lounger and most of the purchasers in the Fakenham weekly market were gathered around the Ford car, from the back of which Joseph was addressing the crowd. In the intervals of his eloquence, Samuel and Reuben were fully occupied in dealing with a line of customers on either side. Presently the oracle recommenced.

"I want you all to understand this," Joseph proceeded. "I want you to get it right here," he added, tapping his forehead. "I am anxious to make my living and to help my son and nephew make their livings, but believe me there's more than that to it. Ancestors of mine have sold medicines — sold them to the rich and given them to the poor — since the days when we Jews lived in Palestine. We make a living by it and a pretty good one, but we sell you good medicines and we sell you medicines which do what we claim for them. Why, I could cover the sides of this car with testimonials received in one morning from people who've been rheumaticcy all their lives and who've thrown away their sticks now and given thanks to the Lord and 'Klask's Remedies.' It ain't miracles we work, but it's something like it. We've kept the secret in our family of how to mix these things and there ain't anybody else can do it just like we do. Is there any one here with corns? Speak to my son Reuben there, and you need never have another. Any one with a bilious attack? Well, we'll keep you free from biliousness for a month. Have you got any form of nerve trouble? We're handling a little preparation behind which beats all the phospherine which was ever made — something which will make a new man of you. Tell us what's the matter with you. Stick to us and we'll cure it. We ain't hucksters. We've been medicine men since the days of the Old Testament and we're proud of it."

A quaint figure Joseph was in the spring sunlight as, for a moment, he lifted his hat — a silk hat, not too elderly, yet which had lost its first glossiness. His untrimmed beard gave him an almost patriarchal appearance, his cheeks sagged no longer, he was thinner by a couple of stone. His pause was the signal for a rush towards the car. He stood there as though enjoying the motley scene, the grey market place, the two comfortable hotels, with their line of carts drawn up in front of each, the market women with their piles of produce, the little County Court Headquarters with its flagged yard and old houses around, almost like some miniature close. And just at that moment a great touring car turned the corner and swung into the London road. Joseph stood there still, a gentle smile upon his lips, one hand stroking his beard, the other holding his hat. Across the little crowd of people Judith looked at him from the car — looked with eager and penetrating eyes, as though seeking to solve the meaning of some startling allegory. She leaned forward in her seat. The last glimpse she caught as the car turned the corner out of the square was of the two young men dispensing their bottles on either side and of an elderly huckster of pleasing appearance, who strongly resembled Joseph Fernham, second Baron Honerton, smiling vaguely across the sunlit space.

"You saw something that interested you?" Paule asked politely.

"I suppose you will think that I am still imaginative," she answered. "I thought that I saw a vision — a quaint vision too, in this old market place."

He held her hands under the wrap. Somehow or other the firm touch of his fingers checked that passionate desire to bid the car stop, to turn round and listen to the old man selling his medicines. She leaned back once more in her place.

"You will laugh at me more than ever when I tell you," she continued. "The old man there and the two young men in the car — they seemed to me like what I have heard of my grandfather and my father when they started selling drugs many years ago. They were nothing but hucksters, you know; they started like that, although it was with packs on their backs instead of even a Ford motor car."

He nodded. There was a quiet smile upon his lips.

"The allegories of life are full of humour," he declared. "Those three, the father and two sons probably, are striving to amass what you to-day have made up your mind to dissipate."

"You think that I am right?" she asked, searching his face.

"For your greater ease of body and mind, without a doubt," he assured her. "The socialists will gibe. It isn't what they want. What does it matter? They don't really count."

"You, at any rate, will keep your word," she murmured.

"I shall keep my word," he promised.

They sped on between flower-starred hedges and hedgerows, past the meadows ripe for the hum of the reaping machine, across a network of streams fringed with marigolds, on to the more open country, the land of gorse and heather, where flowers were few, but the pines shook out their odour in the west wind. They paused for luncheon — a picnic meal — by the side of the road between Newmarket and Royston, in a spot near some village garden where the bees droned and a painted lady flew out from amongst the butterflies. Their chauffeur brought a bunch of wallflowers from the cottage where he asked for some water, and Judith carried them with her to London. As they drew near the outskirts of the city and approached the suburb where the great Works were situated, Judith showed her first sign of nervousness.

"You're coming to see me through it," she reminded him.

"I am coming," he assented. "You know that I cannot stay long. I must catch the boat train to Paris."

"And after Paris?" she murmured.

He made no immediate reply. It was not until they reached the great entrance gates to the huge plot of land on which the factory stood that he spoke again. His tone amazed her. It seemed to her, thirsting so long for something of the sort from him during the last few days, exquisitely human, full of the promise of all that she desired in life.

"After Paris, I set myself to keep my word to you, dear Judith," he announced. "If I fail there will be grave things upon my head. If I fail we shall probably not meet again."

She laughed joyously.

"If you fail!" she repeated, with the supreme confidence of the woman who believes.

It was a specially summoned conference in the great board room of the Works, to which they had come. Samuel was there, very frail and dumb, but gently acquiescent, two members of a famous firm of accountants, the representative of a bank, together with the usual heads of departments, managers and sub-managers. With all these people present, it was Judith who spoke. She stood by Samuel's side, her slender white fingers resting for a moment upon his shoulder, marvellously at her ease, without the least throb of nervousness in her voice. There was not the slightest air of any preparation; her tone was entirely conversational.

"I want to tell you all," she began, "that Mr. Samuel Fernham — my uncle Samuel — and I, who at the present time seem to have become the sole representatives of the firm, have decided to wind up this business. When I told my friend Mr. Lumsden here," she went on, glancing towards the accountant, "that we wished to wipe our hands of it for ever and ever and take our chance of being scolded if what we still ventured to hope should take place, he laughed at me. He wanted us to turn it into a company. He assured me we could get five millions for the business as a going concern, and that this was the proper thing to do. If the business is worth five millions, we do not want the money. It belongs to you who have helped with those others to make it what it is."

There was a moment's spellbound silence. Then Judith continued.

"Of course I haven't any head for details and I shall not attempt to offer them to you. Mr. Lumsden has drawn up the scheme. Every brick and stone of this place, every ounce of drugs and every penny of book debts, belongs to you all in proportion to your length

of service. We Fernhams have all the money we need
or ought to have. Mr. Lumsden tells me that there is
a balance of assets over liabilities of nearly a million
and a half, which he says will easily be sufficient working capital. There is a gentleman from the bank here
who will assure you that any more capital you need
will be yours. I wish you all prosperity. You are,
every one of you, going to be better off by a great deal
when you leave this room. I am glad of it. It is very,
very much better that two thousand of you should be
better off in various degrees than that any more money
should come to my uncle Samuel, to me or to those others who are not here. The business is a present to you
from us all. Work for it, do your best for it, but try to
remember if you can what some of us have forgotten,
that the money you make and the wealth which grows
is worth having not for itself but for what it brings you.
Of course, that is very trite, but most true things are
trite, and the truer they are the more likely we are to
forget them. — And now Mr. Lumsden is going to explain the scheme to you."

There had been rumours of something sensational, but
Judith's offer was so amazing that, for the most part,
every one was stunned. The accountant very wisely
began to deal with the figures almost at once and Judith
slipped away. Paule followed her.

"The newspapers the day after to-morrow should
explain everything to you," he told her, as they stood
in the circular hall outside the conference chamber. "I
shall follow them within twenty-four hours."

"You are very serious," she said, clinging for a moment to his arm, as he walked with her to the entrance.

"I have meddled with a very serious affair," he confessed. "I shall be anxious until the time comes."

He watched her drive off and went back to his rooms where Futoy was packing his clothes for Paris.

"I go with you, Master?" he asked.

"You go with me," Paule assented. "I may need you. Telephone for a taxi."

At Victoria they had a quarter of an hour to wait. Paule was on his way to the barrier when he felt a touch on his arm — a touch, light but ominous. He stiffened with apprehension as he turned his head slowly. It was the one dreaded eventuality — the hundredth chance. Nevertheless he remained outwardly unmoved.

"Can I have a few words with you, Sir Lawrence?" Rodes asked.

"Have you a warrant this time?" was the calm rejoinder.

"Nothing," Rodes confessed. "I am in a position, however ——"

"I must go to Paris by this train," Paule interrupted. "To-morrow I have to speak at a World Congress of Scientists. You may have heard of it — the greatest meeting which has ever been held in Europe. When I have said what I have to say, all those things which you do not understand at present will be made clear to you. Listen — if you interfere now you will do incalculable harm to everybody concerned. Travel down with me to Folkestone and hear my proposition."

"There's a twenty thousand pound reward," Rodes said thoughtfully, "and I know the man who is responsible for their absence."

"I give you my word of honour," Paule promised, "that you shall earn that twenty thousand pounds within ten days."

"I will travel with you to Folkestone," Rodes decided.

There were three Pullmans on the Folkestone train and in one of them Paule found the private compartment at the end disengaged. He ordered refreshments and closed the door. By this time the train was gathering speed, thundering its way across the network of signal lights towards the open country.

" How much exactly do you know? " Paule asked.

" I was at Fakenham when you passed through this morning," Rodes confided. " I have spent quite a lot of time lately in those parts. I was there amongst the crowd, facing the incomprehensible, the ridiculous, the impossible, when I saw Lady Judith's expression as the car passed by. Then I knew that so far as my twenty thousand pounds was concerned, I was home."

" Why have you waited, then? " Paule demanded.

" Because I hate to be beaten. The twenty thousand pounds is offered for the discovery of Lord Honerton, his son Ernest, and his nephew Samuel. Well, there they all are, selling patent medicines under the name of ' Klask ' — their own name, by-the-bye, before they changed it. I've found them all right, but it's an incomplete job and I hate incomplete jobs."

Paule was looking a little anxious.

" Have you spoken to them? " he enquired.

" I spoke to them this morning, after your car had passed," Rodes admitted. " I can tell you I didn't get much for my pains. They wouldn't listen to me — abused me, seemed to think I was out to rob them. They chattered at me like a pack of monkeys, swore they'd never heard of Honerton Chase or the name of Fernham, and either pretended to think or really did think that I wanted to get at their drug business. Anyway they packed up and drove off. I didn't bother. I know where they live in Norwich."

"I am sorry you spoke to them," Paule said, with a troubled frown. "It may make things more difficult. What else have you found out?"

"Just what I have already disclosed to you and Lady Judith. You were only the adopted son of John Paule, the schoolmaster, although you took his name and he was more than a father to you. You were the son of Cecil Fernham and Margaret Heggs. Cecil was murdered, the girl died when you were born, and her father was hanged. It was a stormy entrance into life."

Paule nodded.

"My adopted father," he explained, "was a connection of the Heggses. He had no children and he lived a solitary life. Fortunately I had gifts which appealed to him. He kept my history from me until I went to college."

Rodes took a cigarette from the box which lay open upon the table and lit it. They were rushing now through the darkness at sixty miles an hour.

"This was all ordinary detective work," Rodes continued. "It was easy with the motive discovered. One by one they had disappeared, descendants of old Israel Fernham who, without a doubt, sent your grandfather to hang. There wasn't the faintest doubt but that you were responsible for their disappearance. What had you done with them? I worked at that. Somehow or other I never believed that you had murdered them. I expected to discover them somewhere in confinement, victims of some melodramatic passion for revenge on your part, and, as you know, I discovered nothing of the sort. I discovered them at last, living apparently in the greatest contentment and some apparent prosperity, as quack drug vendors. I have spent months of my time and of my ingenuity trying to trace a single occasion upon

which you have communicated with them, and I can't do
it.   I can't even discover that you have ever been seen
with one of them from the moment they left their homes.
I can't associate you with their abduction or disappearance in any way.   You have beaten me, Sir Lawrence
Paule.   I am going to get that twenty thousand pounds
and I shall hand in my report as to your origin, but,
arrest you I can't — even if I wanted to.   There isn't
evidence enough even for a Bow Street magistrate to
keep you for a night."

Paule was thoughtful for some time.   Presently he
roused himself.

"Your natural course, I suppose, Mr. Rodes," he
said, " is to return to Norwich, attach yourself to these
three men and bring them by hook or by crook into con-
tact with either Lady Honerton or Lady Judith Fernham.   That, at any rate, insures your twenty thousand
pounds."

"It is the only finish of the business that I can see,"
Rodes admitted, "but there's something extraordinarily
crude about it."

"There is also something extraordinarily dangerous,"
Paule assured him earnestly.   "This affair has always
been more or less a sort of duel between us.   You may
recognise the fact that whatever faults I may have or
however much of a criminal I may be, I am a teller of
the truth.   I will sign a paper at this minute, acknowl-
edging that you have discovered the three missing people and are entitled to the reward.   I give you my word
of honour that you shall have the reward, but if you will
bring the matter to an end my way you may save grave
trouble."

"Go on," Rodes invited.

"You will get back to London to-night," Paule con-

tinued. " Motor down to Honerton to-morrow and pre-
pare Lady Judith, but more especially her mother, for
the return of the three missing people. Samuel, the old
man, I know was expected there to-day for a month.
You had better also drop him a hint. Then go into
Norwich and keep your eye upon the Klasks, and on
Wednesday morning read the newspapers."

" The newspapers! " Rodes repeated.

" Read my address to the Congress at Paris," Paule
enjoined deliberately. " You will understand in a minute. Then wait at ' The Maid's Head Hotel ' until I
arrive. It may be two days, it may be three. I shall
come at the earliest possible moment."

" You give me an idea, of course," Rodes admitted.
" I have been to every one of the scientists already,
though, without any result. You weren't even present
when two of them disappeared."

" Wait for the papers," Paule insisted. " You want
them back sane and whole, don't you — not lunatics?
Therefore do as I beg."

They were jolting along down to the docks now. The
detective roused himself from a somewhat prolonged
reverie.

" Well," he observed, " it's an amazing wind-up to
what promised to be one of the most sensational cases
in the world. You seem to have got just a little ahead
of the law, Sir Lawrence — discovered a crime which
isn't entered in the statute book."

Paule smiled grimly. He was handing his things out
of the window to a porter.

" The money is yours, but wait until you understand," was his last injunction to Rodes, as the two men
parted.

CHAPTER VII

SAMUEL looked ruefully over the side of the car and turned to Reuben, who was sitting in front with him.

"We got to have a new outside cover before the autumn," he declared. "Maybe we last until then. I put a beautiful patch on last week."

"These tyres are cruelly expensive," Reuben sighed.

"You lads should worry!" Joseph intervened from the back of the car, where he reclined at his ease with Bessie by his side. "There's no one for saving more than I am, but if a new tyre's wanted we can afford it."

"We don't need to spend money, Dad, just because we can afford it," Reuben retorted.

"Quite right," Joseph assented, "but when the money's got to be spent then it's a comfort to know it's there. What about that advertising?"

"It's a lot of money," Reuben admitted, "but it pays. Did you see our column this morning?"

"It looked beautiful!" Samuel exclaimed enthusiastically.

"Did any of you understand what all this fuss is in the papers this morning about wireless 'hypnosis', or something of the sort?" Bessie demanded. "Whole columns of it — 'Greatest Scientific Discovery of the Age!' they call it."

Joseph shook his head.

"I didn't look for any news," he confessed. "I just read our advertisement. Fine!"

"So did I," Reuben acknowledged. "There ain't any news I like reading as much as that posh Dad's put together about our nerve cure for one and sevenpence ha'penny that costs tuppence farthing. That's news worth reading!"

Bessie scolded her offspring, who showed signs of disquietude, and returned to the subject.

"That's all very well when there ain't any special news," she protested, "but this is a regular eye-opener. It don't seem sense to me. There's a chap in Paris declared that he could give a drug to a person — any one — and let 'em go away wherever they like in reason, and then throw 'em into a state of hypnosis, or whatever the word is — numb his memory and make him do what he wanted. He did it to two chaps who were at the Congress. They drew lots who it should be. Two of them took a little drink and went out without saying where they were going and for the next hour they did exactly what the English doctor or professor or whatever he was said they would. He never went near them, either."

The three men were profoundly uninterested.

"If there's any new trouble coming along of that sort," Reuben observed, "we got to get a drug out quick. 'Take This Three Times a Day and Defy the Hypnotist!' — something of that sort."

Joseph laughed till his stomach shook.

"You lads are all right!" he exclaimed. "Bang up to date — that's what you are!"

"Science ain't any good to us," Samuel declared, looking round. "It's all very well for discoveries like the telephone and telegraph, but it's no use when it comes to the body. Medicine's what's wanted then — good wholesome herb drugs. Wireless hypnosis indeed! Who wants to turn the body into a sort of insulator? Jump down and open the gate, Reuben."

Joseph stroked his beard and looked doubtfully at

the very beautiful lodges and handsome iron gates of Honerton Chase. He brushed the cigar ash from his waistcoat and sat a little more upright.

"We doing right, eh, Reuben?" he asked. "There ain't no mistake about that letter?"

Reuben shook his head.

"Couldn't be," he assured his father. "Plain as posh! The butler or some one here writes that so many of the servants have bought our medicines in Fakenham market that if we pay 'em a call to-day on our way there they'd make it worth our while. I've got the letter with me. There's a P. S.—'Sale of twenty bottles guaranteed.' Worth starting half an hour earlier for. I'll say so!"

"What a beautiful place!" Joseph murmured reverently. "Think what a lot of money it must have cost."

"Think what a lot of money any one must have to live here!" Reuben exclaimed with a note of awe in his tone.

"Everything very well kept too," Samuel observed as they neared the house. "Plenty of money, even amongst the servants, I should say. No need to cut the prices. I wonder which way goes to the back of the house. We'll ask this chap."

An amazed gardener, reading the notices with which the car was besprinkled, directed them. They passed through some smaller iron gates into the very beautiful courtyard. Almost immediately Rodes, in butler's undress, issued from the door and approached them.

"The famous Messrs. Klask, I believe," he said urbanely.

All three raised their hats.

"You got it right," Joseph assented. "We got all

our medicines here. There are two cases fitted on the back. Now, my dear," he added to Bessie, " better let me get out and talk to the gentleman."

The cases were speedily unstrapped and Reuben produced the stand.

" What do you think? " Joseph asked, addressing Rodes confidentially. " You get the servants out here, eh, and I tell them all about what we make and what we cure. Then if we sell a lot we do a little business with you afterwards."

" Not a bad idea," Rodes acquiesced. " Spread the things out just as you please. There's none of the family about to interfere. Hullo, what's this? "

He turned around. One of the indoor servants was approaching with a tray on which were a jug, a decanter, some tumblers and glasses.

" These country servants," Rodes explained indulgently, " give us a lot of trouble. I told them to offer you refreshments after the business was over. P'r'aps they're right, though. You've had a warm ride. I'm sure the lady would like a glass of wine," he concluded anxiously.

" It's a trifle early," Joseph reflected, as he watched an amber stream of liquid being poured into a tumbler, " but it's a warm morning. What do you say, lads? "

The two young men smiled. The idea of refusing a free drink was too ridiculous for discussion. Rodes, who had taken the tray from the servant, served each one of the three. Then he poured out some wine for Bessie.

" I don't know if I wouldn't as soon have the beer," she said.

Rodes shook his head.

" You'll excuse me, madam," he begged. " We don't

offer beer to ladies here. This is a glass of the house-keeper's particular port. She sent it down to you with her special compliments. You won't refuse it, I'm sure."

Bessie sipped her port with much content, and the three men drank their beer. It was a lazy summer day and there seemed to be scarcely any movement about the back of the great house. From a window high up a man stood looking down, his hands gripping the back of a chair, his face white and set. Round the corner of the house, a bath-chair drawn by a little pony had slowly made its appearance. A curious brooding silence reigned everywhere. Rodes had collected the empty glasses and placed them on the tray. The other serv-ant he had motioned back into the kitchen. Joseph made no movement towards the stand which he loved. Reuben was sitting perfectly still with his eyes half closed. Samuel was murmuring inaudible things to him-self. Suddenly Joseph shook himself and stepped out of the car. He turned and shouted to Martin, who was standing in the shadow of the garage. His voice had lost all its cringing quality. He appeared to be vio-lently angry.

"What the hell are you about, Martin," he cried, "to let me come out in a rig like this? What do you mean by it?"

"I'm sorry, your lordship," Martin answered, com-ing forward bravely. "I had a bilious attack and overslept this morning."

"For God's sake put some clothes out and turn on a bath," Joseph directed. "That's all right! I'll come in the back way."

He stumped off. Bessie looked after him, clutching the child, with her mouth wide open.

"Sakes alive!" she exclaimed. "Reuben, what's got the old man?"

Reuben sat up and laughed quite pleasantly.

"I can't think what's got us all," he rejoined, "sitting out here in the sun! Where's the nurse?"

"Where's the what?" Bessie gasped.

Samuel sprang lightly down from the car and started to follow his uncle.

"I say, I'm going to play singles with Joyce this morning!" he told them. "I'm off to change."

Reuben seemed for a moment to falter. Then he turned away.

"I'm going to put on some flannels," he declared. "I can't think what made me get up so early."

Bessie looked helplessly around.

"Crazy!" she muttered to herself. "All three of them! Absolutely crazy! We shall get the chuck from here jolly quick!"

The pony and bath-chair drew up by the side of the car. Rachel leaned over.

"My dear," she said to Bessie, "you are Reuben's wife, aren't you? We used to call him Ernest. I am glad to see you. And this is your baby? May I hold him for a minute, please?"

Bessie, wide-eyed and astounded, descended from the car and handed the child over. There was something very sweet but also very compelling about this elegantly dressed, white-haired woman, with her beautiful eyes and kind voice.

"Those men of mine, ma'am," Bessie complained, "you saw them? They've all gone off. They've beat it into the house. I'm afraid they're crazy. I never heard such talk!"

Rachel Honerton was living in a world of her own.

She was holding the baby tightly in her arms, gazing at him with a rapt expression.

"So this is Reuben's — Reuben's and yours," she murmured, with a sudden instinctive apprehension of the mother standing bewildered by her side.

"What do you know about Reuben?" Bessie demanded.

"My dear," Rachel told her, "Reuben is my son. So this baby is my grandson."

"Your son!" Bessie faltered. "But what is your name?"

"Lady Honerton. You are my daughter, and I am sure we are all going to be very happy together. Wait one moment."

A nurse who had been hovering in the background hurried forward. Rachel handed her the baby.

"You don't mind for a few moments, do you?" she begged, turning to its mother with a delightful smile. "You see, we have to talk. Will you walk by the side of my carriage? I am going to take you to the house."

"You don't mean that you live here?" Bessie asked incredulously.

"Certainly, I do," was the smiling reply. "So are you going to for as long as you like, Bessie dear. You see, I know your name. You look as though you had so much common sense, so much strength. Will you please try to understand?"

"I'll try," Bessie promised. "I'm pretty well dazed, though."

"You must have heard," Rachel continued, her left hand holding Bessie's as they moved slowly towards the avenue, "of the strange disappearance of Ernest or Reuben Fernham and then Samuel Fernham and then Lord Honerton. Well, those are your three men, my dear. The doctors will explain it some day or other. Just now, we have to be very careful. You see, they remembered that this was their home when they got here. We shall have to humour them when we see them again. Don't speak of Norwich, Bessie. Don't seem surprised to be here."

Bessie suddenly began to tremble.

"Reuben may have forgotten that he is married to me," she faltered.

Rachel's beautiful fingers tightened upon the girl's.

"Leave that to me, my dear," she begged. "Reuben will never forget. That is just one thing — one great thing — about all my family and my race. For all our faults, we have fidelity. Reuben's feeling for you and the child would conquer anything else. Only we may have to humour him. You will trust me, please. You will believe me when I tell you that I am very happy to have you for a daughter, and more happy than you could ever imagine about your baby. — Now, my dear, I am going to take you indoors for a little time."

CHAPTER VIII

An intense and almost unnatural silence from all human sources seemed to hover that morning over the great front, the terraces and gardens of Honerton Chase. There were birds twittering on the lawns, some pigeons in the nearer of the two little woods and a whole colony of rooks in the elm trees at the commencement of the park. From the tennis courts came the monotonous sound of the mowing machine and once a peacock on the terrace lifted his head and indulged in his unearthly screech. Judith, who, with Joyce and her uncle Samuel, were reclining in *chaises-longues* under a clump of cedar trees, suddenly caught the former's fingers.

"It is just as though this were the empty stage and the curtain had rung up for the first act of a play or drama," she murmured. "There is something unreal about it all — the silent house, the emptiness out here, whilst we wait, you and I, with our hearts throbbing. He says — Lawrence says — that it all depends upon the next few minutes."

"Lawrence?" Joyce, who was of more phlegmatic temperament, murmured curiously.

"If you didn't know as much as that, you're an idiot," Judith declared. "Sit still, dear. There's some one coming!"

Through the wide-flung doors, opening into the hall, the nurse appeared, wheeling a perambulator. On either side of her were Rachel and Bessie — the latter in a cool white gown of Judith's, which by some miracle fitted her, and a large garden hat. They came slowly down to the terrace, and made for the shade of the cedar trees.

"The woman's all right, anyhow," Judith pronounced. "I like her. She still thinks that either we're all crazy or that she's gone off her head herself, but she's settled down to make the best of it whilst it lasts. — Joyce, here's one of them. Now we shall know!"

Reuben, dressed from head to foot in white flannels, his hands in his pockets, came strolling down the steps. He called out to Judith as he crossed the lawn. Bessie began to shiver. He had not once looked towards her.

"I say, Judith," he suggested lazily, "do you feel like a set? If so, we could have a four to start with and let Joyce and Samuel fight it out afterwards."

Judith rose to her feet and closed the pink parasol she was holding over her head. Her fingers were trembling but her voice was perfectly steady.

"Yes, I'll play, Reuben," she acquiesced.

He turned towards his uncle, who was sitting upright in his chair, his hands clasped upon the ivory handle of his stick.

"Feeling all right this morning, Uncle Samuel?" he asked kindly. "This sunshine ought to do you good."

"I am well," was the hoarse reply. "I am waiting to see Samuel."

"He'll be out directly," Reuben observed. "He began to change before I did."

A servant issued from the house with rackets under his arm. Reuben turned around.

"Just tell Martin to send some cool drinks down to the tennis court in twenty minutes or so," he directed. "And you might let Mr. Samuel know that we're waiting."

He strolled deliberately across towards the little
group gathered round the perambulator. Rachel
gripped the back of her chair. It seemed to Bessie
that, notwithstanding the sun, the colour was all ebbing
away from her cheeks. Surely there was something
strange about this young man, suddenly more debonair,
suddenly free from a dozen small affectations. He
seemed to have slipped back with such amazing ease into
the consciousness of his altered position.

"New gown, Bess," he remarked approvingly. "Jolly
sensible too, this weather!"

"I——"

He looked at the nurse and for the first time the
slightest trace of surprise showed itself in his face. It
passed, however, almost at once.

"Can I have the kid for a moment, nurse?" he asked.
"I won't take him into the sun."

The child sat up and crowed. Reuben took it into his
arms, a bundle of white swansdown and indefiniteness.
He talked absurdities for several moments, and they
listened to him, the two women, as though he had drawn
aside the veil before paradise.

"Hullo, here's Samuel!" he declared, looking back
towards the house. "We'll have to start. Are you
coming down to watch us, Mother? You must come
anyhow, Bessie. — Put the child back, nurse," he added,
handing him over.

Samuel had paused on the top of the steps to light a
cigarette.

"I say," he shouted, "some one's taken my racket
out of the press. I put it in myself the last time I
used it. Foul play, I suspect. Hullo, Dad!"

Samuel opened his lips but no sound came. His eyes
were riveted upon his son. There was wonder in his

gaze and an amazing tenderness. The young man crossed the lawn and leaned over his chair.

"You're looking fine this morning, Dad," he declared. "Being here always seems to do you good. Are you coming down to watch us play tennis?"

"Presently — I'll come presently," was the subdued, yet eager reply. "You're looking better, my boy — much better!"

"I'm tophole!" Samuel answered frankly. "'Neurota' must have done the trick! I'm rather thinking of writing a testimonial for the firm. — I must go and talk to Joyce."

He approached her chair, smiling but without undue excitement.

"Forgive my going to speak to Dad first," he begged, as he held out his hands to lift her from her chair. "Come on down to the courts before the others. I want to hear from your own lips that you haven't changed your mind."

"I can tell you that before we start," she laughed. "I wish I could think that being engaged is going to have the same effect upon me as it has upon you," she added, studying him wonderingly. "I never saw you look so well!"

He passed his arm through hers.

"Don't hurry, you people," he called out, glancing over his shoulder. "Remember we're young and that sort of thing! — How ripping you look in tennis clothes, Joyce," he continued. "I thought you could never look sweeter than you did in that blue gown you wore at dinner last night, but I like you even better in this white kit."

Reuben stepped back to meet Bessie and drew her attention to the two.

"I say," he asked, "were we ever so bad as that?"

Then, through the open doors came Joseph, also in flannels, with a long cigar in the corner of his mouth.

"Any one seen Martin?" he demanded. "Where the devil is the fellow?"

Martin hurried across from the tennis courts, and Joseph indignantly held out the top of his trousers for inspection.

"Look here!" he exclaimed. "You must have put out some one else's trousers for me. They're all too large. Rachel, look at this! I haven't lost six inches in the night, have I?"

Martin was speechless. Judith came up, laughing softly.

"Why, my dear Dad," she declared, "you've been getting thinner and more sylphlike all the summer. I wondered when you'd notice it. Those are your trousers, all right. You'll have to have them taken in and another hole made in your belt."

Joseph surveyed his decreased dimensions with obvious pleasure.

"To think I never noticed it!" he muttered. "I had an idea I was getting thinner, too. What do you think of this, Rachel?" he went on, turning again towards his wife. "I shall have to go and see my tailor the first day I'm in town!"

"You will indeed, my dear," she assented.

Bessie, to whom he had not yet spoken, glanced at him anxiously. He returned her gaze and removed his cigar for a moment from his mouth.

"Hullo, what's wrong with you, Bessie?" he enquired. "Kid not behaving? You little rascal!" he proceeded. "Hold my cigar for a minute, nurse."

There were more amenities with the baby, after which

Joseph returned it to the nurse and took up his cigar again with satisfaction.

"These Laranagas improve every day," he confided to Samuel. "Never tasted anything better than this one. I wish you smoked, old chap. I'm going to sit here and enjoy it. Keep little Reuben on the other side, nurse. There isn't much wind, but I don't want the smoke to get in his eyes."

Judith suddenly raised her head and listened. From somewhere in the stable yard there was the sound of the soft purring of an engine. She turned to Reuben.

"I'm going into the house for a few minutes," she announced. "We must give Samuel and Joyce a chance!"

"They've gone into the chalet to look for balls," Reuben grinned. "All right, don't hurry so far as I'm concerned."

Judith skirted the side of the house rapidly and passed through into the courtyard. A car was standing there with Futoy at the wheel.

"Are you waiting for Sir Lawrence?" she asked.

Futoy signified his grave assent. Judith turned back into the house. She met Martin in the hall.

"Can you tell me where Sir Lawrence is?" she enquired quickly.

"In the front library, my lady," Martin replied. "He is writing a note."

Judith breathed a sigh of relief as she opened the door of the room and found him there. He rose from the table almost at her entrance, a letter in his hand.

"I have just been writing down a little advice," he explained at once, "to help you to deal with any emergency."

"And I have come to give you a little advice," she

retorted, closing the door firmly behind her. " The first part of it is ———"

" Well? "

" That you come and kiss me at once."

He threw the letter on the table. She moved a step towards him. There was something absolutely steely in his demeanour, forbidding in the gesture with which his whole being seemed to stiffen.

" You are a very emotional person, Lady Judith," he said curtly, " and you are carried away just now by a tide of feeling. You see the end of all your troubles and you are grateful. You forget that it was I who was responsible for those troubles."

" Go on, please," she invited pleasantly. " Say it all."

" You have to remember," he continued, his tone becoming harsher, " who I am — Heggs' grandson, the man who was hung. You have to remember that it was I who in a spirit of vengeance deliberately risked the lives and the reason of three members of your family."

She nodded.

" I understand all that," she assented. " I should be inclined to forgive a great deal, though, for the simple reason that you have shown such excellent taste in avoiding melodrama. You might easily have made lunatics of all three, or have killed them with scarcely any fear of detection. Then you could have revealed your identity and gloated. I should have hated that! "

She paused. For the moment he had nothing to say.

"As it is," she went on, " what have you done? As a family, when you found us, we were a decadent lot. Israel, my grandfather, was the prototype of all that was best in us, and there wasn't one of us who was fit to hold a candle to him. Ever since his passing we have sucked up wealth and luxury until our men were becoming rotters and I — well, I am not proud of the life I lived for a few years. Remember what they were, those three, when you drove them out! Dad hadn't a thought but for his money. He ate too much, he drank too much, he smoked too much. Look at him to-day. He looks ten years younger. He has done some solid work. He may forget it but the good it did him is there, written in his face. Look at Reuben! He has a touch of my grandfather Israel in his expression already. He's harder. He'll never fall back. And Samuel! He's as much improved as any of them. A year ago I couldn't have pointed out a more selfish young man. Yet his first thought when he arrived here was not for Joyce but for his father. — You haven't done any one any harm, Lawrence. We're really all very much obliged to you. I'm the only one you seem to treat badly."

" You? " he queried.

" Yes, you're keeping me waiting such a long time."

" For what? "

" For everything! " she murmured, with upstretched arms.

" Of course, if you're going to be this kind of a lover," she declared, a little later, " I shall have to give up wearing these ethereal sort of clothes. Please pull yourself together now and come out on the lawn whilst I make the great announcement. After all, it's much better to have you in the family. If anything goes wrong at any time, you will be on the spot. Tell me," she went on, passing her arm through his affectionately, and leading him towards the door, " what happened to the great prescription which numbs the brain and makes the subject so amenable to hypnosis? I tried to read the whole account of the proceedings, but it was terribly difficult."

" .The president of the Society," he told her, " has locked it up with two other formulæ which scientists have evolved at different times, and which we have decided are too dangerous to be of practical use to humanity at present.   One, I may tell you, would make war at any time absolutely impossible.   The other would protect us in case of unexpected attack from the possible inhabitants of one of the planets we have been watching. Mine is the third of the discoveries which it has been decided are too dangerous to be given to the world.   In the words of the president — ' the publication of this formula could lead only to confusion and distress.' "

" That's all those stupid scientists know about it!" she murmured, as they passed out into the hall.

THE END